'I SHOULD LIKE THESE DATES A LITTLE CLEARER'

A CHRONOLOGICAL STUDY OF THE RECORDED CASES OF SHERLOCK HOLMES

'I SHOULD LIKE THESE DATES A LITTLE CLEARER'

A CHRONOLOGICAL STUDY OF THE RECORDED CASES OF SHERLOCK HOLMES

A. R. Colpo

For C.C., my Stamford

First Edition published in 2021
Reprinted with minor revisions in March 2023

Copyright © 2021 Alec R. Colpo

The right of Alec R. Colpo to be identified as the Author of this work has been asserted in accordance with the Copyright, Designs, and Patents Act 1988.

All Rights Reserved. No part of this publication may be reproduced, stored in a retrieval system, or transmitted, in any form or by any means, electronic, mechanical, photocopying, recording, or otherwise, without the prior written permission of the Copyright owner.

ISBN 979 8 5932 2445 3 (paperback)

Cover illustration by Sidney Paget

Table of Contents

Introduction ix
Facts, Assumptions, and Tenets xv
Four-Letter Case Abbreviations xix
PART I: AN ANALYSIS OF DATES 1
1. A Study in Scarlet 3
2. The Sign of Four 8
3. A Scandal in Bohemia 20
4. The Red-Headed League 24
5. A Case of Identity 30
6. The Boscombe Valley Mystery 35
7. The Five Orange Pips 37
8. The Man with the Twisted Lip 42
9. The Blue Carbuncle 44
10. The Speckled Band 47
11. The Engineer's Thumb 49
12. The Noble Bachelor 53
13. The Beryl Coronet 56
14. The Copper Beeches 59
15. Silver Blaze 64

Table of Contents

16. The Cardboard Box 69
17. The Yellow Face 73
18. The Stock-Broker's Clerk 76
19. The "Gloria Scott" 79
20. The Musgrave Ritual 84
21. The Reigate Squires 92
22. The Crooked Man 94
23. The Resident Patient 96
24. The Greek Interpreter 101
25. The Naval Treaty 104
26. The Final Problem 107
27. The Hound of the Baskervilles 111
28. The Empty House 130
29. The Norwood Builder 132
30. The Dancing Men 134
31. The Solitary Cyclist 137
32. The Priory School 138
33. Black Peter 141
34. Charles Augustus Milverton 143
35. The Six Napoleons 147
36. The Three Students 151
37. The Golden Pince-Nez 153
38. The Missing Three-Quarter 155
39. The Abbey Grange 157

Table of Contents

40. The Second Stain 159
41. Wisteria Lodge 172
42. The Bruce-Partington Plans 176
43. The Devil's Foot 178
44. The Red Circle 180
45. The Disappearance of Lady Frances Carfax 184
46. The Dying Detective 187
47. The Valley of Fear 189
48. His Last Bow 196
49. The Mazarin Stone 197
50. The Problem of Thor Bridge 200
51. The Creeping Man 203
52. The Sussex Vampire 208
53. The Three Garridebs 211
54. The Illustrious Client 212
55. The Three Gables 215
56. The Blanched Soldier 217
57. The Lion's Mane 221
58. The Retired Colourman 223
59. The Veiled Lodger 225
60. Shoscombe Old Place 230

PART II: A BIOGRAPHY 235

The Lives of Mr Sherlock Holmes and Dr John H. Watson 237

Table of Contents

Conclusion 280
Appendix I: Chronological Table 284
Appendix II: Comparative Chronology 294
Appendix III: A Note on Holmes's University 322
Bibliography 324

Introduction

Since the publication of *Shoscombe Old Place* by Sir Arthur Conan Doyle, the literary agent of Dr John H. Watson, in March 1927, the conundrum of determining the precise date of each of the sixty recorded cases of Mr Sherlock Holmes has been an intriguing subject of study for students of the Canon. There are now a significant number of complete chronologies of the cases, yet there is limited agreement amongst their creators as to the dates of the cases. In the hope that we may settle some of the uncertain and disputed points of chronology and present convincing alternatives for dates previously believed to be settled, we now proffer our own observations and conclusions.

Before permitting the reader to progress to the analysis, we would offer some words of explanation as to its structure and methodology. The book is divided into two parts. The first is arranged as a series of commentaries on the dates of the sixty cases. They are presented in their order of publication, according to the first date of publication; thus the cases of the collections *His Last Bow* and *The Case-Book of Sherlock Holmes* do not appear in the order in which they were gathered in those collections, but rather in the order in which they were originally published serially in magazine form. Similarly, *The Cardboard Box* is in its original place immediately after *Silver Blaze*. The copy-text which we used for our analysis and references was the original British two-volume edition of the collected cases: *The Complete Sherlock*

Introduction

Holmes, Long Stories (London: John Murray, 1929) and *The Complete Sherlock Holmes, Short Stories* (London: John Murray, 1928). We regard this as the truest edition of the cases for several reasons. The original *Strand* magazine editions of the cases contain a number of minor errors which were later admitted and corrected by Watson, and these modifications are reflected in the British book edition published by John Murray. The American magazine editions suffer from the same objections as those of the *Strand*, as well as the further detriment—shared by the collected American book edition, first published by Doubleday and Company in 1930—that their integrity is compromised by the rather liberal editorial alterations made in consideration of the cultural sensibilities of contemporaneous Americans.[1]

The second part of the book is a biography of the life of Sherlock Holmes which provides a sort of recapitulation of our conclusions, the cases being presented in chronological order throughout the broader delineation of Holmes's and Watson's lives. Having made some effort in our individual analyses to explain what occurred in the gaps of time between the cases, we reiterate these insights in the biography as their coherence is more marked when thus arranged as a continuous narrative. The second part of the book will accordingly serve above all else to demonstrate that the cases, when arranged according to the dates which we have selected, fall into a sensible and smooth sequence. In the appendices the reader will find a chronological table listing the cases and their dates, as well as a comparative chronology which juxtaposes the dates chosen by us with those favoured by the other chronologists for each of the sixty cases.

---

[1] See our discussion of *The Resident Patient* for more on this.

Introduction

As to the matter of evidence, the facts derived directly from each narrative are given the greatest weight in the analysis of that case. When these facts conflict with one another or with those of another case, those which cannot be substantiated with facts from elsewhere in the Canon or from outside sources are discounted. Secondary importance is given to historical facts, notably those which we have found in contemporary newspaper articles. Tertiarily, the evidence of both the monthly phases of the moon and the time of sunrise, sunset, and twilight[1] is sometimes used for determining the time of the month and corroborating statements made by Watson, and while we cannot presume that Watson's descriptions of the moon and sun are in every case precise, we may trust that he had no reason to seriously and regularly falsify this information. The fourth source of evidence which is taken into consideration for a select number of cases is the meteorological conditions described in the narratives. This type of evidence is, however, far from decisive, given the transient nature of the weather, the limited availability of meteorological records, and the dubiousness of the value of any such records due to the vast disparity of weather conditions throughout even the relatively small area of London on any given day. Some chronologists rely, we think, far too heavily upon weather as evidence, especially in certain cases where they regard meteorological evidence as superior to textual or historical facts. Nevertheless, we admit that the weather can be a helpful guide if a case offers no better evidence.

Our procedure with regard to references has been to refrain from citing any quotations taken from the case being discussed,

---

[1] We determined the moon phases, the sunrise, sunset, and twilight times, and the day of the week of dates using the calendar database at https://www.timeanddate.com/.

Introduction

as doing so would result in an overwhelmingly excessive number of footnotes; these quotations are accordingly indicated only by the single quotation marks which surround them. For quotations that are not from the case in question, we adopt the practice of citing using the formats of (Long, [case abbreviation], [page]) and (Short, [case abbreviation], [page]) for the *Long Stories* and *Short Stories*, respectively. Other sources, such as newspaper articles and the works of other chronologists, are cited in Turabian format.

As a sort of disclaimer, we would like to note that, in writing this chronology, we initially avoided consulting any works of Holmesian chronological scholarship in order to develop entirely original arguments and dates and to be able to claim them as our own. If, therefore, any of our analyses seem to closely reflect the opinions, conclusions, or reasoning of any other chronologist (and no reference is made to such chronologist's work), this is the consequence of our having fortuitously arrived at an analogous notion entirely on our own. Having completed our chronology in this sort of isolation, we then proceeded to analyse it within the context of the nine traditional chronologies which were accessible at the time of writing.[1] While we did not exhaustively compare and evaluate the extant chronologies, we did analyse their contents, noting when their arguments supported our conclusions and when our evidence disproved the theories for alternative dates proposed by others. This process resulted in our altering or refining some of our original dates

---

[1] The nine chronologies which we were able to consult were those of Bell, Blakeney, Christ, Brend, Baring-Gould, Zeisler, Dakin, McQueen, and Hall. The only other complete chronology that we were aware of was that of Folsom, but his work was privately printed and thus was not available on the market at the time of writing.

Introduction

based upon the findings of others; in all such instances, we have explicitly referenced the works that influenced us.

The creation of a chronology is no mean task, but for the true scholar it is one of great pleasure. The chronological problems of the Canon are a stimulant that drives the student ever onwards until he has acquired such a penchant for the solving of these conundrums that he cannot but feel some little regret upon the completion of his chronological researches. There are, of course, other avenues of study left to him, but none that is at one and the same time quite so intriguing, frustrating, and gratifying. We hope that the reader may derive as much pleasure from the perusal of our work as we enjoyed in the creation of it. Inspector Alec MacDonald, though speaking of another matter entirely, best expressed the driving desire of every chronologist when he said 'I should like these dates a little clearer'.[1]

---

[1] Long, VALL, 505.

Facts, Assumptions, and Tenets

Listed below are some facts about travel and language usage, as well as assumptions we made when beginning our analysis and tenets which we established throughout the course of our research.

Rates of travel:
1. A horse carriage travels at highly variable speeds depending on the horses, roads, and length of journey. The average speed when walking is four miles per hour and when trotting is twelve miles per hour, so in our analyses we use eight miles per hour as an overall average, considering that most journeys would involve a combination of varying speeds.
2. A steam train of the late Victorian Era travels between thirty and forty miles per hour.

Time references current in the phraseology of the late Victorian Era:
1. *Ultimo* refers to the previous month.
2. *Inst* refers to the current month.
3. *Prox* refers to the following month.
4. When Watson uses a phrase such as 'Monday next' or 'last Tuesday', he means the very next Monday or most recently passed Tuesday, not the Monday of the

following week or Tuesday of the previous one, as is made clear by the usage of such phrases in, notably, *The Final Problem* and *The Three Garridebs*.

Canonical assumptions:
1. We tentatively accepted from the outset of our analysis that Holmes was born in 1854. The basis of this supposition was the description of him as a 'man of sixty'[1] at the time of *His Last Bow*, a case which indubitably occurred in 1914. We encountered nothing to contest this in our researches and now consider it to be a tenet.
2. We originally speculated that Watson was born in the mid-1850s. Although there is very little evidence in the Canon regarding the year of his birth, we know that he was roughly the same age as Holmes and that he received his Doctor of Medicine degree in 1878. After completing our chronology, we encountered the theory of S.C. Roberts that Watson was born in 1852 because a famous physician of his time who was also born in 1852 began studying in the same year as Watson and received his own Doctor of Medicine degree in 1878.[2] As we did not discover anything to contradict this, we now consider Watson's being born in 1852 to be a tenet.
3. Sir Arthur Conan Doyle acted as Watson's literary agent beginning in 1887 and arranged for the publication of all of the sixty accounts which constitute the Canon.

---

[1] Short, LAST, 1,076.
[2] S.C. Roberts, *Holmes & Watson: A Miscellany* (London: Oxford University Press, 1953), 61.

Facts, Assumptions, and Tenets

Canonical tenets:
1. When referring to other cases within a given account, particularly when trying to prove a point, Watson has a tendency to insert references to those cases which he has already published—even if they occurred at a later date than the case whose account he is writing (though obviously before its date of publication)—rather than the ones actually mentioned by Holmes and him in their original conversation, evidently believing his readers will be better able to appreciate the import of the conversation if he refers to cases with which they are familiar.
2. Watson by his own admission occasionally takes the liberty of altering the actual dialogue of individuals in his accounts in order to clarify some point for the reader (as with Cyril Overton in *The Missing Three-Quarter*[1] and with Mrs Lucca in *The Red Circle*[2]). He even modifies the words of Holmes himself in *The Illustrious Client*.[3] Thus we know that he does not relate everything that was spoken verbatim, and this may be the cause of some of the inconsistencies.
3. The descriptions Watson gives of the clothing that various individuals wear throughout the Canon are not to be relied upon for such purposes as, for example,

---

[1] Short, MISS, 811. Cyril Overton spoke, Watson says, 'with many repetitions and obscurities which I may omit from this narrative'.
[2] Short, REDC, 964. Watson says of Mrs Lucca that 'She spoke in rapid and fluent but very unconventional English, which, for the sake of clearness, I will make grammatical'.
[3] Short, ILLU, 1,102. Watson says that Holmes 'told the story, which I would repeat in this way. His hard, dry statement needs some little editing to soften it into the terms of real life.'

determining the time of year based upon the appearance of an overcoat. Both because we do not think that Watson was especially diligent in taking precise notes of attire, and because of how changeable the weather is and how often it does not comply with our general expectations for any given time of year, we feel that clothing is hardly defensible evidence for any given date.

Four-Letter Case Abbreviations

STUD	*A Study in Scarlet*
SIGN	*The Sign of Four*
SCAN	*A Scandal in Bohemia*
REDH	*The Red-Headed League*
IDEN	*A Case of Identity*
BOSC	*The Boscombe Valley Mystery*
FIVE	*The Five Orange Pips*
TWIS	*The Man with the Twisted Lip*
BLUE	*The Blue Carbuncle*
SPEC	*The Speckled Band*
ENGR	*The Engineer's Thumb*
NOBL	*The Noble Bachelor*
BERY	*The Beryl Coronet*
COPP	*The Copper Beeches*
SILV	*Silver Blaze*
CARD	*The Cardboard Box*
YELL	*The Yellow Face*
STOC	*The Stock-Broker's Clerk*
GLOR	*The "Gloria Scott"*
MUSG	*The Musgrave Ritual*
REIG	*The Reigate Squires*
CROO	*The Crooked Man*
RESI	*The Resident Patient*
GREE	*The Greek Interpreter*

Abbreviations

NAVA	The Naval Treaty
FINA	The Final Problem
HOUN	The Hound of the Baskervilles
EMPT	The Empty House
NORW	The Norwood Builder
DANC	The Dancing Men
SOLI	The Solitary Cyclist
PRIO	The Priory School
BLAC	Black Peter
CHAS	Charles Augustus Milverton
SIXN	The Six Napoleons
3STU	The Three Students
GOLD	The Golden Pince-Nez
MISS	The Missing Three-Quarter
ABBE	The Abbey Grange
SECO	The Second Stain
WIST	Wisteria Lodge
BRUC	The Bruce-Partington Plans
DEVI	The Devil's Foot
REDC	The Red Circle
LADY	Lady Frances Carfax
DYIN	The Dying Detective
VALL	The Valley of Fear
LAST	His Last Bow
MAZA	The Mazarin Stone
THOR	The Problem of Thor Bridge
CREE	The Creeping Man
SUSS	The Sussex Vampire
3GAR	The Three Garridebs
ILLU	The Illustrious Client
3GAB	The Three Gables

Abbreviations

BLAN	*The Blanched Soldier*
LION	*The Lion's Mane*
RETI	*The Retired Colourman*
VEIL	*The Veiled Lodger*
SHOS	*Shoscombe Old Place*

PART I: AN ANALYSIS OF DATES

1. A Study in Scarlet

First published December 1887

This case, the first in which Watson acted as Holmes's biographer, and fittingly enough the first which he published, is certainly the simplest of the four novellas for which to ascertain the date. Disagreement exists, of course, but a close examination of the facts shows that only one date is possible.

Dr Watson was present at the ill-fated Battle of Maiwand, fought on 27 July 1880 during the Second Anglo-Afghan War, where he was seemingly wounded not only in the shoulder but also in the leg.[1] It is our belief, substantiated below, that while a bullet very clearly struck his leg and left him with lingering pain for many years, his shoulder injury was more likely something less chronic, such as a broken bone or a torn ligament. In any case, Watson was sent back to Peshawar to recover, but just as he was beginning to do, he was struck with enteric fever. This was probably in late August 1880, and 'for months' he was at death's door. Eventually he began to recover and returned to England, whereupon he went to London and spent 'some time' at a private hotel until one fateful day he was introduced by his old associate Stamford to Mr Sherlock Holmes.

---

[1] Watson refers to his shoulder injury in this account, but in *The Sign of Four* he speaks of his leg that was hit by a jezail bullet (Long, SIGN, 146). Thus he appears to have suffered two injuries while on campaign.

A Study in Scarlet

Christ[1] and McQueen[2] have argued that all of these events would have occupied so much time that Watson could not possibly have returned to London by January 1881, but all of Watson's statements regarding lengths of time here are rather vague, and the matter ought to be considered as settled by Mr Percy Metcalfe's discovery[3] that the troopship *Orontes* did in fact make the passage from India to Britain during October and November of 1880, which necessarily puts Watson in London by the New Year. Zeisler, in fact, provides a highly satisfactory tabulation of the weeks that Watson spent recovering from wounds and illness which agrees precisely with the departure of the *Orontes* mentioned above (a fact of which he does not appear to have been aware, as he does not mention it).[4]

Stamford, having lunched with Watson, took his former associate to the hospital to meet Holmes, with whom Watson agreed on the following day to share rooms at 221B Baker Street. As to the date of this historic meeting, Zeisler cites the emptiness of the hospital as proof that it took place on a holiday, which could only have been 1 January 1881.[5] 'Weeks went by' during which Watson learnt nothing of Holmes's occupation until, on 4 March 1881, Holmes asked him to accompany him to Lauriston Gardens, and Watson caught his first glimpse of his fellow lodger's unique profession.

---

[1] Jay Finley Christ, *An Irregular Chronology of Sherlock Holmes of Baker Street* (New York: Magico Magazine, 1947), 1-2.
[2] Ian McQueen, *Sherlock Holmes Detected: The Problems of the Long Stories* (New York: Drake Publishers, 1974), 18-20.
[3] D. Martin Dakin, *A Sherlock Holmes Commentary* (Newton Abbot: David & Charles, 1972), 10.
[4] Ernest Bloomfield Zeisler, *Baker Street Chronology: Commentaries on The Sacred Writings of Dr. John H. Watson* (New York: Magico Magazine, 1983), 7.
[5] Zeisler, 7-8.

A Study in Scarlet

Watson notes that the 4 March was 'a foggy, cloudy morning, and a dun-coloured veil' covered the city. Holmes remarked that 'up to last night, we have had no rain for a week'. *Bell's Life in London* for Saturday 5 March 1881 notes that it rained during the night and morning of Friday 4 March.[1] *Lloyd's Weekly Newspaper* records in its weather column that from 27 February to 5 March it rained or snowed on three days, a total of .76 inches, but a majority of .47 inches of this precipitation occurred on Friday 4 March in the form of rain.[2] Furthermore, there was precipitation on the 27th and 28th in the form of snow, so it did not *rain* for a week before 4 March.[3] This strongly corroborates the year 1881.

On the afternoon of the 4th Holmes expressed his wish to attend a concert in which Norman-Néruda was to play a violin solo composed by Chopin. This statement raises several issues, and has been used variously by chronologists to shift both the days and the year of this case.[4] As there is no evidence in contemporaneous newspapers to corroborate that Norman-Néruda gave a performance of any kind on or near Friday 4 March 1881, and as Chopin never composed a violin solo, we must seek an explanation for these erroneous details.

The Friday 11 February 1881 edition of *Brief: The Week's News* contains the following excerpt: 'At the afternoon performance of Saturday's [5 February 1881] Popular Concerts, Herr Ignaz Brüll made his first appearance this season, and played in Goldmark's "suite" (in E major) for pianoforte and violin—with

---

[1] 'Grand Military and Household Brigade Steeple Chases', *Bell's Life in London and Sporting Chronicle,* 5 March 1881, No. 3,166, page 7.
[2] 'Remarks on the weather from Feb. 27 to March 5', *Lloyd's Weekly London Newspaper,* 6 March 1881, No. 1,198, page 3.
[3] 'Remarks on the weather from Feb. 27 to March 5', page 3.
[4] See Christ's, Baring-Gould's, and McQueen's discussions of the dating of *A Study in Scarlet.*

A Study in Scarlet

Madame Norman-Néruda at the latter instrument—and in some studies of Chopin for pianoforte alone'.[1] It would appear, then, that Holmes had attended this concert in February, shortly after Watson and he had moved into Baker Street—doubtless mentioning that Norman-Néruda would be playing and that Chopin would be played (by someone)—and that it was some other concert which Holmes attended on 4 March. Watson, when composing the manuscript for *A Study in Scarlet*, apparently conflated whichever concert Holmes attended on 4 March with the one which he attended on 5 February. The fact that Watson did not himself attend the concert on 4 March—because he 'was tired out in the afternoon'—explains why he did not remember the details of the performance.

On the morning of Saturday 5 March, Watson presented his own 'condensation' of several newspapers' articles about the crime. His summary of the *Standard* asserted that Drebber and Stangerson had left for Euston Station 'upon Tuesday, the 4th inst.' As the 4th was a Friday in 1881, however, an issue arises—an issue, by the way, which cannot be solved by selecting 1882, the only other conceivable year. According to the statement of the landlady herself, Drebber left his lodgings for the station about 8 p.m. on the 3rd. Lestrade's remark that Drebber and Stangerson 'had been seen together at Euston Station about half-past eight on the evening of the third' corroborates the landlady's statement, showing that the 3rd is the true date. Thus it would appear that the newspaper, or Watson's account of it, was wrong about both the day and the date. It was a Thursday, not a Tuesday; presumably this was the result of Watson's writing 'T'

---

[1] 'Music and the Drama', *Brief: the Week's News*, 11 February 1881, Vol. VII, No. 172, page 146.

A Study in Scarlet

(or some other such vague indicator) when making notes of the articles, and, when later consulting them, not checking if it was a Tuesday or a Thursday. We suspect that he mistakenly wrote 'the 4th' instead of 'the 3rd' as a result of noting that the murder was actually committed in the small hours of the morning of the 4th.

At the end of the narrative, we learn that Jefferson Hope died of an aneurism before he could be sentenced for his crimes. McQueen seizes upon this incident to object to 1881 as the correct year, arguing that the case could not have been solved on a Saturday (as in 1881) because Hope, before dying of his aneurism, was sentenced to appear before a magistrate, and this sentencing would not have been done on a Sunday.[1] What he overlooks is the fact that this was strictly a two-day case, and that Hope died 'On the very night after his capture', not the night of the day after his capture, which nullifies his argument, for it shows that Hope's sentencing would only have occurred on a Sunday if the year were 1882. Clearly the inspector at the police station—who, when Hope was first brought to him on Saturday the 5th, said that Hope 'will be put before the magistrates in the course of the week'—proceeded to have his associates arrange for Hope's trial to occur on the following Thursday while Hope was recounting his tale, after the conclusion of which the inspector informed Holmes and Watson that on Thursday 'your attendance will be required'.

A Study in Scarlet began on Friday 4 March 1881 and concluded on Saturday 5 March. Holmes and Watson's discussion of the case occurred on the following evening, 6 March.

---

[1] McQueen, 20-21.

2. The Sign of Four

First published February 1890

The events of *The Sign of Four* must necessarily have occurred prior to February 1890, when the account was first published. The pieces of evidence throughout the narrative conflict, some suggesting a date early in the 1880s, others a date towards the end of that decade. Inevitably there is disagreement amongst the chronologists; they argue generally for 1887 or 1888. The date of this case critically affects the dating of many subsequent ones, so we must weigh all of the available evidence in order to definitively establish its date.

Evidence for an Earlier Case

Watson remarks that his 'constitution has not got over the Afghan campaign yet'. He served, as noted above, until being wounded at Maiwand on 27 July 1880. This would seem to suggest that the case occurred within a few years of his service. He later adds that he was nursing his wounded leg, hit by a jezail bullet 'some time before'. This injury could only have been sustained during the Battle of Maiwand, his last military action, and as it was still aching with 'every change of the weather', this also favours a date within a few years of July 1880.

The Sign of Four

The apparent surprise with which Watson still regarded Holmes's powers—a demonstration of observation and deduction regarding Watson's sending a telegram and inferences from the appearance of Watson's watch—suggests an earlier date, not too long after the events of *A Study in Scarlet*.

Watson speaks of marvelling at Holmes's solution to the Jefferson Hope murder. This too suggests a date shortly after *A Study in Scarlet*, before many other cases had occurred, as he would not have been likely to refer to it with such admiration six or seven years after the fact and after having witnessed the solution of more remarkable cases.

When Mrs Hudson informed Holmes and Watson that Miss Morstan had arrived, Holmes said, 'Don't go, doctor. I should prefer that you remain.' He later said that 'He [Watson] and I have worked together before'. These statements seem to suggest that Watson had only joined Holmes on a few occasions thus far, indicating again a date in the early '80s when they were still in the initial stages of their partnership.

Evidence for a Later Case

Watson mentions 'the years that I had lived with him in Baker Street'. Such a phrase necessitates the passing of at least a few years, but more likely upwards of five, since *A Study in Scarlet*.

Watson remarks of Holmes that 'I had never known him to be wrong'. This points to a date before *The Yellow Face* of 3 April 1886, *The Five Orange Pips* of 23–24 September 1887, and *A Scandal in Bohemia* of 20–22 March 1888, in all of which cases Holmes was wrong to varying degrees.[1] It equally suggests that

---

[1] See our discussions of these three cases for the evidence for their dates.

Watson had seen Holmes solve quite a few cases, so it favours early 1886 most strongly. However, as we will see below, the case could not have occurred in 1886, so it seems that this comment was a bit of hyperbolic bluster by a Watson desirous of championing his friend to his readers, and it should not therefore be given much consideration as a piece of chronological evidence.

Jonathan Small says that he returned to England 'some three or four years ago'. Major Sholto died on 28 April 1882 after seeing Small at his window, having recently been notified in a letter from India (which had arrived no earlier than the beginning of that year) of something which caused him great alarm—evidently, as Holmes supposed, news of Small's escape. The treasure was not found for years after Sholto's death. All of this puts the case definitely no earlier than 1885.

While Small might have been able to reach England shortly after the aforementioned letter if he had sailed directly there, he specifically states that he was drawn hither and thither by events and his arrival in England thus considerably delayed. It is clear, therefore, that the letter was also delayed, either in being sent or in arriving, as that is the only possible explanation for the fact that although it took Small a long time to return to England, he still arrived within a few months of the letter. This is no unlikely supposition when we consider who would have been left at the Andaman Islands to tell Sholto of Small's escape. It must have been some old acquaintance, perhaps 'Lieutenant Bromley Brown', who informed Sholto that the prisoner had fled, and there is no reason to suppose that he had made any haste to send the letter—probably he was entirely unaware of its significance. Further delay would have been caused by the fact that the post apparently only left the Andaman Islands once per month on the 'relief-boat'.

Holmes asked if Watson's leg would stand 'a six-mile trudge', and later he again referred to 'a six-mile limp for a half-pay officer with a damaged tendo Achillis'. If this case had occurred in the first year or two of the partnership, Watson would not have been likely to briskly walk one mile, let alone six, as his leg was still definitely wounded at that time. We must interpret all of the references to the leg to indicate a lingering discomfort at the old site of the wound, though not something so serious as to prevent his taking some exercise.

Earlier or Later?

On the whole this evidence suggests that the case occurred in the late 1880s. The evidence in favour of an earlier date is limited and not absolute, while certain other evidence, including the mere presence of the pearls that Miss Morstan received for six years (see below, '1887 or 1888?'), definitively demonstrates that the case could not have taken place before 1887. The evidence for an earlier date, furthermore, may be discounted as follows.

Watson speaks of his leg wound later in the narrative as if it were no longer a fresh wound, but rather a lingering injury: 'an army surgeon with a weak leg', not a wounded leg. The wound in his leg seems at this point, then, to have been mostly healed. Perhaps it was flaring up and particularly bothering Watson, due to some change in the weather, either at the time of the case or when he penned the manuscript.

It is not unreasonable to suppose that, when he was writing the manuscript for *The Sign of Four*, Watson wished to commence the tale with an exciting anecdote and accordingly extrapolated one—the incident with the watch—which he certainly would not have forgotten from his early days with Holmes. No doubt he felt that this would not seem too out of place to his readers, for whom this would be only the second published case they would read.

Regarding Watson's expression of admiration for Holmes's deductions in *A Study in Scarlet,* we suspect not that he was more impressed by that case than by any intervening one, but rather that he wished to refer back to his only other published case (*A Study in Scarlet*) so that his readers could appreciate the reference. He certainly could have mentioned some other instance in which Holmes had made more remarkable deductions, but he would then have had to have provided a summary of that case so that his readers could understand just how insightful Holmes had been, and this would have been an awkward interruption to the flow of the narrative. Besides, it is only natural that Watson would take advantage of an opportunity to refer to his other published work as a means of advertising it.

We interpret Holmes's request that Watson remain for the interview and Watson's evident discomfort as mere joviality on the part of Holmes. Holmes may have noticed his friend's evident attraction to Miss Morstan and accordingly orchestrated for him to remain. Watson, presumably, expressed that he ought to leave not because he was unaccustomed to working with Holmes, but rather because he was discomfited by his attraction to Miss Morstan.

1887 or 1888?

Miss Morstan said that her father had obtained twelve months' leave in the year 1878. The fact that 'He disappeared upon the

The Sign of Four

3rd of December, 1878—nearly ten years ago'—would seem to put the events of *The Sign of Four* in autumn 1888. She then stated that 'About six years ago—to be exact, upon the 4th of May, 1882—an advertisement appeared in the *Times*'. This, conversely, suggests a date in late spring or summer 1888, probably sometime between April and August.

Thus far, the evidence favours 1888, but Miss Morstan noted that she responded to the advertisement posted by Thaddeus Sholto on 4 May 1882 and on the same day received a lustrous pearl, and that every year since then she had received another. She then opened a flat box which contained *six* of these pearls. She received one on the first year, 1882; thus the sixth pearl would have been received on 4 May *1887*. The 4 May 1888 cannot yet have happened, therefore, which places the case between 4 May 1887 and 3 May 1888. Blakeney offers the explanation that Miss Morstan may have had one of her pearls made into jewellery or otherwise separated it from the rest in the box,[1] but if this were the case, and the year were 1888, Holmes surely would have asked about the absent pearl, and Miss Morstan would have clarified its whereabouts.

This leaves us to conclude that when Miss Morstan said 'about six years ago', as noted above, her thoughts were already moving ahead to the approaching new year. Supposing that *The Sign of Four* occurred in autumn 1887, this is by no means an abnormal manner of thinking, especially given that nearly five and a half years had in fact passed and that saying either 'about five' or 'about six' would be equally imprecise. Hall similarly reasons that Miss Morstan's statement that she had received the

---

[1] T.S. Blakeney, *Sherlock Holmes: Fact or Fiction?* (London: John Murray, 1932), 63.

first pearl six years ago was a natural miscalculation caused by her looking at the six pearls and, remembering she had received one each year, thinking six years had passed.[1] Anyone might have made this simple mistake, and she was more likely than most given that she was obviously attracted to Watson, just as he was to her, and consequently would not have been thinking with full clarity of the matter at hand.

When Miss Morstan referred to a time period of about nine years as 'nearly ten', she was similarly anticipating that in the following year a decade would have passed. In further explanation of this statement, Bell believes that the grief and anxiety that Miss Morstan must have been feeling during this period would have made the time seem longer to her than it really was.[2] We think this quite probable, and we would add that her continued distress, when combined with the distraction of Watson's presence, could very well have led her to make imprecise statements.

Watson refers to his 'small brochure' entitled *A Study in Scarlet,* first published via his literary agent, Arthur Conan Doyle, in magazine form in December 1887 and as a book in July 1888. He had, therefore, by this time presumably drawn up the manuscript for that case. The fact that he refers to it as a brochure would seem to suggest that it was probably not yet published, and certainly had not been published as a book, thus indicating a date before July 1888 and likely prior to December 1887. Holmes, however, remarked that he had to investigate in a

---

[1] John Hall, *"I Remember the Date Very Well": A chronology of the Sherlock Holmes stories of Arthur Conan Doyle* (Romford, Essex: Ian Henry Publications, 1993), 31.
[2] H.W. Bell, *Sherlock Holmes and Dr Watson: The Chronology of their Adventures* (New York: Magico Magazine, 1984), 54.

disguise, as many of the criminal classes were beginning to recognize him, 'especially since our friend here took to publishing some of my cases'. This would seem to indicate a date after *A Study in Scarlet,* and possibly some other cases, had been published—and read by some of Holmes's adversaries. We speculate that this remark was made by Holmes in anticipation of the consequences that he feared would result from Watson's publishing *A Study in Scarlet* at the end of the year.

Holmes said of the Sholto brothers 'that they were six years looking for it [the treasure]'. As they began seeking the treasure in April 1882, it seems that the date of the case would be no sooner than the end of 1887. While autumn 1887 is only five and a half years, Holmes had an interest in emphasising the length of the search, and may have exaggerated somewhat. This hyperbole would also explain Watson's comment that it was strange that Thaddeus Sholto should write to Miss Morstan 'now, rather than six years ago', which phrase Blakeney uses in conjunction with the other references to years noted above in his argument for 1888.[1] His theory relies far too heavily upon these statements about elapsed times, which are only ever approximate at best; indeed, there is an example within *The Sign of Four* itself of such an imprecision when Holmes says that Major Sholto's death 'upon the 28th of April, 1882' was 'Four years later' than the death of Captain Morstan 'upon the 3rd of December, 1878', for this period of time is scarcely greater than three years. Thus we see that Holmes was given to exaggeration, and our supposition of hyperbole, which has the merit of acquitting Watson of having committed careless errors, is substantiated.

---

[1] Blakeney, 57.

The Sign of Four

Small said that he arrived in England three or four years ago. Four years, even from 1887, would put his arrival in 1883, yet he was definitely in Norwood on 28 April 1882. Evidently, then, Small did not accurately recall how long it had been since he had arrived. The earlier year of 1887 is more probable than 1888, for if it were 1887 then he would have been wrong by only one year, a more believable mistake than referring to a period of six years as three or four.

The points in favour of 1888, then, are Miss Morstan's two statements about the number of years that had elapsed; Holmes's comment about Watson publishing cases; and the number of years that the Sholto brothers spent seeking the treasure. The evidence for 1887, meanwhile, includes the number of pearls which Miss Morstan had received; the reference to *A Study in Scarlet* as a brochure; and the amount of time Jonathan Small was in England. The evidence of the pearls and the brochure is far more convincing than the remarks about years by Miss Morstan, which cannot be considered any more definite than those by Small, and for which we have given satisfactory explanations.

The Month and the Day

The events of *The Sign of Four* spanned five days in 1887. On the fourth day Watson read an article which stated that 'about three o'clock last Tuesday morning' Mordecai Smith left in the *Aurora*. When Holmes talked to Mrs Smith on the second day of the case, she said that her husband had 'been away since yesterday mornin''. The day on which the case began—when Miss Morstan called at Baker Street, and Thaddeus Sholto led Holmes, Watson, and Miss Morstan to Pondicherry Lodge—was, therefore, a Tuesday. The previous night Tonga had killed Bartholomew

The Sign of Four

Sholto, who had not been seen all day, and Small had absconded with the treasure in the *Aurora*. The river chase on the Thames occurred on the following Friday, and the case concluded on the Saturday morning, when Small told his story to Holmes, Watson, and Jones.

Miss Morstan received a letter postmarked 7 July on the day of her interview with Holmes and Watson, apparently establishing that as the date when the adventure began. This date, however, is impossible. Watson states that when they went to meet Sholto later on that first day 'It was a September evening'. It was not yet 7 p.m., but the street lamps were already lit; this would not have happened in July, as the sun would not have set until about 8:30, and twilight would have lasted past 9. On the night of the river chase, the 'last rays of the sun' were shining upon St Paul's about 7:15; again, this is more characteristic of a September sun. It most precisely matches April, which month Zeisler chooses,[1] but it is only by an overly literal interpretation of the ten years and six years mentioned by Miss Morstan, and an unjustifiable rejection of the patent references to September, that he arrives at this date. We believe that a bit of inaccuracy with regard to the precise time of the sunset is more likely than a blatant misstatement of the month.

Athelney Jones remarked that 'It is very hot for the time of year'. This is an unlikely statement if the case occurred in July, as it would have to have been exceptionally hot to warrant his saying this, whereas if it were in September, the day may very easily have been unusually hot. Bell[2] and McQueen,[3] each of whom also opts for a September date, both note that the meal

---

[1] Zeisler, 5.
[2] Bell, 50.
[3] McQueen, 82.

of oysters and grouse offered by Holmes to Athelney Jones would not have been available in July, and the 7 July date is definitively ruled out by the fact that, in 1887, 7 July was a Thursday (and in 1888 it was a Saturday), and as we have shown above, the first day must be a Tuesday.

Watson remarks in the small hours of the morning of the second day (Wednesday) that there was 'half a moon' showing. He further notes 'a moonbeam' and 'the moonshine' illuminating the features of Pondicherry Lodge. In the year 1887, the waning half-moon occurred on Saturday 10 September, three days after Watson made his remark (tentatively on Wednesday 7 September). The moon on the Wednesday would, then, have been gibbous and waning, closer to a half than full, and less than three quarters. It is hardly unreasonable to imagine that Watson would refer to a two-thirds-full moon as 'half a moon'. The date of 7 July is again ruled out by the fact that 5 July was the full moon, and it would still have been virtually full two days later. We acknowledge that 1888 is attractive insofar as there was a half-moon on Wednesday 12 September, and the case might fit nicely from Tuesday 11th through Saturday 15th, but in other respects 1888 is far less probable, as explained above.

In light of all of this, it is evident that the case occurred in September. That the 7 July date was in fact a misprint is confirmed by the following: Watson's literary agent, no doubt at Watson's instigation, wrote to the editor of *Lippincott's Magazine* on 6 March 1890 to say that 'there is one very obvious mistake which must be corrected in book form—in the second chapter the letter is headed July 7th'.[1] Why this directive was not heeded and future editions not amended is another mystery altogether.

In which week in September 1887 did the events occur? As noted above, the Friday of the river chase was referred to by Jones as an uncharacteristically warm day for the season. An unusually warm day in September is far more likely in the first half of the month than the second; thus we must opt to use the half-moon which occurred on the 10th, not the 24th (also a Saturday and therefore no more attractive with regard to the moon), as our guide, and we are able to state with certainty that, because Wednesday 7 September (Wednesday being the morning upon which Watson noted a half-moon) was only three days before a half-moon, this was the week of the case.

The events of *The Sign of Four*, therefore, began on Tuesday 6 September 1887 and concluded in the small hours of the morning of Saturday 10 September 1887. It is well worth noting that Watson became engaged to Mary Morstan late on the night of Friday the 9th.

---

[1] Arthur Conan Doyle, *The New Annotated Sherlock Holmes*, vol. 3, *The Novels*, ed. Leslie S. Klinger (New York: W.W. Norton & Company, 2006), 234.

3. A Scandal in Bohemia

First published July 1891

Watson states plainly that this case began on 20 March 1888. He was in civil practice at this time and also married, and he talks of the 'home-centred interests which rise up around the man who first finds himself master of his own establishment'. This suggests that he had only been married for a short time as of March 1888. Conversely, his statement that his marriage had caused Holmes and him to drift apart indicates at least a few months' time since the nuptials. Watson further notes that he heard 'From time to time' of cases in which Holmes was involved, including 'his summons to Odessa in the case of the Trepoff murder', 'the singular tragedy of the Atkinson brothers at Trincomalee', 'and the mission which he had accomplished so delicately and successfully for the reigning family of Holland'. This succession of three international cases is further evidence that several months have passed.

Watson, as noted above, became engaged to Mary Morstan on 9 September 1887. They would have had little reason to delay the marriage any lengthy amount of time, given both their mutual dearth of relations to accommodate and the fact that, as McQueen further argues, the two lovers were already relatively advanced in years and would have been eager to enter matrimony.[1] Watson would, however, have needed some time to set up in practice and be in a position to make a living before marrying, and thus we may suppose that they were married two or three months after their engagement, in November or December 1887. This would allow three or four clear months for Watson and Holmes to drift apart and at least as long for Holmes to solve his three international cases.

Watson mentions his wooing of Mary Morstan and the case which he entitled *A Study in Scarlet*. The dates selected for these above are therefore corroborated by the fact that they had already occurred by this time. The fact that he did not use the actual title *The Sign of Four* suggests that this case occurred before February 1890 (when *The Sign of Four* was first published), while his use of the title *A Study in Scarlet* confirms that December 1887 was in the past.

One possible objection to a date in the late 1880s for this case is that when the hereditary King of Bohemia arrived, Watson said, 'I think that I had better go, Holmes'. This is satisfactorily explained, however, when we consider how natural it would have been for Watson, after not seeing his friend or helping him with a case for an extended period of time, to have felt at least somewhat out of place intruding upon a private consultation— especially given the mysterious and secretive nature of the client. What is more, it is only natural that his conscience would urge him, as a newly-wed man, to be responsible, return to his home and wife, and not become entangled once again in adventures with his erstwhile associate. In any case, Holmes commanded his friend to stay, delighted to have such a fortuitous opportunity of having him once more at his side.

---

[1] McQueen, 78.

A Scandal in Bohemia

As to the precise date of the case, in 1888 20 March was a Tuesday. Baring-Gould objects to this year because Holmes remarked that he had three days to solve the case and that the betrothal (of Wilhelm Gottsreich Sigismond von Ormstein, Grand Duke of Cassel-Falstein, and hereditary King of Bohemia, to Clotilde Lothman von Saxe-Meningen, second daughter of the King of Scandinavia) was to be publicly announced on the following Monday, leading him to conclude that the first day of the case must have been a Friday.[1] Zeisler, following similar reasoning, also chooses a Friday,[2] while Bell interprets Holmes's comment to mean three full days and accordingly says that the first day was a Thursday.[3] Blakeney, meanwhile, argues that the case was on Wednesday 20 March 1889 because Holmes would not have counted the Wednesday or the Sunday as one of the three days,[4] but he gives no reason for why Holmes would not have intended to work on a Sunday with such an important case on hand, and he also disregards Watson's explicitly stated year of 1888 without any justification.

That so many astute chronologists should have let this statement lead them astray is shocking when one considers that it does not, in fact, contradict a Tuesday as the first day. As McQueen explains, although the hereditary King of Bohemia implied—ambiguously—that Adler would send the photograph on Monday, the day of the betrothal, she would actually have had to have sent the photograph away several days before the Monday if she wanted it to arrive on Monday and affect or

---

[1] William S. Baring-Gould, *Sherlock Holmes of Baker Street: A Life of The World's First Consulting Detective* (New York: Bramhall House, 1962), 73.
[2] Zeisler, 73. He selects 1889 as the year due to his erroneously putting Watson's marriage in January of that year.
[3] Bell, 56.
[4] Blakeney, 59.

A Scandal in Bohemia

prevent the announcement.¹ Holmes, it would seem, predicted that she would have to send the photograph away on Saturday morning in order for it to arrive at its international destination on the following Monday, and, as it was already after 8 p.m. on Tuesday when he mentioned that 'we have three days yet' to solve the case, he was clearly indicating that he had Wednesday, Thursday, and Friday to recover the photograph before Adler sent it away.

The case began, then, on Tuesday 20 March 1888. Watson returned at 3 p.m. the following day, Wednesday 21 March. The lamps were being lit at 6:50 p.m.; this is appropriate for March. On the morning of Thursday 22 March, they repaired to Briony Lodge to find that Irene Adler had flown, and the case concluded.

---

¹ McQueen, 109-110.

4. The Red-Headed League

First published August 1891

This case presents a number of difficulties, arising primarily from the conflicting dates that Watson presents to the reader. By establishing what evidence is substantiated by facts, however, we can definitively date this troublesome case.

Watson claims that it occurred 'in the autumn of last year', which would be (from the time of publication) autumn 1890, and we can accept this as the correct year for a number of reasons. Firstly, Holmes commented that Watson had helped him in 'many of my most successful cases' and that he had 'chronicle[d]' many of these, both of which facts suggest a date after February 1890, after the publication of at least *A Study in Scarlet* and *The Sign of Four*. Secondly, the *Morning Chronicle* which contained the Red-Headed League advertisement which Jabez Wilson consulted was unequivocally said to be dated 'April 27, 1890', a Sunday 'Just two months ago', and there is no reason to doubt the accuracy of this statement.[1] The argument might be made that it would have been highly irregular for a job interview to

---

[1] Brend claims that the *Morning Chronicle* would not have been published on a Sunday (Gavin Brend, *My Dear Holmes: A Study in Sherlock* [London: George Allen & Unwin Ltd, 1951], 93). He appears to have been unaware that its publication was indefinitely suspended in 1865. Watson clearly did not record the name of the paper and made a guess when composing the narrative for publication.

have been held on a Sunday; we would reply that if it were any other day there would hardly have been so many red-headed men not working and able to spend their day waiting to apply to such an extraordinary position, not to mention the fact that it is not at all surprising that such an exceptional institution, which was in any case fake, would choose not to operate during normal business hours. Thirdly, Watson married in late 1887, as we have shown above, and he informs us that he called upon Holmes, indicating that he was no longer living at Baker Street. He makes no mention of his wife, but he does refer to his medical practice and his 'house in Kensington', so we may be sure that he was married to Mary Watson, *née* Morstan, at this time. Lastly, Watson explains that his practice 'is never very absorbing'; he says similarly at the time of *The Final Problem*—indisputably April 1891—that 'The practice is quiet',[1] rendering 1890 more likely than any earlier year.

Wilson stated that he worked for the league for eight weeks. Given that his interview was on the day of the advertisement (Sunday 27 April) and that he began working the very next day, the eighth week would have been the 16–21 June. McQueen argues that Wilson was not paid for his last week of work and thus, since he received thirty-two pounds in total, he must have worked nine weeks,[2] while Blakeney insists that Watson incorrectly recorded the total earnings of Wilson.[3] Both of these explanations, besides flagrantly disregarding Wilson's explicit statement, are compromised by their baseless assumption that Clay was so parsimonious as to not leave Wilson his final week's wages along with the note of dissolution. There is no evidence

---

[1] Short, FINA, 545.
[2] McQueen, 114.
[3] Blakeney, 78.

The Red-Headed League

to suggest that he would not or did not do this; in fact, there is proof to the contrary, for we can be sure that the rather petulant Wilson would have told Holmes if he had been cheated of his final four pounds as part of this 'expensive joke' (whereas, having received it with the note, he would have had no special cause for mentioning it). Thus far it appears that the case occurred on Saturday 21 June.

There is, however, an objection to accepting that the case occurred in June, arising from the fact that Wilson, on the day of his visit to Holmes, produced the card-board which he had found that morning on the door of his erstwhile office announcing that 'THE RED-HEADED LEAGUE IS DISSOLVED. OCT. 9, 1890.' This supposed date of dissolution is supported by Watson's earlier statement that the case occurred in the autumn, but it is completely irreconcilable with the fact that the newspaper advertisement from eight weeks earlier had a date of 27 April. We must now proceed to a deeper analysis of the facts to finally determine which date is correct.

Holmes says on the first day of the case that 'To-day is Saturday', and this day of the week is corroborated repeatedly throughout the account. In 1890, 9 October was a Thursday; 21 June, conversely, was a Saturday, supporting this as the correct date of Holmes's entrance into the case. Wilson says specifically that Vincent Spaulding showed him the *Morning Chronicle* advertisement at the shop 'just this day eight weeks'. Since 27 April was a Sunday, this suggests that the day of the case should be a Sunday as well, but we know that Holmes, not Wilson, was correct because the bank was closed on the day following the attempted robbery, and banks were only closed on Sundays.

The chronologists who maintain that the 9 October date is somehow more absolute than the 27 April date are compelled to resort to some questionable explanations as to how Watson's handwriting compromised both the 27 April date and (because it is not a Saturday) the very 9 October date upon which their position is based. Dakin, citing Sayers for support, asserts that the respective dates ought to be 4 August and 11 October[1]; this, however, results in a separation of nearly ten weeks—far too long to fit with Wilson's eight weeks. Part of his evidence is that Wilson would not wear both an overcoat and a frock coat in June,[2] but it is far more reasonable to suppose that there was a cool day in June than that Watson allowed two incorrect dates to be sent to the publishers. Bell, meanwhile, selects 9 August and 4 October but offers no explanation for the many conflicting dates that he alters save that Watson read a '4' for a '9',[3] and, though this is in itself possible (though not probable), the many issues that he leaves unaddressed negate his theory.

In the hope of dispelling any further doubt as to the validity of the 27 April date, we now submit a hitherto overlooked piece of substantiating evidence. Holmes made a remark about attending the Sarasate concert at St James's Hall 'this [Saturday] afternoon', and the *Standard* of London of Thursday 19 June 1890 does indeed announce 'SARASATE'S THIRD and LAST CONCERT, St. James's Hall, Saturday Afternoon Next, at 3.0'.[4] The programme included music by Max Bruch—German, as Holmes notes—but also Mackenzie (presumably Alexander), who was influenced by German composers, and "Le Chant du Rossignol".[5] This could mean either Saturday 21 June or

---

[1] Dakin, 49-50.
[2] Dakin, 49.
[3] Bell, 70-71.
[4] 'Sarasate', *The Standard*, 19 June 1890, No. 20, 576, page 1.
[5] 'Sarasate', page 1.

Saturday 28 June, depending on the intended usage of the modifier 'next' by the newspaper; it is evident, however, from the contextual evidence of other passages in this newspaper that it is 21 June.

Newspaper sources show that Sarasate played again at St James's Hall on the afternoon of Saturday 18 October 1890, but not at any time closer than that to 9 October, and the 18th has no merit as a possible date for the case. We would further note that our supposition that Watson conflated the details of two concerts, referring erroneously to an earlier one, in *A Study in Scarlet* was based upon the fact that he did not attend it and therefore had no reason to remember or even to have known its details. The circumstances in this instance are quite different as Watson did attend, rendering him far less likely to have made a similar error and effectively precluding the possibility of his having conflated the concert of 18 October with some other one that they attended on the day of the case. October is, therefore, conclusively rejected in favour of June, leaving us to explain the inconsistencies, namely the references to autumn and 9 October.

The date of 9 October which was posted on the door of the dissolved League is decidedly inaccurate. Perhaps it was a final jest at the expense of Jabez Wilson which his phoney employers could not resist. Having already arranged that he would be given a false address for the new premises and, upon setting forth in search of them, find himself at 'a manufactory of artificial knee-caps', they proceeded to further befuddle the pawnbroker by posting a future date upon the notice of dissolution, giving him some little false hope that the League was not yet fully dissolved. Holmes and Watson's 'roar of laughter' at 'the comical side of the affair' upon Wilson's showing them the notice of dissolution may be quite satisfactorily explained by such an interpretation.

The Red-Headed League

The reference to autumn is obviously a blatant error on the part of Watson, as there is no evidence in the account to suggest that it occurred in autumn, while there is strong proof that it occurred in June. The precise cause of this error may never be known, but we may surmise that Watson simply conflated the season of this case with that of another. Perhaps he forgot to record the date and, seeing his note about the placard stating 9 October, rather carelessly wrote that the case occurred in autumn without due reflection.

The most bizarre and singular case of the League of Red-Headed Men occurred on Saturday 21 June 1890. This is one of only three recorded cases from this year.[1]

---

[1] Short, FINA, 537. For our discussion of the connection of this case with *A Case of Identity*, see the following chapter.

5. A Case of Identity

First published September 1891

At the commencement of this case a series of comments leads the reader to believe that the date was a few weeks after the events recorded in *A Scandal in Bohemia*. Watson was living away from Baker Street, and Holmes remarked to him that 'I forgot that I had not seen you for some weeks'. He showed him a golden snuffbox which was 'a little souvenir from the King of Bohemia in return for my assistance in the case of the Irene Adler papers'. The king had presumably given Holmes this gift not long after Adler's case, so *A Case of Identity* would appear to have occurred in April 1888. This supposition may be strengthened by the fact that Holmes mentioned a recent case for 'the reigning family of Holland', for it is possible that this is a reference to the same 'mission which he had accomplished so delicately and successfully for the reigning family of Holland'[1] shortly before *A Scandal in Bohemia*.

Watson remarks of Holmes that 'Only once had I known him to fail, in the case of the King of Bohemia and of the Irene Adler photograph'. This confirms what was already beyond a doubt, namely that *A Case of Identity* occurred after *A Scandal in Bohemia*. It also shows us that Watson did not consider either *The Yellow*

---

[1] Short, SCAN, 4.

A Case of Identity

Face of 1886 or *The Five Orange Pips* of 1887[1] to be a failure for Holmes. With regard to the former case this is understandable, for although Holmes had an erroneous theory and was therefore wrong, neither he nor anyone else suffered for it; as to the latter, though Holmes was guilty of negligence insofar as he underestimated the danger to his client with dire consequences, Watson apparently did not consider that he was ever really involved enough to have personally failed.

The evidence so far favours a spring 1888 date, but there are two issues which contradict this. The first objection is that in *The Red-Headed League* Holmes referred to a conversation that he had with Watson 'the other day, just before we went into the very simple problem presented by Miss Mary Sutherland',[2] about the relative eccentricity of life and fiction. That conversation is in fact the very one which constitutes the opening pages of this account, and which begins with Holmes remarking that 'life is infinitely stranger than anything which the mind of man could invent'. This piece of evidence would place the case in mid-June 1890.

The other issue is that Miss Sutherland advertised for her missing groom 'in last Saturday's *Chronicle*', which states that 'on the morning of the 14th, a gentleman named Hosmer Angel' went missing. This was the morning of the wedding, which 'was last Friday', and in 1888 the only months in which the 14th was a Friday were September and December, while in 1890 only February, March, and November had a Friday the 14th. Hall[3] and McQueen[4] both put the case in the week of 17 September 1888,

---

[1] See our discussions of these two cases for the evidence for their dates.
[2] Short, REDH, 30.
[3] Hall, 16.
[4] McQueen, 111.

but cite no evidence beyond that of the advertisement. Dakin opts for 1889 and argues for September by noting that Holmes and Watson 'sat on either side of the fire'[1]; but McQueen, despite choosing September himself, undermines this evidence by noting that the fire may very well not have been lit.[2]

We are left to determine which of these three sets of facts is the most definite. The wedding being on a Friday seems quite certain, as Holmes and Miss Sutherland both confirmed it. Watson might have incorrectly copied the newspaper advertisement, and thus the reference to the Friday of the wedding being the 14th of the month may be inaccurate. The fact that Watson had not yet seen the snuffbox which Holmes received from the King of Bohemia, as well as the repeated reference to the reigning family of Holland, both strongly suggest that this case occurred a few weeks after *A Scandal in Bohemia*, but, as we will see below, Watson was very busy in spring 1888 and scarcely saw Holmes before June. We may be sure that the dialogue given by Watson, or something very much like it, actually passed between the two friends on one of his rare visits that spring, but, as this case from 1890 was meant to be one of the first cases published after *A Scandal in Bohemia*, Watson, wishing to share with his readers the gifts which Holmes had received, took the liberty of referring to them out of context, as the cases of the King of Bohemia and the reigning family of Holland would be fresh in his readers' minds.

Besides Holmes's remark in *The Red-Headed League*, there is further evidence for an 1890 date in Watson's reference in this account to 'the case of the King of Bohemia and of the Irene

---

[1] Dakin, 55.
[2] McQueen, 111.

A Case of Identity

Adler photograph...the weird business of the Sign of Four, and the extraordinary circumstances connected with the Study in Scarlet'. The fact that Watson referred to *The Sign of Four* by its publication title, while he had no formal title yet for *A Scandal in Bohemia*, indicates that the case occurred after the first publication of *The Sign of Four* in February 1890. Furthermore, Miss Sutherland's use of a typewriter to supplement her income indubitably favours as late a date as possible, given that the first typewriter dealership in Britain opened only in 1886.

In view of our hypothesis, explained above, that Watson's practice was rather slow in June 1890, we must address his seemingly contradictory comment in this account that 'A professional case of great gravity was engaging my own attention at the time, and the whole of the next day I was busy at the bedside of the sufferer'. Though it may seem to suggest that he was generally busy at this time, this statement does not actually indicate anything more than that Watson happened to have a demanding patient just at this moment; he may very well have had little to do before and after this.

Supposing that Holmes's statements in *The Red-Headed League* regarding the case of Miss Mary Sutherland are accurate—and, after all, they are more to be relied upon than the references to gifts—this case must have occurred in mid-June 1890. Christ observes that throughout the case only warm-weather clothing is mentioned[1]; this effectively eliminates October through April, strongly supporting June as the month. Given that in June 1890 the 14th was a Saturday, it appears that Watson made a minor error in translating his notes into a full narrative, and that the date of the *Chronicle* advertisement itself, not of the wedding, was

---

[1] Christ, 11.

the 14th. Miss Sutherland did not consult Holmes on Sunday the 15th, for if she had she would not have said 'last Saturday'. She heard of Holmes 'from Mrs. Etherege', probably on Saturday or Sunday; she argued with her step-father before consulting him; and she declared that she 'can't sleep a wink at night'. All of this indicates the passing of a few days and nights since the wedding on Friday. Given how anxious the young woman was about the situation, however, we can imagine that her frustration at receiving no reply to her advertisement on Saturday or Sunday would have led her to consult Holmes on Monday.

We can say with certainty that the case occurred early in the week of 16 June, and we believe that Monday 16 June 1890 was the first day and that it ended the following day with the interview with Mr Windibank.

6. The Boscombe Valley Mystery

First published October 1891

This case is, for our purposes, remarkable only for the fact that some chronologists must needs dispute its patently indicated date. It opens with Watson and his wife, Mary, discussing whether he could spare the time to join Holmes in investigating the Boscombe Valley tragedy. Watson asserted that his practice was quite demanding at the moment, to which his wife replied that 'Anstruther would do your work for you'. The events of this case, then, must have happened after Watson's marriage in late 1887, but before June 1890, by which time Watson's patients had diminished considerably.[1]

Holmes stated that 'On June 3—that is, on Monday last—' the murder occurred. In 1889, but not in 1888, 1890, or any subsequent year until 1895 (four years after the publication of the case), 3 June was a Monday, so 1889 must be the year. The inquest was held on Tuesday the 4th, and the case was 'on Wednesday brought before the magistrates at Ross, who have referred the case to the next assizes'. Holmes apparently was not called in to the case on the Thursday, for if he had been, he would, as Bell sensibly observes, have referred to Wednesday as 'yesterday'.[2] It would seem, then, that Holmes was summoned

---

[1] As noted in our discussions of *The Red-Headed League* and *A Case of Identity*.
[2] Bell, 65.

on Friday the 7th. On the following day he, along with Watson (who had, in the end, joined him), visited Boscombe Pool, the scene of the murder, then had a private interview with John Turner in which Holmes uncovered the whole truth of the affair, bringing the case to a successful conclusion.

This case lasted from Friday 7 June to Saturday 8 June 1889.

7. The Five Orange Pips

First published November 1891

The task of dating the case of John Openshaw and the five orange pips is no easy one. Watson begins by informing us that 'between the years '82 and '90, I am faced by so many [cases] which present strange and interesting features, that it is no easy matter to know which to choose and which to leave'. He then proceeds to list a series of notable cases which occurred during 'The year '87' and concludes by stating that he chose to present this one due to its 'singular features'.

Thus far we are safely in the year 1887. Further evidence in support of this is that John Openshaw told Holmes that 'It was in January, '85, that my poor father met his end, and two years and eight months have elapsed since then'. This definitely places the case in September 1887, as does Watson's statement that it was in 'the latter days of September'. Given his repeated references to the 'equinoctial gales', we may presume with some confidence that it occurred close to 23 September, the day of the equinox. This day itself was a Friday, which would enable Watson to be busy working on the following day, Saturday. It would appear, then, that Openshaw consulted Holmes on Friday 23 September 1887 and that Holmes spent Saturday the 24th searching for his murderers.

Unfortunately, Watson does not leave us with these facts alone. He adds the notice that 'My wife was on a visit to her aunt's,[1] and for a few days I was a dweller once more in my old quarters at Baker Street'. Here we encounter multiple issues. In the first place, we must recall that Mary Morstan, at the commencement of the case entitled *The Sign of Four*, told Holmes that 'My father...sent me home when I was quite a child. My mother was dead, and I had no relative in England.'[2] The explanation of this contradiction may lie in the fact that Mary, being very fond of Mrs Cecil Forrester—who, Watson notes, acted very 'motherly'[3] towards her—was in the habit of referring to her affectionately as 'aunt', which phraseology would no doubt have been adopted by Watson after their marriage. Alternatively, and perhaps more likely, it may be that Mary was visiting an aunt on the Continent or elsewhere; note well that she told Holmes that she had no relative *in England*, but said nothing of the rest of the world. It would be natural, too, that if this aunt were her closest living relative, she should wish to consult her about the approaching wedding.

The second point of controversy in the aforementioned sentence is that Watson refers to Mary as his wife. Surely, if this case did indeed occur in late September 1887, he would not yet have been married, having only become engaged on 9 September. His writing 'wife' instead of '*fiancée*' in the manuscript which he submitted to the publisher was doubtless the result of his writing this account several years after being married, at

---

[1] The original *Strand* magazine text has her not at her aunt's but 'on a visit to her mother's' (Arthur Conan Doyle, *The Original Illustrated Sherlock Holmes* [Secaucus: Castle Books, 1981], 69). This obvious error was corrected in later editions.
[2] Long, SIGN, 153.
[3] Long, SIGN, 193.

which point he was firmly in the habit of referring to her as his wife.

Another difficulty which presents itself is that on the second day of the case Watson states that 'All day I was engaged in my professional work'. It is evident from this that sometime in mid-September he secured a job as a doctor in some capacity, obviously in order to prepare to support himself and Mary after their impending marriage. It is consonant with Watson's chivalrous character that he would feel the need to be well-established in life and wholly able to support Miss Morstan before he would marry her. At this time, he was probably working for another doctor, perhaps on an as-needed basis, for he did not work every day.[1] In any case, he would soon after marriage acquire his own practice.[2]

The final issue—that Watson was apparently on a visit to Baker Street—is a formidable one, for we know that on Friday 7 October 1887 Watson was definitely still living at Baker Street.[3] It is unrealistic to suppose that he moved away and back within a two-week period, so we must accept the only alternative, however improbable it may seem—namely that he was in fact neither married nor living anywhere but at 221B Baker Street at the time of this case—and seek an explanation for this incongruity.

The sentence which gives rise to this problem does not flow naturally with the rest of the paragraph, and reads almost as an

---

[1] Short, NOBL, 224-225. Not long after this case, Watson says that 'I had remained indoors all day' and 'lay listless', clearly not the activities of a doctor in regular practice.
[2] Short, STOC, 354. 'Shortly after my marriage I had bought a connection in the Paddington district.'
[3] See our discussion of *The Noble Bachelor*, which has more substantial evidence for dating than this case does.

added afterthought. We believe that the publishing editor, fearing that readers of the cases being serialised in the *Strand* magazine would be confused by Watson's apparently sudden return to living at Baker Street without explanation following the first four adventures in which he specifically mentioned living elsewhere, asked Watson to provide a statement to clarify his living situation at the time. Watson, we surmise, replied succinctly with some such remark as 'I was at Baker Street and my wife at her aunt's'. The publisher, unacquainted with the details of Watson's personal life and marriage, then wrongly assumed that he was married at the time of this case and misunderstood this to mean that he and Mary had both left their new marital home, the former to visit Holmes and the latter to visit her aunt, whereas in truth Watson was still living with Holmes, and Mary was either still living with her 'aunt' Mrs Forrester (she would not, after all, have left her employer without giving her sufficient notice to find a new governess) or visiting a true aunt abroad. The fact that Watson had started practicing again as noted above would only have further misled the editor into thinking he had left Baker Street.

One last point of note in this case is Holmes's comment that 'I have been beaten four times—three times by men and once by a woman'. We need not follow Bell,[1] Blakeney,[2] Christ,[3] Zeisler,[4] and Dakin[5] in subscribing to the fallacy that Holmes could only be referring to Irene Adler, and that this case must therefore have occurred after *A Scandal in Bohemia*. Effie Munro successfully hid

---

[1] Bell, 55.
[2] Blakeney, 59.
[3] Christ, 13.
[4] Zeisler, 78.
[5] Dakin, 62.

The Five Orange Pips

her secret from everyone, including Holmes, with her child's yellow mask in April 1886,[1] and though Holmes was not 'beaten' (in the sense that he was not directly competing with Effie Munro in the same way as with Irene Adler) but rather outwitted, he was nonetheless upset enough about his erroneous deductions to ask Watson to use the case as a warning to him against overconfidence in the future. Conclusive as this is, it is nevertheless worth adding that, even if this were not the defeat at the hands of a woman referred to by Holmes, there are sufficient unrecorded cases prior to 1887 that one of them could certainly contain an instance of some other woman beating him. Besides, if the woman referred to here were in fact Irene Adler, Holmes would no doubt have called her *the* woman, not *a* woman.

Having shown that the conflicts which arise from placing this case in 1887 may be reasonably explained, we have happily obviated the need to consider any other years, an odious eventuality which would have led to great difficulties in seeking to explain the multiple patent references to 1887. We may, therefore, confidently declare that Holmes and Watson were engaged on this case on 23 and 24 September 1887.

---

[1] See our discussion of *The Yellow Face* for the evidence for its date.

8. The Man with the Twisted Lip

First published December 1891

Watson tells us at the beginning of the account that this case began 'One night—it was in June, '89'. He was living with his wife, Mary, and he was engaged in professional practice, for he remarks that he 'was newly come back from a weary day' of patients. This agrees completely with his 'fairly long list' of patients which he had on 6 June 1889.[1]

Watson told Isa Whitney that it was the night of 'Friday, June 19'. This is a problem, for in 1889 19 June was a Wednesday. It was not a Friday until 1891, but by June 1891 Holmes was supposedly dead and certainly not solving cases in London.[2] It is, however, certain that the day of the case could not have been a Wednesday because it was 'Last Monday' that Neville St Clair disappeared, and when Holmes told him that his wife did not receive his letter until 'yesterday', St Clair bemoaned 'What a week she must have spent' worrying. He obviously would not have referred to two days as a week, so Wednesday the 19th is eliminated, and it cannot be Wednesday the 26th because then 'Last Monday' would no longer be the day of St Clair's disappearance, and the phrase 'on Monday', used repeatedly by

---

[1] Short, BOSC, 75.
[2] See our discussion of *The Final Problem*.

The Man with the Twisted Lip

Holmes in his conversation with Mrs St Clair, would refer to the 24th, the wrong Monday.

Evidently, then, Watson mistook his dates when writing the manuscript for this case. After he told Whitney that it was Friday the 19th, the latter protested with 'Good heavens! I thought it was Wednesday. It *is* Wednesday.' Probably what actually passed between the two men was that Watson said simply 'It is Friday', and Whitney, who was delirious from the effects of his opium usage, replied by declaring that 'I thought it was Wednesday. It *is* Wednesday, June 19'. Watson, when writing the manuscript two years later, apparently failed to check his dates, and misallocated Whitney's words to himself.

Thus the case began on the night of Friday 21 June 1889. Its events continued into the following day, so it concluded on Saturday 22 June.

9. The Blue Carbuncle

First published January 1892

'I had called upon my friend Sherlock Holmes upon the second morning after Christmas', Watson remarks. This must be a Christmas after his marriage, for Holmes told him that 'When I see you, my dear Watson, with a week's accumulation of dust upon your hat, and when your wife allows you to go out in such a state, I shall fear that you also have been unfortunate enough to lose your wife's affection'. Watson was, furthermore, practicing as a doctor, for he said that 'In that case I shall continue my professional round'.

The case must, therefore, have been on 27 December in a year between 1887 and 1890, for by December 1891 Holmes was presumed dead.[1] It could not have been 1890, for in the winter of 1890–1891 Holmes was busy with a case for the French Government.[2] It likewise could not have been 27 December 1889, for in *The Valley of Fear* of early January 1890 Watson states that 'A long series of sterile weeks lay behind us'.[3] It seems highly improbable that it occurred in 1887, for in March 1888 Watson stated that he had hardly seen Holmes since his marriage, only

---

[1] Again, see our discussion of *The Final Problem*.
[2] Short, FINA, 537.
[3] Long, VALL, 476. See our discussion of this case for the evidence for its date.

The Blue Carbuncle

hearing occasionally from secondary sources of some of his cases, and Holmes remarked to Watson that he was not aware that he had returned to civil practice. A further point against 1887 is that *A Study in Scarlet* was published in the *Beeton's Christmas Annual* of that year, and we may be sure that Watson would not have failed to show his first literary endeavour to Holmes had he visited him that December.[1] It is quite clear, then, that this case could only have occurred in 1888. Christ supposes that the theft of the blue carbuncle, which occurred on 'the 22nd inst.', must have been on a weekday, since Horner had gone to the hotel on a professional call and Breckenridge was open for business at the market.[2] In 1888, 22 December was a Saturday, but there is no reason to suppose that Horner would not have worked on a Saturday, and, given that this was the busy Christmas season, it would have been only natural for Breckenridge to be open at the market on a Saturday.

Watson remarked that 'of the last six cases which I have added to my notes, three have been entirely free of any legal crime'. Holmes proceeded to confirm that these three cases were *A Scandal in Bohemia*, *A Case of Identity*, and *The Man with the Twisted Lip*, though he did not use any of their publication titles but rather named the cases by referring to their principal actors. This would seem to suggest that this case occurred sometime after the latest of the three named by Holmes, but *A Case of Identity* occurred in June 1890, and we know that this case could not have happened in December 1890. Therefore, this statement of Holmes's must be understood to be a fabrication of Watson's in

---

[1] Baring-Gould, who puts the case in 1887, claims that this happened (92), but offers no explanation as to why it was not mentioned in the account, thus inadvertently raising an objection to his own chosen year.
[2] Christ, 14.

which he conveniently referred back to the first six cases of the series then in the process of being published (this case being the seventh) in order to prove a point about the nature of the cases that he was presenting to the public. Again, he is referring to cases with which his readers would be familiar to ensure that they would be able to appreciate the references.

The case of the blue carbuncle occurred on Thursday 27 December 1888. In selecting this date, we are alone amongst the chronologists, and we trust that we have fulfilled Brend's 'secret hope that the next writer on this subject will unearth some evidence to show that we are all wrong and that *The Blue Carbuncle* in fact occurred in some other year [than 1889]'.[1]

---

[1] Brend, 92.

10. The Speckled Band

First published February 1892

At the beginning of this account Watson tells us that he has 'notes of the seventy odd cases in which I have during the last eight years studied the methods of my friend Sherlock Holmes'. This manuscript, then, appears to have been completed by Watson in 1889, given that his partnership with Holmes began in 1881; this fact is quite useful in progressing with the chronology, as it proves that sometimes the comments in the introductory paragraphs of Watson's accounts were not written in the year of publication.

Watson explains that 'The events in question occurred in the early days of my association with Holmes, when we were sharing rooms as bachelors, in Baker Street'. He then continues: 'It was early in April, in the year '83'. His descriptions of trees and bushes 'throwing out their first green shoots' and of 'the sweet promise of the spring' corroborate this season. McQueen argues (in favour of an 1882 date for *A Study in Scarlet*) that if the partnership began in 1881, 1883 would not be considered 'the early days'.[1] We must remember, however, what McQueen clearly forgets, namely that Watson was writing from the viewpoint of the late '80s, when anything which occurred before

---

[1] McQueen, 20.

The Speckled Band

his marriage would have seemed to him to be from an altogether different epoch of his life.[1]

The Speckled Band occurred in early April 1883. Lacking any more precise evidence for determining the date of the case, we accept the 'general agreement that 4 April is the day'.[2] Though most of the events occurred on that day, the conclusion did not come until the small hours of the following morning, so this was actually a two-day case that continued into the 5th.

---

[1] Note how he specifically refers to their days as bachelors.
[2] Dakin, 75.

11. The Engineer's Thumb

First published March 1892

Watson first tells us concerning this case that 'At the time the circumstances made a deep impression upon me, and the lapse of two years has hardly served to weaken the effect'. This suggests a date in 1890, given that the account was published in 1892. In the very next sentence, however, he continues, 'It was in the summer of '89, not long after my marriage, that the events occurred which I am now about to summarize'. This statement not only contradicts the previous one, but also is itself erroneous, for summer 1888, not 1889, was the first summer succeeding his marriage.[1] It would seem that Watson originally wrote the manuscript in 1890 and failed to update the phrase 'lapse of two years' when publication did not occur until 1892, and that he carelessly allowed the '89 to be published in place of the correct '88.

Watson then proceeds to inform us that he 'had returned to civil practice, and had finally abandoned Holmes in his Baker Street rooms, although I continually visited him, and occasionally even persuaded him to forego his Bohemian habits so far as to

---

[1] The evidence in other cases for placing the marriage in late 1887, rather than 1888, is stronger than any indicators to the contrary here.

The Engineer's Thumb

come and visit us'.[1] This is definitely indicative of a time shortly after Watson's marriage, which places the case in summer 1888. As Watson acquired his practice in March 1888 and did not see much if anything of Holmes for three months after that, the case cannot have occurred before June.[2] The statement about continually visiting Holmes conflicts, however, with the evidence of *The Stock-Broker's Clerk*, and the only explanation that makes sense of that statement is that this case occurred some weeks after *The Stock-Broker's Clerk* (which was in June 1888) and that, between that case—the first time Watson had joined Holmes for a case since *A Scandal in Bohemia*—and this one, the two men had begun once again to see a great deal of one another.

Watson further remarks that 'My practice had steadily increased', which would be the natural result of his three months or more of assiduous work since acquiring it in March. He also notes that 'I happened to live at no very great distance from Paddington Station', thereby showing us that the practice which he had purchased from Mr Farquhar earlier in the year served also as his home.[3]

On the night of Hatherley's adventure, the moon was bright enough for the unfortunate engineer to comment that 'through the window [of a bedroom] the moon was shining brightly'. He then further stated that upon looking out of the window, he reflected upon 'How quiet and sweet and wholesome the garden looked in the moonlight'. If the moon were bright enough to cast light through a window and for Hatherley to clearly see the garden below him by its light, it must have been very nearly full.

---

[1] The first time that Holmes visited Watson was at the time of *The Stock-Broker's Clerk*, and he went again shortly afterwards for *The Crooked Man*.
[2] See our discussion of *The Stock-Broker's Clerk*.
[3] Short, STOC, 354.

In June 1888 the full moon was on the 23rd, in July it was again on the 23rd, and in August it was on the 21st. We must now determine upon which of these three summer dates the case occurred.

When Hatherley awoke the next morning, 'the moon had sunk and a bright morning was breaking'. This describes daybreak, when civil twilight begins, which is about forty minutes before sunrise. He walked to the station, and since he could see it from where he lay, we can suppose that he would have arrived in five to ten minutes. There was a train to Reading in less than an hour, so by the time he boarded it, about an hour would have already passed since he awoke. The train would be travelling thirty to forty miles per hour, and, as the distance between Reading and Paddington is forty miles, that portion of the journey must have taken over one hour with stops, while the initial seven miles to get from Eyford Station in Berkshire to Reading would have taken about fifteen minutes. Thus, allowing at least five minutes for switching trains, a minimum of two and a half hours elapsed from the time Hatherley awoke to the time he found himself in London.

He told Watson that he arrived in London 'a little past six'. As two and one half hours is the shortest elapsed time possible, 3:45 a.m. is the latest he could have awoken, and it is more likely that he awoke and saw the dawn breaking fifteen or twenty minutes before that. On 23 June, civil twilight begins at 2:59,[1] which is too early. Besides, Watson says that the case occurred in the summer, and although summer technically begins at the end of June, the implication of his remark is, in all probability,

---

[1] The practice of Daylight Saving was not instituted until 1916, so all times are given in standard GMT and, regardless of the time of year, are not affected by the changes now caused by British Summer Time.

that the case was in July or August. On 23 July, civil twilight starts at 3:31, and on 21 August it commences at 4:21. The latter time is certainly too late, but the former fits nicely. Hatherley would have awoken about 3:45, fifteen minutes into civil twilight and about thirty minutes before the sun rose at 4:15, and he would have seen the morning light on the horizon.

The case occurred, then, on Monday 23 July 1888.

12. The Noble Bachelor

First published April 1892

Watson refers to the events of this case as a 'four-year-old drama'. This may indicate four years since the time of publication, which would place it in 1888; but the manuscript may have been written some years prior to publication, as we have seen in other instances, so this does not in fact determine the date.

'It was a few weeks before my own marriage, during the days when I was still sharing rooms with Holmes in Baker Street',[1] Watson says, that this case occurred.[2] Since the marriage could not have been earlier than November 1887, this statement shows us that this case was in October 1887 (as is substantiated by the

---

[1] As noted in our discussion of *The Five Orange Pips*, Watson was still living with Holmes until his marriage in November, but he had started practicing again in mid-September. Evidently he did not work every day, for he informs us that on the day of this case he 'had remained indoors all day' and 'lay listless'.

[2] This is one of several pivotal cases which reference Watson's marriage and purport to take place in 1887. The chronologists who date *The Sign of Four* later than 1887 are confronted with the difficulty of explaining why these cases must have actually occurred later than Watson says, and some, such as Baring-Gould, resort to the direful expedient of alleging that Watson had a wife *before* Mary Morstan. In addition to lacking any factual basis, this claim is inherently flawed as it conflicts with the many statements in Watson's account of *The Sign of Four* that betray the emotions of a man falling in love for the first time.

reference to 4 October, discussed below). It also enables us to isolate Watson's marriage to a few weeks later in early November. Watson mentions 'high autumnal winds', just as he did in *The Five Orange Pips*, so this case probably occurred about the same time. Furthermore, he says that 'the jezail bullet which I had brought back in one of my limbs as a relic of my Afghan campaign, throbbed with dull persistency'. This is very much the same sort of pain of which he complained in *The Sign of Four*, further corroborating this as a contemporaneous case.

Holmes computes that Lord St Simon was 'forty-one years of age' from the fact that he was 'Born in 1846'; this agrees with, and even favours, our chosen year of 1887. Dakin, who puts Watson's marriage in 1888, insists that if St Simon were born in December 1846, the year for this case could conceivably be 1888.[1] This hypothesis is, however, inherently improbable, and, as Hall rightly says, it is based upon faulty reasoning, for when computing ages, as Holmes was doing, the proper method is to subtract the year of birth from the current year,[2] yielding, in this instance, forty-one. If Holmes's reference book had specified St Simon's age, rather than his year of birth, Dakin's theory would be plausible, but because Holmes computed the age based upon the year of birth, the current year was definitely 1887.

Watson recited an announcement in a newspaper stating that 'on Wednesday last…the wedding had taken place'. Miss Doran disappeared on this same Wednesday morning. He then read from an 'article of a morning newspaper of yesterday', which said that 'The ceremony, as shortly announced in the papers of

---

[1] Dakin, 84. Dakin (and the others who put the case in 1888) run into many awkward difficulties with regard to the date and the day of the week. These are non-existent when the case is placed in 1887.
[2] Hall, 12.

The Noble Bachelor

yesterday, occurred on the previous morning'. The day when the case was brought to Holmes was, then, a Friday.

Holmes remarked that it was significant 'to know that within a week he [Francis Moulton] had settled his bill at one of the most select London hotels'. The date of that bill, upon the reverse of which was written Moulton's message to Miss Doran, was 'Oct. 4th'. On that day, a Tuesday in 1887, he left his posh lodgings for some more modest ones 'in Gordon Square', whither he took his long-time bride after she joined him on the morning of 5 October following the wedding. On the Friday, Holmes told Watson that Moulton had left the expensive hotel 'only the day before', which would mean that Moulton had been there until Thursday 6 October, but this is clearly impossible as it would have defeated Moulton's entire purpose for moving to less ostentatious rooms. Holmes must have actually said 'only the day before *the wedding*', Watson accidentally omitting that last essential phrase when writing his manuscript.

It is worth noting that the choice of 1888 causes serious difficulties since in that year 4 October was a Thursday, resulting in the unlikely scenario that, the wedding being on a Wednesday and Moulton having the bill to write upon on that morning, he would have had to have left the hotel not on the day before the wedding but rather a full six days before it, the wedding necessarily being on Wednesday 10 October. As Holmes would thus have been investigating on the 12th, this choice of year also makes nonsense of his remark that Moulton had left the hotel 'within a week'. Besides proving 1887 to be the year of this case, this is evidence for an 1887 date for *The Sign of Four*.

Holmes was consulted two days after the wedding, on Friday 7 October 1887.

13. The Beryl Coronet

First published May 1892

Watson states very clearly that 'It was a bright, crisp February morning, and the snow of the day before still lay deep upon the ground'. This was the first day of the case, when Holmes and Watson were watching a man stumble along Baker Street towards their rooms. Watson refers to 'our bow-window' and 'our room' and was at Baker Street early in the morning. He later again remarks that 'we found ourselves in our room once more', so this is manifestly a case that occurred before Watson left the Baker Street rooms in November 1887.

It seems likely that it was an early case given some of Watson's statements. He remarks that 'My friend insisted upon my accompanying them in their expedition, which I was eager enough to do, for my curiosity and sympathy were deeply stirred by the story to which we had listened'. This suggests a time shortly after *A Study in Scarlet* when Watson was not yet in the habit of accompanying Holmes on all of his cases. Holmes, furthermore, refrained from revealing any of his conclusions to Watson, even less than was usual in later cases, and Watson makes the observation that 'It was no uncommon thing for him to be away for days and nights on end when he was hot upon a scent, so that his lateness caused me no surprise'. Again, this comment seems to resemble those that Watson made at the

The Beryl Coronet

beginning of his partnership with Holmes, and to betray a certain fascination with Holmes's irregular habits that Watson no longer focusses upon in later accounts. The most probable year for the case, then, is 1882. The only other plausible year, 1883, is discounted by the fact that, as Dakin observes, there was no snow, which is integral to this case, in February of that year.[1]

As to the day, the illustrious client who deposited the beryl coronet as security for his loan stated that he would certainly 'be able in four days to reclaim it', and he then said that 'I shall call for it in person on Monday morning'. The day upon which he left it with Alexander Holder, then, was a Thursday, and Holder related that it was stolen from him on the very first night that he had it in his possession. He called upon Holmes the next morning—that of Friday—and solicited his services, and the case concluded on Saturday morning, when Holder returned to Baker Street for an explanation of the extraordinary affair.

Having established that the case occurred in February 1882, we must now attempt to determine the dates. On the night of the theft—Thursday night or early Friday morning—Arthur Holder, upon jumping outside through the window, was able to 'see a dark figure in the moonlight' at the end of the lane. The moon must have been fairly full if there were sufficient light for Arthur to discern someone at a distance; but as he only saw a 'dark figure', not the clear outline of Sir George Burnwell, and as the snow on the ground would have accentuated whatever light the moon was producing, it seems unlikely that it was completely full.

In 1882, Friday 3 February was the full moon, so this was not the night of the theft. Saturday the 11th and Friday the 24th were

---

[1] Dakin, 88.

The Beryl Coronet

both half-moons, so it must have occurred on either Friday 10 February or Friday 24 February. Zeisler admits that the moon on the 10th is appropriate but rejects the day because there was very little sunshine which, he believes, contradicts Watson's remark that the snow was 'shimmering brightly in the wintry sun'.[1] Christ, meanwhile, insists that the case could not have occurred until the latter part of February since Arthur Holder had already entreated his father to give him money three times during the current month.[2]

These reasonable observations eliminate the 10th, leaving us to conclude that the case occurred from Friday 24 to Saturday 25 February 1882.

---

[1] Zeisler, 68.
[2] Christ, 18.

14. The Copper Beeches

First published June 1892

This account opens with Holmes offering some rather scathing criticism of Watson's literary efforts. He told Watson that 'in these little records of our cases which you have been good enough to draw up' he had been guilty of embellishing the accounts with a tinge of romanticism. The specific cases mentioned by Holmes include 'The small matter in which I endeavoured to help the King of Bohemia, the singular experience of Miss Mary Sutherland, the problem connected with the man with the twisted lip, and the incident of the noble bachelor'. Watson also later mentions 'the affair of the blue carbuncle'. This might mean that this case occurred after the latest of the above mentioned, which is *A Case of Identity* of 16–17 June 1890, or it may be an instance of literary license such as we have seen before.

Watson says that on 'a cold morning of the early spring' he and Holmes 'sat after breakfast on either side of a cheery fire in the old room in Baker Street'. This retrospective view of the rooms might suggest that Watson was no longer living at Baker Street when this case occurred, though it is equally likely that, as this statement is not dialogue, he wrote it from the perspective of no longer living there when he penned the manuscript.

The Copper Beeches

Indeed, in spite of the above evidence in favour of a later date, it is evident that this case occurred while Watson was still living with Holmes. Watson refers to watching Holmes's moods, he mentions a telegram which 'we' received just before he was 'thinking of turning in', and he says he came down to breakfast in the morning. Any argument that Watson might have been visiting Holmes for a few days, furthermore, is effectively nullified by the fact that Watson did not mention having either a practice or a wife. This evidence proves that the case occurred sometime between 1882 and 1887.

The explanation of the references to the other cases is that Watson, thinking that his readers would not be overly concerned with the niceties of chronology, inserted the references to the aforementioned cases of 1887–1890—which actually occurred after *The Copper Beeches*—when penning this manuscript sometime in the early 1890s for the simple reason that, having made a note of Holmes commenting about certain cases, he, not remembering precisely which cases Holmes had mentioned, deemed it meet to insert cases with which his readers would be familiar. Watson had a predilection for doing this, as we have seen elsewhere.[1] This explanation is far more plausible than any which might be proffered against the evidence clearly demonstrating that Watson was living at Baker Street.

Additional evidence supporting an earlier date rests in the concluding paragraph of the account in which Watson provides a summary of the subsequent lives of the principal actors in the case. He says that Mr Rucastle 'was always a broken man' and that he and his wife 'still live with their old servants', while Miss Violet Hunter, at the head of a private school, 'has met with

---

[1] See our discussion of *The Blue Carbuncle*.

considerable success'. All of these statements tend to imply that a considerable number of years passed between the events of the case and Watson's writing the manuscript, again placing it no later than about 1887. It is worth noting that there is, in any case, no viable year subsequent to all of the cases referred to, for the latest, *A Case of Identity*, was in June 1890, so *The Copper Beeches*, which occurred in early spring, could not have been in that year, and the only remaining year, 1891, is eliminated by the fact that Holmes was working on a case in France early that spring.[1]

Holmes remarked to Miss Hunter that 'your little problem promises to be the most interesting which has come my way for some months'. This suggests that no other case of any real note—certainly no case actually published by Watson—occurred in the first three months of the year preceding this case. As *The Beryl Coronet* occurred in February 1882, that year may be eliminated. The year 1883 is also unlikely, given that *The Speckled Band* occurred on 4–5 April and that that case and this one do not in any way refer to one another. Furthermore, since this case definitely occurred after 5 April (see below), Holmes could not have bemoaned that there were no cases of interest preceding it in 1883. Similarly, 1887 is not tenable, given the fact that from mid-February to mid-April of that year Holmes was working on a case that led ultimately to his 'lying ill in the Hotel Dulong'[2] in Lyons.

Since the case began in early spring, we must consider a March or April in 1884, 1885, or 1886. After Miss Hunter consulted Holmes, 'A fortnight went by' before she sent a telegram requesting his presence 'at the Black Swan Hotel at

---

[1] Short, FINA, 537.
[2] Short, REIG, 417.

The Copper Beeches

Winchester at midday to-morrow'. Thus the case continued fifteen days after it began, and this day 'was an ideal spring day'.

More importantly, on Miss Hunter's third night at the Copper Beeches—three days after she first consulted Holmes—'It was a beautiful moonlight night, and the lawn in front of the house was silvered over and almost as bright as day'. This clearly shows that there was a full or nearly full moon that night. Twelve days later, on the final day of the case when Holmes and Watson went to the Copper Beeches, Watson declares that 'it was just seven when we reached the Copper Beeches' and that 'The group of trees...[were] shining like burnished metal in the light of the setting sun'. The sun was, therefore, setting about 7 p.m. on this last day.

As there was no British Summer Time, the sun would have set at 7 p.m. on 15 April in Winchester. Watson's phrase is 'the light of the setting sun', which could very well refer to the lighting anywhere between roughly twenty minutes before sunset and the actual moment when the sun drops below the horizon, so this could conceivably refer to any day in the second half of April (as the sun would have set about 7:26 on the 30th of the month). What we must find, then, are the years in which the full moon was in early April and about twelve days before a date in the second half of the month. In 1884, the full moon was on the 10th, which makes it a plausible year; in 1885, it was on the 29th, obviating further speculation for that year; and in 1886, it was on the 18th, rendering that year untenable since the case would have begun on the 15th, which is hardly in 'the early spring'. If further proof were needed to negate 1883, it exists in the fact that the full moon in that year was on 22 April.

The year 1884 is, then, the only one in which the full moon was in the first half of April, so this must be the year in which

The Copper Beeches

the case occurred. As Miss Hunter described the lawn in the night-time as 'almost as bright as day', we may safely presume that this was the night of the full moon. This night—10 April—was the night of the third day after she had consulted Holmes, which means that the case began on Monday 7 April 1884. It resumed fifteen days later, on Tuesday 22 April, and concluded on the same night. On that evening, the sun set at 7:12 p.m.

15. Silver Blaze

First published December 1892

Holmes and Watson 'sat down together to our breakfast one morning'. Watson observed Holmes as he brooded over the case of the missing horse 'For a whole day', showing that he was living with Holmes and thus placing the case before November 1887. Holmes remarked that 'I made a blunder, my dear Watson—which is, I am afraid, a more common occurrence than any one would think who only knew me through your memoirs'. Although this seems to suggest a date after a number of cases had been published, it cannot have been post-1887, and this statement must ultimately be regarded as another instance of Watson inserting either whole dialogue or particular references to cases which actually occurred at a later date. Perhaps Holmes had made a critical comment to him about one of his recently published accounts while he was writing the manuscript for this case, and, rankling from the affront, he seized the opportunity to insert a statement which served as a veiled gibe.

It is necessary with this case to begin by determining the days and to work from there towards the year. The tragedy occurred 'last Monday night'; Holmes received telegrams entreating his assistance on the following day, Tuesday; he mulled over the case on Wednesday; and on Thursday morning he and Watson set out for Dartmoor, returning to London the same day. The following

Silver Blaze

Tuesday they went to Winchester for the race and returned by the evening train.

The setting of the sun is in this case, as in a number of others, of vital importance in determining the date. Watson says that it was evening (which could not have been any earlier than 5 p.m.) before they arrived at the Tavistock station on the Thursday, yet it was early enough that they had sufficient remaining daylight to visit the scene of the crime before it was too dark—in spite of the fact that the drive to King's Pyland from Tavistock was two miles and that immediately after arriving they went into the sitting room to see what the dead man had had in his pockets, which must have taken at least ten minutes, before finally walking to the hollow. After a short inspection there, Holmes and Watson began to walk across the moor as 'The sun was beginning to sink behind the stables of Capleton'.[1] After a somewhat lengthy but brisk walk on the moor and twenty minutes' conversation between Holmes and Silas Brown, the sun was gone and 'the reds had all faded into greys'.

It seems reasonable to suppose that it was about 5:30 p.m. when they arrived in Tavistock—Watson does say that it was evening *before*, not *when*, they arrived, suggesting evening had already begun. If the horse carriage had moved at the moderate rate of eight miles per hour, the drive of two miles to King's Pyland would have taken about fifteen minutes, putting their arrival about 5:45. The interlude observing the dead man's effects in the sitting room and speaking to Mrs Straker likely occupied ten minutes, and the short walk to the hollow another five. Holmes probably spent about fifteen minutes investigating

---

[1] It is Mapleton in the *Strand* text (*The Original Illustrated Sherlock Holmes*, 185-200).

Silver Blaze

the scene of the crime, so it was roughly 6:15 p.m. when Holmes and Watson began their stroll and the sun was low enough for the Capleton stables to appear in front of it on the horizon. This would have been a few minutes before actual sunset (which is, precisely, the moment when the top of the sun disappears completely below the horizon). What is required, then, is a Thursday upon which the sun sets on Dartmoor just after 6:15 p.m. On both 14 March and 19 September, the sun sets at 6:19, so these dates may be tentatively considered, though, allowing for variations in our above computations, any day within a week of either one is equally plausible.

Holmes and Watson's trek to reach the Capleton stables began with a brisk walk during a brief conversation, then they 'passed over a quarter of a mile of dry, hard turf', followed by another half-mile which brought them 'quite close to Capleton'. Though they were searching for tracks and began to follow one back the way they had come, they were walking quickly, and as a brisk walking pace is about three miles per hour, the walk must have taken about twenty minutes. Therefore it was about 6:35 when Holmes began his interview with Silas Brown, and about 6:55 when he emerged from it and the sky had turned grey. When the sun sets at 6:19, the end of civil twilight is at 6:52. If civil twilight had already ended by the time Holmes returned, the sky would have been mostly devoid of light and there would not have been much grey left. Watson does not, however, say that the sky was still grey, but rather that 'the reds had all faded into greys *before* [emphasis added] Holmes and the trainer reappeared'. He is simply noting an atmospheric phenomenon that he observed at some point during his vigil waiting for Holmes.

There is meaningful evidence elsewhere in the narrative corroborating a September date. Inspector Gregory said that 'He

Silver Blaze

[Simpson] has twice lodged at Tavistock in the summer'. Looking back at the summer as this statement does, it confirms a date after summer has ended, or at least is in its final days. The moor was 'bronze-coloured from the fading ferns', again suggesting a date in autumn. Zeisler boldly claims that the only horse race in Winchester (where Holmes and Watson went for the 'Wessex Cup' and the climax of the case) in all of the years between 1881 and 1903 was on 17 July 1888, and that the case must have thus occurred at that time.[1] How thoroughly he researched this point we do not know, but we have shown July to be impossible, and in any case we cannot reasonably believe that anyone went to the trouble of constructing a horse-racing venue only to use it but once in a period of fifteen years or more.

Having, then, established that the case occurred in late September, and not in March, we must now determine in what year. An earlier rather than a later date is suggested by Watson's tentative offer to accompany Holmes to Dartmoor—'I should be most happy to go down with you if I should not be in the way'—and Holmes's response: 'My dear Watson, you would confer a great favour upon me by coming. And I think that your time will not be mis-spent.' This exchange of words is not what one would expect if Watson had already developed the definite habit of accompanying Holmes. Contrarily, Watson's familiarity with Holmes's mannerisms, namely the 'gleam in his eyes' which betrayed that he had found a clue, suggests a later case. Yet none of this evidence is definitive, whereas it is a fact that the year could not have been earlier than 1887, for Silver Blaze was 'from the Isonomy stock' and 'now in his fifth year', and Isonomy only

---

[1] Zeisler, 88.

Silver Blaze

began breeding in 1881.[1] Watson makes no mention of his *fiancée*, which is a point against 1887, but he is similarly remiss about this in other accounts as well.

We know that this case began on a Thursday, and in 1887 the closest Thursday to the 19 September was the 22nd. On this day, the sun set at 6:13 p.m. and civil twilight ended at 6:45, so our computation above was off by about five minutes, clearly the result either of their having arrived in Tavistock slightly earlier, or of their having progressed through the subsequent events more quickly, than estimated. Having, then, begun on Thursday 22 September, the case continued and ended on Tuesday the 27th. Watson, as we have seen above, had recently begun working, though his days and hours were irregular. The fact that Holmes did not ask him to go to Dartmoor, but rather that Watson himself offered, supports this theory, as Holmes would no longer have been able to assume that Watson would invariably be free to accompany him.

---

[1] Brend, 79; Dakin, 95; McQueen, 86.

16. The Cardboard Box

First published January 1893[1]

Watson opens this narrative by stating that 'It was a blazing hot day in August' with the 'thermometer at 90'. Holmes said on the day of the case that 'To-day is Friday. The packet was posted on Thursday morning.' There is no reason to doubt the veracity of any of these statements, or that the case concluded when 'Two days later he [Holmes] received a bulky envelope, which contained a short note' from Lestrade along with the typewritten statement of the criminal.

Watson makes a number of comments which confirm that he was living at Baker Street at the time: he remarks how strange a contrast it was 'to believe that these were the same walls which loomed so gloomily through the fogs of winter'; he says 'Our blinds were half-drawn', suggesting he still regarded himself as a tenant; and he states that 'A depleted bank account had caused me to postpone my holiday', making no mention of his wife being part of these plans. He was, furthermore, obviously not in practice, for when Holmes asked if he was willing to join him for the case, he replied that he 'was longing for something to do'. Lastly, towards the end of the account, he refers to 'our rooms

---

[1] This case belongs here according to our practice of arranging the cases in the order of their first date of publication; in our copy text, however, it appears much later as the second instalment in *His Last Bow*.

The Cardboard Box

at Baker Street'. The case, then, would seem to have occurred sometime before September 1887.

There is, however, a statement made by Holmes during the evening retrospection at Baker Street on the first day of the case which conflicts with an early date. He compared this case to 'the investigations which you have chronicled under the names of the 'Study in Scarlet' and of the 'Sign of Four,' [in which] we have been compelled to reason back-ward from effects to causes'. These cases were not published with these titles until December 1887 for the former and February 1890 for the latter, but even by the earlier time Watson was married and working. The events of *The Sign of Four*, meanwhile, did not even occur until September 1887. This reference to the two above-mentioned cases must, then, have been another literary liberty on the part of Watson, such as those we have seen before. Again, we stress that it should not come as a surprise that Watson would choose to refer to cases that his readers would be familiar with when using them as examples of reasoning, especially as he had no especial reason for respecting strict chronological accuracy. Watson states at the beginning of the account that 'I shall turn to my notes' for this case, suggesting that he probably wrote the notes just after it occurred, and was now, much later, consulting them to compose the manuscript, which he probably did not complete until late 1892. Thus, he must have once again deemed it appropriate to insert a reference to two of his earliest-published and most well-known cases, both of which happened to serve as examples of the type of case he remembered Holmes having discussed on this occasion. Holmes had doubtless referred to two obscure cases which Watson did not wish to have to summarise for his readers.

The Cardboard Box

Early in the case Holmes asked Watson if he would 'run down to Croydon with me on the off chance of a case for your annals?' This statement does not necessarily indicate a date after Watson had begun to publish these annals; it merely serves to confirm what we already knew, namely that, even in the earlier years of the partnership, Watson was actively taking notes of the cases in which he participated.

Knowing that the case occurred on a Friday and a Sunday in August, we are faced with the task of determining in what year. One need not look beyond the walls of Baker Street to find the answer: Watson had recently hung a 'newly framed picture of General Gordon'. General Charles George Gordon, of Khartoum fame, met his untimely end at the hands of the Mahdi on 26 January 1885, which tragic fate immediately solidified him in the popular mind of the time as a martyr of the nation. More than likely it was in the immediate wake of the general's death that Watson acquired his portrait, and we may presume that it had been lying unframed (doubtless due to his 'depleted bank account') for some time, like his 'unframed portrait of Henry Ward Beecher', until he at last had it framed in August 1885.

Hall cites the evidence of Tim Owen—that there was no railway line as far as New Brighton proper until 1888—as proof that the case must have been in that year, since, according to Jim Browner's statement, Mary Browner and Alec Fairbairn purchased railway tickets to travel from Liverpool to New Brighton.[1] This apparently sound deduction is unfortunately contradicted by the far more forceful evidence that Watson was unmarried, not in practice, and living at Baker Street at this time, meaning that the case necessarily occurred before 1888. The

---

[1] Hall, 52.

most likely explanation would seem to be that Jim Browner simply omitted some details from his statement. Although New Brighton was not connected by rail in 1885, it was possible to purchase train tickets to travel from the James Street station in Liverpool under the river to the Green Lane station in Birkenhead, from where the journey to New Brighton could have easily been completed by cab. Evidently Browner saw no need to mention these minor logistical details in his confession, feeling it was sufficient to indicate that they bought tickets, boarded a train, and ended up in New Brighton.

Upon which Friday in August the case occurred there is no way of knowing, but what can be said is that it began on Friday 7, 14, 21, or 28 August in the year 1885, and that it continued and concluded on the Sunday two days later.

17. The Yellow Face

First published February 1893

This case began, Watson tells us, 'One day in early spring' when 'the first faint shoots of green were breaking out upon the elms, and the sticky spearheads of the chestnuts were just beginning to burst into their five-fold leaves'. This suggests early April, and as Watson was without doubt living with Holmes, since they had leisure to go for a two-hour walk in the park, the case must have occurred before November 1887.

Watson continues by saying that their two-hour walk 'befits two men who know each other intimately'; this statement would not have been made in the first couple of years of their partnership. Similarly, Holmes said to Mr Grant Munro during their first meeting that 'my friend and I have listened to many strange secrets in this room, and that we have had the good fortune to bring peace to many troubled souls'. He could not have realistically said this any time before 1883.

Another statement which warrants an explanation is Watson's reference to 'the affair of the second stain, and that which I am now about to recount' as two cases in which Holmes 'erred'. This may appear to suggest that the case that Watson published some years later as *The Second Stain* occurred prior to this case, but *The Second Stain* is clearly not the same case as the one Watson is referring to here, for in the published account Holmes in no way

The Yellow Face

'erred'.[1] Evidently Watson in his notes used the same title for multiple cases, only one of which was ever published.

Mr Munro's troubles began 'last Monday'. He saw the yellow face that evening, and the next day he saw his wife at the cottage. 'On the third day' after this—Friday—he entered the cottage but found nothing. He told Holmes that that was yesterday, so the day on which he consulted Holmes was a Saturday. It 'was a very dark night and a thin rain began to fall'. These rain clouds would have largely blocked the light of any type of moon, but the fact that it was exceptionally dark suggests that the moon was probably closer to new than full.

When Holmes and Watson returned from their walk in the park and discovered that a client had called while they were gone, Holmes complained that 'It's very annoying though, Watson. I was badly in need of a case.' This shows plainly that Holmes had not had any cases for at least a few weeks, if not longer, as of the time of this case. Since this case occurred in early April, the earliest imaginable year—1883—thus becomes impossible, for *The Speckled Band* occurred on 4–5 April 1883. We can discount later April 1884 for the same reason since in mid-April of that year *The Copper Beeches* occurred, and earlier April 1884 is eliminated by the fact that, at the time of the events of *The Copper Beeches*, Holmes remarked that he had had no cases of any great interest for several months.[2] Neither could it have been 1887, for from February to late April of that year Holmes was on the Continent.[3]

---

[1] Nor is it the 'Second Stain' case referred to at the time of *The Naval Treaty*, as we demonstrate in our discussion of that case.
[2] Short, COPP, 283.
[3] Short, REIG, 417.

The Yellow Face

This leaves us with 1885 and 1886, and looking at when the new moon fell near a Saturday in early April, we can suppose that the case occurred on either 11 April 1885 or 3 April 1886, both Saturdays. The new moon was on 15 April in 1885, four days from the closest Saturday, whereas it was on 4 April in 1886, only one day after Saturday the 3rd, so 1886 is more likely. The indications noted above that Holmes and Watson had been working and living together for a considerable amount of time favour the later year as well, so we may conclude that Saturday 3 April 1886 is the date.

18. The Stock-Broker's Clerk

First published March 1893

'Shortly after my marriage I had bought a connection in the Paddington district.' Watson opens the account with this statement, which leads the reader to presume that, given that Watson was married in November 1887, this case probably occurred in the first few months of 1888. A few sentences later he asserts that 'For three months after taking over the practice I was kept very closely at work, and saw little of my friend Sherlock Holmes, for I was too busy to visit Baker Street, and he seldom went anywhere himself save upon professional business'. This suggests that the case occurred before *A Scandal in Bohemia* of March 1888, yet in the very next sentence Watson assures us that it was 'one morning in June' that Holmes appeared at his practice (where he lived) and the case began. This is substantiated by the fact that Holmes referred to 'Summer colds' and remarked that the present June was very wet. Watson, then, must have taken over the practice—which he purchased from 'Old Mr. Farquhar'—in March 1888, as that would be three months before this June.

The difficulty is thus to explain how it is possible that, if Watson bought the practice in March 1888, he scarcely saw Holmes for three months, and that Holmes had never visited him at this new residence of his. *A Scandal in Bohemia* definitely

The Stock-Broker's Clerk

occurred on 20 March 1888, and Watson tells us at that time that he 'had seen little of Holmes lately'.[1] Holmes apparently did not know that Watson had gone into practice, as he proceeded to deduce this fact on 20 March 1888.[2] Watson had partially returned to medical practice in September 1887, however, and it is inconceivable that Holmes could not have known this.

As discussed above, Watson did not have his own practice in autumn 1887, but rather was in a partnership with or working for someone else. Quite probably he purchased the practice of Mr Farquhar in early March 1888, sometime shortly before *A Scandal in Bohemia* and thus 'shortly after' his marriage. Holmes would then have been able to sensibly deduce in *A Scandal in Bohemia* that Watson had returned to practice—his acquisition of his own practice would result in his showing the signs of more demanding work—as Watson would likely not have had time to see him before 20 March to inform him. *A Scandal in Bohemia* occurred just after Watson bought his practice, and thus it is one of a very few visits to Baker Street he found the time for during those 'three months after taking over the practice'.[3]

This agrees with our dating of *The Engineer's Thumb* as the case currently in question included Holmes's first visit to Watson's residence, after which the partnership was to a degree revived, and following which Holmes and Watson saw a great deal more of each other prior to the aforementioned case. Of note is that the practice near Paddington which he speaks of at the time of

---

[1] Short, SCAN, 3.
[2] Short, SCAN, 5.
[3] During a second visit in April 1888, Holmes showed Watson the golden snuffbox given to him by the King of Bohemia. As noted in our discussion of *A Case of Identity*, this incident was detailed by Watson in his account of that case, though it had actually occurred two years earlier.

The Stock-Broker's Clerk

The Engineer's Thumb[1] is in fact the practice which he purchased from Farquhar.

There remains one difficulty in the following remark made by Holmes: 'I trust that Mrs. Watson has entirely recovered from all the little excitements connected with our adventure of the 'Sign of Four'?' This statement seems like one which ought to have been made by Holmes the first time he saw Watson after he had married Miss Morstan, apparently at the time of *A Scandal in Bohemia*. The only explanation for this remark is that Holmes, in his usual eccentric manner, put the superfluous fact of Mary's existence out of his mind, and thus it did not occur to him to ask Watson how she was feeling at the time of *A Scandal in Bohemia*. Then, when he visited Watson's own practice, where his wife lived with him, for the first time in June 1888, the facts associated with Mary Morstan and her case were recalled to his memory, and he—rather awkwardly, as it was so belated—asked if she had recovered from the stress of that case. Watson, in his usual polite manner, simply responded that they were 'both very well'.

This case occurred on a Saturday—Mr Hall Pycroft finished his list of hardware sellers on 'Friday—that is, yesterday'—in June in the year 1888. Based upon Watson's statement of 'three months' and the conclusion that he bought his practice in mid-March, it was evidently Saturday 16 June 1888.

---

[1] Short, ENGR, 201.

19. The "Gloria Scott"

First published April 1893

This case, Holmes said, 'was the first in which I was ever engaged'. He went to visit Victor Trevor, his only friend from university, at Donnithorpe 'for a month of the long vacation'. This was evidently the vacation of July-September, between his two years at university.[1] After spending the month at Donnithorpe, Holmes repaired to London and 'spent seven weeks working out a few experiments in organic chemistry. One day, however, when the autumn was far advanced and the vacation drawing to a close,' Victor Trevor telegrammed for him to return to Donnithorpe.

Since the long vacation ended in early October, it is strange that Holmes referred to the autumn as 'far advanced'. There is, however, further evidence to support the fact that the 'long vacation' referred to was during the later summer and early autumn: during the first month of the vacation, which would have been July, Holmes remarked that he, Victor Trevor, and Mr Trevor 'were sitting out upon the lawn on garden chairs, the three of us, basking in the sun and admiring the view across the

---

[1] Holmes himself refers very clearly to 'the two years that I was at college'. His other reference to 'my last years at the university' (Short, MUSG, 399) might suggest that he spent more than two years studying, but this is a less explicit statement, and we must accept the superiority of the former evidence.

The "Gloria Scott"

Broads'. This is something which would have been done at the end of July, seven weeks before the end of the case in September, not something which would have been done at the end of September, as would be true if the case ended in November. Evidently, then, Holmes was exaggerating when he declared that autumn was nearly over, actuated, perhaps, by that innate aversion to the resumption of studies so characteristic of students.

With regard to the year of this case, there are a number of statements throughout the account that contradict one another. Hudson, upon appearing at the house of Mr Trevor, declared that 'it's thirty year and more since I saw you last', and Mr Trevor, in the beginning of the statement that he wrote for his son, remarked that 'the laws were more harshly administered thirty years ago than now', referring to the time when he was convicted shortly before meeting Hudson. According to Mr Trevor, the convict ship on which he met Hudson left Falmouth on 8 October and foundered on 6 November in 'the year '55, when the Crimean War was at its height', but as this would mean that the case could not have occurred before 1885, clearly an impossible date, either the references to thirty years must be incorrect, or the ship must have foundered in an earlier year.

Bell argues that it must have sunk in the 1840s because Holmes could not have referred to Mr Trevor as an 'old man' about 1875 if Mr Trevor had been, as he claimed, only twenty-three in 1855.[1] Blakeney strengthens this hypothesis by noting that if the ship sank in 1855, Victor Trevor, who scarcely could have been born before 1857, would have been too young to be

---

[1] Bell, 8-10. He takes his theory too far, we think, in claiming that the entire narrative that Mr Trevor wrote for his son was a fabrication to hide some serious crime in which he had been involved.

at university at the same time as Holmes.[1] In explanation of how the date came to be erroneously recorded, Dakin offers that in Mr Trevor's frantically written statement to his son the numbers "44" looked to Watson like "55", and that he accordingly took the liberty of exhibiting his knowledge of military history by adding a reference to the Crimean War.[2] While this is certainly a plausible explanation, we think it more probable that Mr Trevor, who was, according to his son, quite nervous and distracted at the time of writing, recorded the wrong date in his statement, and Watson, who had been given the original document by Holmes, very understandably made no attempt to correct it.

While it is clear that the convict ship sank before 1855, there is nevertheless a serious flaw in the argument that it happened in the 1840s. Mr Trevor declared in his statement that upon arriving in Sydney on the ship that rescued them, he and Evans 'changed our names and made our way to the diggings' and 'we prospered, we travelled, we came back as rich colonials to England', clearly indicating that one of the many Australian gold rushes was in full progress at the time when they arrived. The difficulty lies in the fact that the first gold rush in Australia did not begin until May 1851, so the earliest possible date for the sinking of the *Gloria Scott* is 6 November 1851. As the arguments of Bell and Blakeney are both quite sound, we must see if they can agree with such a date.

If Mr Trevor were twenty-three in 1851, he would have been forty-seven in 1875; Holmes would have been only twenty-one, so it would not have been unreasonable for him to regard Mr Trevor as 'old'. Having dispelled any reservations Bell might

---

[1] Blakeney, 47.
[2] Dakin, 108-109.

have had, we may turn to Blakeney. Supposing Mr Trevor arrived in Australia sometime in late 1851 or early 1852, he would have been able to earn his fortune at the gold fields by the end of 1852. He and Evans travelled, probably for a year or so, before returning to England, whereupon they both doubtless married very quickly. Victor Trevor, then, may very well have been born in 1854 or 1855, putting him at university at the same time as Holmes. This agrees with the fact that Mr Trevor, in his statement to his son, claimed that 'For more than twenty years we have led peaceful and useful lives', which would be true if their arrival in Australia had taken place in 1852.

If the above hypothesis is to be believed, two statements which conflict with it must be explained. As we have observed above, in his statement to his son Mr Trevor said that the laws of England were harsher thirty years ago than at present. As Mr Trevor's statement was recited to Watson by Holmes verbatim, and as Watson had the actual document at his disposal when writing his account, we can hardly suppose that any errors were committed by Watson regarding statements about years. Mr Trevor himself may have made a mistake when writing, as with his erroneous reference to the Crimean War, and intended the 'thirty' to be a 'twenty', or he may have simply been using 'thirty' hyperbolically (it was, after all, more than twenty) to emphasise how long ago the events seemed.

The other claim that thirty years had passed since the sinking of the *Gloria Scott* came from Hudson, who probably last saw Mr Trevor and Evans when they all arrived at the port of Sydney. It would seem that Hudson must have actually meant 'twenty', as this would align with Mr Trevor's similar remark of 'more than twenty years'. The explanation of how it came to be recorded by Watson as 'thirty' may be as follows: Hudson really said 'many a year', and Holmes told Watson this, but Watson, wishing to add more precision when writing the manuscript, saw the hyperbolic 'thirty' in Mr Trevor's statement and carelessly inserted the same number of years into Hudson's statement without realising that it made nonsense of the timeline of events and also contradicted Mr Trevor's remark about 'twenty years' at the end of his statement.

Though this hypothesis requires some degree of speculation on these points, it complies with the definite fact that the sinking of the convict ship could not have been before the first gold rush in 1851. Furthermore, it places Victor Trevor at university in 1872 or 1873, which fits with the fact that Holmes, born in 1854,[1] would likely have started 'at college' in 1872 at the age of eighteen, placing this case a year later.

The most that we can assert, then, is that the case began in the month of July in the year 1873, following Holmes's first year at university which began in 1872, and that it concluded on a day about seven weeks later in September 1873.

---

[1] Short, LAST, 1,076. This is widely accepted as the year of his birth on the evidence of *His Last Bow*. At the time of that case, which indisputably occurred in 1914, Holmes was described as a 'man of sixty'. While this may of course be an approximation of his age, our hypothesis that he started at university in 1872 has the additional merit of Holmes turning sixty in 1914.

20. The Musgrave Ritual

First published May 1893

Holmes had spent his time since leaving university 'studying all those branches of science which might make me more efficient'; as he did this in London, he presumably moved into his 'room in Montague Street' very soon after quitting his formal education. Dakin claims that Holmes must have been at university for three years,[1] and indeed he could not have graduated if he had not been; but we argue that he had no need to graduate once he decided, sometime after his involvement in *The "Gloria Scott"*, that he would pursue a career in detection, and that he could best educate himself to this end independently of any structured university learning. It would appear that Holmes received either an allowance or an inheritance from his parents sufficient for him to live frugally at this time, but cases were not plentiful, and it was a long time before his reputation began to grow. Most of his early cases were brought by 'old fellow-students', and the third such was that of Reginald Musgrave, of whom Holmes said that 'For four years I had seen nothing of him, until one morning he walked into my room in Montague Street'.

If Holmes began his time at university in 1872 and remained there for two years, as we determined in our discussion of *The*

---

[1] Dakin, 106.

The Musgrave Ritual

"*Gloria Scott*", he must have left the university sometime in 1874. Presumably he saw Reginald Musgrave at some point during his last months there, so four years later would place this case in 1878. We may safely presume that he had not seen him since his time at university given that Holmes had only 'some slight acquaintance with him', suggesting that no social calls would have been paid in the interim.

Holmes had only had two other cases from former students before this one, and as most of his cases were from this source, he could not have had many, if any, other cases in those four years. He remarked that it was from the time of the case of Musgrave that 'I trace my first stride towards the position which I now hold'. From this point until *A Study in Scarlet* in early March 1881 is about three years, which would be sufficient time for him to have 'already established a considerable, though not a very lucrative, connection', as he told Watson he had done.

A point against any later date for this case is that Holmes mentioned 'the record of the Tarleton murders, and the case of Vamberry, the wine merchant, and the adventure of the old Russian woman, and the singular affair of the aluminium crutch, as well as a full account of Ricoletti of the club foot and his abominable wife' as cases of which he had records from before Watson's time. Holmes also helped Mrs Farintosh 'in the hour of her sore need',[1] Mortimer Maberley was one of his 'early clients',[2] and shortly before *A Study in Scarlet* Lestrade 'got himself into a fog recently over a forgery case'[3] about which he consulted Holmes. It is most likely that this considerable number of cases, which are probably not the only ones which Holmes

---

[1] Short, SPEC, 175-176.
[2] Short, 3GAB, 1161.
[3] Long, STUD, 21-22.

handled before 1881 but which must be mostly if not wholly subsequent to *The Musgrave Ritual*, were spread throughout a longer rather than a shorter range of years, so an earlier date for *The Musgrave Ritual* is preferable.

As to the events of the case in question, Brunton the butler was surprised in the study on a Thursday night, and he was discovered to be missing on a Sunday morning. Rachel Howells was missing on the following Wednesday morning, following the third night after Brunton's disappearance. Musgrave said that they searched for her 'yesterday', so he consulted Holmes on a Thursday, and he and Holmes went to Hurlstone that afternoon.

Holmes stated that he had not seen Musgrave for four years, and as he most likely left the university in June this would most accurately, though by no means definitely, place the case about that month. If we move it slightly and place it in July it agrees with the Musgrave Ritual's statement that the month was 'The sixth from the first'. Bell, however, alternatively suggests that this statement refers to September since, at the time when the Ritual was written, the year legally began on 25 March.[1] Which month is correct may be best determined by considering the position of the sun.

Holmes arrived at Hurlstone on the Thursday in the afternoon, and immediately began to analyse the oak and the elm. About this time the sun 'was low in the heavens', suggesting that this must have been close to the end of the afternoon, after 4 p.m. in either month. At whatever precise time this was, Holmes found that a six-foot pole cast a shadow of nine feet. The sun would, then, have to have had an altitude of precisely 33.7 degrees. The scar in the ground left by the fallen elm was

---

[1] Bell, 13.

between the house and the oak, suggesting that these two trees must have once stood in a line very nearly perpendicular to the house. The end of the shadow of the elm, as computed by Holmes and Brunton, was close to the wall of the house. This must be the long side of the old wing (running north-south) of the L-shaped manor. Holmes walked along the wall north ten by ten, then he turned east and walked five by five. The ten eastward steps brought him close to the centre of the north face (a short side) of the house, and from there he turned south two by two, and these few paces brought him to the very threshold of 'the low, heavy-lintelled door, in the centre of this old part [of the house]'. (This all shows that the new wing was attached perpendicularly to the southern end of the old one.) From there he turned west down a passage that extended to the western exterior wall, in which there was a window through which the 'setting sun shone full upon the passage floor'. Because this old portion of the house had 'enormously thick walls and tiny windows', the sun at this time must have been low on the horizon—which we already know was true—and also very nearly due west.

Let us suppose that it was about 4:30 p.m. when Holmes entered the old wing. He insisted upon calling in the local police and awaiting their arrival before proceeding to investigate in the cellar underneath, and as it probably took about an hour for them to arrive, the discovery of Brunton's body would have occurred about 5:30. After the opening of the chambre Holmes mused for twenty minutes, until at least 6 p.m. Presumably only after the body was removed and the police had left, Holmes and Musgrave repaired to the new wing and Holmes explained to Musgrave the 'long chain of surmise and of proof' that had led him to the solution of the mystery. All of this must have taken at least an hour, so it was after 7 p.m. when he finished. It is quite possible of course that the interval waiting for the police took longer, and that Holmes waxed eloquent while explaining his reasoning, and thus it may have been as late as 8 p.m. It is important to note that by the time Holmes had finished his explanation, 'twilight had closed in and the moon was shining brightly in the sky'.

To determine the date of the case we must find, then, at what time of year the sun is 33 degrees above the horizon and also close to due west while at this altitude, and then see if the result agrees with our estimation of the timeline of events. As to the former, any time in June or July, on either side of the summer solstice, is plausible. Christ claims that the week immediately surrounding the solstice is the only one during the year when these conditions could have been met,[1] and although this is the time when they would have been most nearly met, June is too early to agree with the ritual, and we think that July is the correct month. September is too late in the year for the sun to be anything close to due west at the necessary altitude and can thus be eliminated. If 'the sixth from the first' means the first of the legal year, as Bell notes, then July makes no sense, but we believe that the date from which the six months was computed is 30 January, the date of King Charles I's execution. This event not only marked the end of an era for English Royalists, but also was regarded by them as the day of accession of the new king, Charles II, 'whose advent was already foreseen'. It was only natural, therefore, for the Royalists who hid the fragments of the crown to choose to date their ritual from 30 January. The day which Brunton realised the ritual referred to was, then, 30 July.

---

[1] Christ, 29.

The Musgrave Ritual

When Musgrave discovered Brunton in the library and told him he must leave his service immediately, Brunton asked to remain for 'a month'. Why should he have demanded so much time, if not because 30 July was still several weeks away? Musgrave told him he could have 'a week'; Brunton, 'in a despairing voice', begged for 'at least a fortnight'. As Zeisler notes, he could not have known beforehand that a few weeks either way would have made little difference because he did not know that his destination was a door and not a spot of earth.[1] Brunton no doubt initially asked for more time than he needed both so he could avoid arousing suspicion by leaving right after finding what he thought was a treasure, and because he expected that his first request would be denied by Musgrave. The 30th was probably about two weeks away from the Thursday night when he was discovered, and the fortnight was the actual amount of time he needed. He was only given a week, however, and decided to test the ritual two days later. Ultimately all of this suggests that the Thursday night when Brunton implored Musgrave for leave to remain for a fortnight was either 11 July or 18 July. Holmes arrived on the scene a week later, either the 18th or the 25th. The former is far more likely given Holmes's comment that the 'moon was shining brightly' and the fact that the full moon in July 1878 was on the 14th. This leaves us to conclude that the case for Holmes occurred on Thursday 18 July 1878.

Having determined the date of the case, we must now see if it agrees with the tentative timeline we delineated above. The precise time on 18 July 1878 when the sun was at an altitude of 33 degrees 31 minutes with an azimuth of 262 degrees 4 minutes—very close to due west—was 4:15 p.m. This, then, was

---

[1] Zeisler, 30.

the time of day when Holmes performed his experiment with the shadow of the pole. The sun would have been falling in the sky by this time as Holmes noted. Holmes referred to the light on the passage floor from the 'setting sun' shortly thereafter, not later than 4:30 p.m., which is, incidentally, the time we proposed above before making our calculations. Even in July, the sun might technically, if unconventionally, be described as setting at this hour, especially when referring to sunlight that was streaming through a small window at an angle. As we speculated above, the police apparently made no haste in going to Hurlstone when they were summoned—or Holmes talked with Musgrave significantly longer than he indicated to Watson—because the sun did not set until 8:07 p.m. on this day. Admittedly a September sunset would be a better fit in these respects, but the other evidence definitely precludes that month, so we must accept these plausible explanations.

Holmes said that the windows of the old part of the house were small and the walls thick and that this was one of the motivating factors in the construction of the new wing. These dingy apertures may, of course, have been updated and enlarged since the time when the new wing was built a century ago, and thus any argument concerning them may be irrelevant. It is worthwhile to present the following explanation, however, if only to pre-empt counterargument. If the window on the west wall was two feet tall and two feet wide, located six feet above the ground in a wall that was one and one-half feet thick—a reasonable estimate for what was not dissimilar to a feudal keep in style—then at 4:30 p.m. on 18 July 1878 the sun would have shone a square of light on the passage floor at the distance of 11 feet 4 inches to 13 feet 3 inches from the west wall. Ten paces eastward on the outside of the north wall followed by four paces southward had brought Holmes to the door, and inside to his right—'Two steps to the west'—the light was shining 'upon the passage floor'. The sunlight as computed would be shining in a square of about two feet by two feet on this very passage floor, illuminating 'the old foot-worn grey stones' as Holmes said. Thus, even if the windows had not changed over the years, there still would have been sunlight upon the passage floor entering from the window in the west wall.

The final task is then to explain why it was not until 4:15 p.m. that Holmes measured the shadow of the pole since Musgrave called upon him in the morning. Evidently Musgrave arrived no earlier than 11 a.m. He would have discussed the case with Holmes until about noon, after which they took the 'first train'—as of that time—which was probably no sooner than 1 p.m. They would have alighted from the train after 2, and it probably took half an hour to drive to Hurlstone. This leaves about an hour and a half of time to be accounted for, and the most likely explanation seems to be that the trains were delayed for any of a number of reasons. This is certainly preferable to Zeisler's illogical assertion that Holmes duly arrived at Hurlstone early and measured the shadow just after 1 p.m. but proceeded to spend an incredible three hours making the paces given in the Ritual, not arriving at the old door until 4 p.m.[1]

This case occurred on 18 July 1878.

---

[1] Zeisler, 38.

21. The Reigate Squires[1]

First published June 1893

This case, Watson tells us plainly, was the one which 'in the spring of '87' caused Holmes to suffer a constitutional breakdown. Watson states that 'on the 14th of April...I received a telegram from Lyons, which informed me that Holmes was lying ill in the Hotel Dulong'. Holmes had spent the previous two months, since mid-February, working on a case which had baffled 'the police of three countries'. Watson arrived in Lyons on the 15th, and 'Three days later we were back in Baker Street together'. Hoping that a change of scenery would help Holmes to recover, Watson took him to visit Colonel Hayter 'a week after our return from Lyons'. They arrived at his house on the 25 April, which was a Monday in 1887, and that very night the Colonel told them that 'Old Acton, who is one of our county magnates, had his house broken into last Monday', the night of the 18th.

The next morning, they learnt of the reported burglary at the Cunninghams' house, and Holmes evinced surprise that the burglars, who were supposed to be the same men who had rifled

---

[1] The original title in the *Strand* magazine was *The Reigate Squire*. This lack of plurality was corrected in the British book edition. The American editors, however—intent, it would seem, upon effacing this reference to class distinction—altered it to *The Reigate Puzzle*.

Acton's house, would burgle another house so close and 'within a few days'. As there was a week between the two robberies, this statement is a bit imprecise, but, given the context, it is not unreasonable to suppose that Holmes used hyperbole to emphasise the unusually short period of time which had apparently elapsed between the robberies.

Holmes later wrote a brief summary of the incident to be used in the advertisement for a reward, and it stated that 'about a quarter to one on Tuesday morning' the burglary was attempted. This, of course, corroborates the date of Monday the 25th as the day when Holmes and Watson arrived at the Colonel's house, for it was during the small hours of the following morning—Tuesday morning—that the attempted burglary occurred.

The case itself, then, occurred on Tuesday 26 April 1887.

22. The Crooked Man

First published July 1893

'One summer night, a few months after my marriage, I was seated by my own hearth smoking a last pipe and nodding over a novel, for my day's work had been an exhausting one.' With this statement Watson begins this account, and from it we can deduce both that Watson was not living at Baker Street and that he was in active medical practice. As he was married sometime in November 1887, this must refer to summer 1888. These two dates, in the overall scheme of a life, are really not very far apart, so it need elicit no surprise that Watson refers to about seven months as merely 'a few'. The year 1888 is further supported by the fact that, as McQueen observes,[1] the Barclays were married after the relief of 'Bhurtee' in 1857 during the Indian Mutiny and had 'been married for upwards of thirty years'.

Holmes referred to 'these little sketches' that Watson wrote when explaining to him that it was by withholding information from the reader that he rendered the accounts remarkable and dramatic. The referenced writings were not necessarily published cases, for no titles or descriptions are given; it is equally likely that they were manuscripts which Watson had prepared for his own amusement, possibly with the hope of future publication.

---

[1] McQueen, 76-77.

The Crooked Man

The mention of the reader, meanwhile, could have been merely figurative, so Watson may not have had as yet any public audience for his writings.

This case occurred between *The Stock-Broker's Clerk* and *The Engineer's Thumb*. At the time of the former Watson had not seen Holmes for quite some time, and Holmes visited Watson's house for the first time. By the time of the latter, Watson was once again frequenting 221B, and Holmes even occasionally visited Watson. Noting the plural implication of Holmes's visits, it is apparent that *The Stock-Broker's Clerk* and this case are the occasions referred to and that this case occurred sometime between 16 June and 23 July 1888.

Colonel Barclay was murdered 'on the evening of last Monday', and Holmes said that the facts of the case 'are only two days old'. Holmes, then, called upon Watson at 11:45 on a Wednesday night. Holmes had already begun investigating 'upon the Tuesday morning', and on the Thursday the two men visited Henry Wood, Watson having assured Holmes that 'Jackson would take my practice'. There are five weeks in which the case might have occurred, and the earliest date possible must be preferred given Watson's remark that it was 'a few months after my marriage', which we know was in November 1887. Thus Holmes's investigation lasted from Tuesday 19 June to Thursday 21 June 1888.

23. The Resident Patient

First published August 1893

With this case it is necessary in the first place to begin by offering some description of the sullied publication history of Watson's account. The original text as written by Watson was first published in the *Strand* in August 1893, but in the subsequent book edition of the cases—the *Memoirs*—a gross addition was made in the form of a large block of text taken from *The Cardboard Box* (which case either Watson or Doyle considered inappropriate for contemporaneous readers and did not publish with the other eleven in the *Memoirs*) in which Holmes deduces Watson's train of thought. The text extracted from *The Cardboard Box* was inserted after the first paragraph of the original narrative, and replaced what was formerly a rather enlightening second paragraph, reproduced below, in which Watson makes several important statements:

> I cannot be sure of the exact date, for some of my memoranda upon the matter have been mislaid, but it must have been towards the end of the first year during which Holmes and I shared chambers in Baker Street. It was boisterous October weather, and we had both remained indoors all day, I because I feared with my shaken health to face the keen autumn wind, while he was deep in some of those abstruse chemical investigations which absorbed him utterly as long as he was engaged

upon them. Towards evening, however, the breaking of a test-tube brought his research to a premature ending, and he sprang up from his chair with an exclamation of impatience and a clouded brow.

"A day's work ruined, Watson," said he, striding across to the window. "Ha! the stars are out and the wind has fallen. What do you say to a ramble through London?"[1]

Interestingly, although the extracted mindreading episode was returned to *The Cardboard Box* when it was published in the collection *His Last Bow* and subsequent collected book editions, *The Resident Patient* was not restored to its original state to include the above paragraphs. The American editors, incomprehensibly, elected to leave it unaltered from its modified state and thus to publish the same identical block of text in both *The Resident Patient* and *The Cardboard Box*. The British editors, meanwhile, removed the intrusive paragraphs, but they did not restore Watson's original text as quoted above, preferring instead to insert the following morsel:

> It had been a close, rainy day in October. "Unhealthy weather, Watson," said my friend. ["]But the evening has brought a breeze with it. What do you say to a ramble through London?"[2]

This truncation is as strange as it is senseless, as it merely presents less information without including anything new which might suggest that the original facts had been erroneous. For this reason, we hold the original text from the *Strand* to be the truest account of this case. Presumably the editorial decisions to retain the text from *The Cardboard Box* or to insert altogether new text

---

[1] *The Original Illustrated Sherlock Holmes*, 282.
[2] Short, RESI, 459.

were made without Watson's knowledge when the collected book editions were being prepared for publication.

Watson, then, tells us that 'I cannot be sure of the exact date, for some of my memoranda upon the matter have been mislaid, but it must have been towards the end of the first year during which Holmes and I shared chambers in Baker Street'. He further declares that 'It was boisterous October weather', which puts the date in October 1881. The fact that he was still complaining about his 'shaken health' supports this, as does his statement that Holmes's 'talk, with its keen observance of detail and subtle power of inference, held me amused and enthralled'. Watson was certainly always impressed by his friend's abilities, even into the final years of their partnership, but he would have felt these emotions most strongly in the first months of their association. The fact that he then says that he 'was sufficiently conversant with Holmes' methods to be able to follow his reasoning' as to the medical nature of their client may at first seem contrary to an early date, but in fact he had had by October 1881 six months of acting with Holmes in which to study his methods, and, being a medical man himself, he would not have had much difficulty recognizing the accoutrements of his own profession.

'At half-past seven next morning, in the first dim glimmer of daylight', Watson says, the case brought to them the previous night by Percy Trevelyan came to a dramatic conclusion. This clearly indicates a time before actual sunrise, yet even on 31 October the sun rises as early as 6:53 a.m., and civil twilight begins at 6:16. It is not until 23 November that sunrise is at 7:31 and the end of December that civil twilight begins about 7:26. The case, then, would seem to have occurred towards the end of November, certainly after the 23rd. It is important to note that

The Resident Patient

Watson speaks at the beginning of the case of October *weather*, not necessarily of the month itself, and it is perfectly natural for him to refer to certain weather experienced in November as being exemplary of what is typical for October. It is also possible that Watson simply indicated the wrong month; he does admit, after all, that some of his notes were lost.

Some explanation is required with regard to the statement that the bank robbery in which Sutton took part occurred in 1875. Biddle, Hayward, and Moffat—who murdered Sutton—were sentenced to fifteen years in prison, and thus they ought not to have been released until 1890. Holmes said that 'When they got out the other day...[it] was some years before their full term'. Some years indeed: if this case occurred in 1881, they were released a full nine years early—meaning that more than half of their sentence was dropped. Hall believes that the case occurred in 1887, as such an early release would have been highly unlikely at that time,[1] but he disregards Watson's statement that this was during his first year living at Baker Street, perhaps because he used the American edition for his analysis. Bell, meanwhile, also places the case in 1887, insisting that Watson's original version was incorrect about the case being in his first year with Holmes as a result of his mislaying his memoranda,[2] but this reasoning would require us to believe that Watson had such a terrible memory that he had dated the case a full six years before its proper time, and this is simply not credible even if Watson had had no notes in front of him. Thus Watson must have incorrectly remembered the term of the prison sentence—not surprising given that, as Christ notes, it was an obscure fact from the past,

---

[1] Hall, 21.
[2] Bell, 44-45.

not personally relevant to Watson[1]—for there is ample evidence to confirm that the case did occur in the first year of Watson's residence with Holmes. We would emphasise that it is far more likely that Watson would accurately remember the date of his own involvement in the case than that he would precisely recall the details of the robbers' prison sentence.

We may assert, then, that the case occurred in late November 1881, though we lack the data necessary to determine precisely the two days.

---

[1] Christ, 32.

24. The Greek Interpreter

First published September 1893

'During my long and intimate acquaintance with Mr. Sherlock Holmes I had never heard him refer to his relations, and hardly ever to his own early life.' This statement, with which Watson begins the account, is in the past perfect tense, and accordingly indicates that, since Holmes had never once alluded to his relations before this case, Watson had known Holmes for quite a long while by this time. Brend, evidently overlooking this fact, places the case in summer 1882 simply because he does not believe that Holmes would have said of any later year than this that 'I did not know you quite so well in those days',[1] which was his reason for not telling Watson more specifically what Mycroft's role in the government was.[2] The very fact that Watson was surprised to have never before heard about Mycroft suggests in itself, however, that they had been living together for considerably more than a year. We may, furthermore, be sure that Mycroft Holmes was not the sort of man who would permit his brother to trust anyone, even a colleague of five or six years, with his rather confidential occupation, though he eventually relented after many years of Holmes and Watson collaborating and undergoing the ordeal of Holmes's apparent death.

---

[1] Short, BRUC, 970.
[2] Brend, 59-60.

The Greek Interpreter

'It was after tea on a summer evening' that the conversation at last turned into such a channel as to induce Holmes to mention his brother. Watson was neither married nor in practice, as he was having afternoon tea with Holmes and was ready enough to go visit Mycroft in the evening, apparently having no other duties to withhold him. Further confirmation of this fact lies in Watson's statement that 'We had reached *our* [emphasis added] house in Baker Street'. The case occurred definitely before November, and probably before September, 1887, then, and, given the opening statement by Watson, it most probably was in 1886 or 1887. Knowing that it was in the summer allows us to eliminate 1887, for during that summer Holmes was experiencing a dearth of cases.[1]

The fact that Mycroft said to Watson that 'I hear of Sherlock everywhere since you became his chronicler' is seized upon by Bell,[2] Christ,[3] and Hall[4] as proof that the case must have occurred after the publication of some of Watson's accounts, and they place it in 1890. Regrettably, in doing so they wilfully disregard— without a convincing explanation—the fact that Watson was clearly neither married nor in practice at the time of this case. We subscribe to Dakin's supposition that Mycroft's statement was probably made at some later date and simply inserted by Watson here, presumably for dramatic effect.[5]

---

[1] Long, SIGN, 143. We deduce this from the fact that, prior to *The Sign of Four,* which began on 6 September 1887, Holmes used cocaine 'Three times a day for many months', and he specifically explained to Watson that he only had need of artificial stimulants when he had no cases to occupy him.
[2] Bell, 69.
[3] Christ, 33.
[4] Hall, 16.
[5] Dakin, 127.

The Greek Interpreter

Given that it was mostly dark outside at 'ten minutes to nine' when Mr Melas reached the house of his clients on the first night, but that there was sufficient light for him to have 'a vague impression of a lawn and trees on each side' of him, we may deduce that civil twilight ended about 9 p.m. It ends at precisely 9 on 11 July, but in 1886 this was a Sunday, and Mr Melas said that his first visit to the house had occurred 'on Monday night'. On Monday 12 July 1886 civil twilight would have ended about 8:58, but the full moon was on the 16th of the month, so the 12th would not have been as dark as Melas indicated. This leads us to conclude that Melas's first visit was on the night of Monday 5 July. Holmes became involved two days later: Melas, when he met Holmes, said that 'This is Wednesday evening'.

Wednesday 7 July 1886, when civil twilight ended at 9:04 and there was still some twilight left at 8:50, was the day of the case.

25. The Naval Treaty

First published October 1893

'The July which immediately succeeded my marriage was made memorable by three cases of interest in which I had the privilege of being associated with Sherlock Holmes, and of studying his methods. I find them recorded in my notes under the headings of "The Adventure of the Second Stain,"[1] "The Adventure of the Naval Treaty," and "The Adventure of the Tired Captain."' Watson thus begins his account of this case, and from this first statement we know at once that it occurred in July 1888. The fact that *The Engineer's Thumb* also occurred in this month is not an issue, for Watson does not say that the 'three cases of interest' which he mentions were the *only* three cases in this month, and it is probable that he did not consider *The Engineer's Thumb* especially interesting (even if its singularity 'made a deep impression upon'[2] him), for Holmes was not very involved and

---

[1] Holmes was highly successful in the 'Second Stain' case which Watson describes here, and thus it cannot be the same one in which Holmes erred, mentioned in *The Yellow Face*. It is also clearly not *The Second Stain* actually published by Watson, for that case involved neither 'Monsieur Dubuque, of the Paris police', nor 'Fritz von Waldbaum, the well-known specialist of Dantzig'. Evidently Watson was extremely partial to this title and used it three times.
[2] Short, ENGR, 201.

The Naval Treaty

had little need 'for those deductive methods of reasoning by which he achieved such remarkable results'.[1]

In confirmation of the fact that he was married, Watson records that 'my wife agreed with me that not a moment should be lost in laying the matter before' Holmes; that he was 'back once more in the old rooms in Baker Street'; and that he had a practice which 'could get along very well for a day or two [without him], since it is the slackest time in the year'. With regard to his qualification of July as 'immediately' succeeding his marriage, he is clearly using this phrase to convey that it was the first *July* after his marriage; if he had meant the first month after his marriage, it would have been far more natural for him to have said 'the *month* which immediately succeeded my marriage'.

Percy Phelps said that 23 May was 'nearly ten weeks ago'. Ten weeks later precisely would have been 1 August, so the date was a few days before this. He would not have said nearly ten weeks if it were only a day or two into the tenth week, so the case must have occurred sometime between 28 and 31 July. Inspector Forbes, conversely, referred to the interval of time as 'all these nine weeks', but as he was referring to whole weeks, he evidently omitted the tenth week because it was not yet completed.

On the same day that they called upon Phelps, Holmes and Watson found 'that Lord Holdhurst was still in his chambers at Downing Street'. As they had arrived in London at 'twenty-past three' and had gone to Scotland Yard and talked with Inspector Forbes before driving to Downing Street, it must have been well after 4 p.m. when they arrived. Given that Lord Holdhurst was still at his office at that hour, this was certainly a week-day, so we may rule out 28 and 29 July. These two days are also eliminated

---

[1] Short, ENGR, 201.

The Naval Treaty

by the fact that Watson and his wife discussed how his practice would not suffer if he left it 'for a day or two', a comment (made on the first day of the case) which would have been unnecessary and illogical if spoken on or immediately before a Sunday, when he would not have been working in any case. As noted above, 26 or 27 July as the first day would not work as both Holmes and Phelps stated that 'nearly ten weeks' had passed since the document was stolen, and those would be only a day or two after the ninth full week. We are left, then, with the 30th and the 31st as possibilities for the first day of the case.

The events occurred over the course of three days. Holmes and Watson went to Briarbrae and consulted Forbes and Lord Holdhurst on the first day; they went back to Briarbrae on the second day, and Phelps returned to London with Watson while Holmes remained that night at Woking; and Holmes returned the treaty to Phelps on the morning of the third day. As Watson states that this case occurred in July, it must have occurred more in July than in August; therefore, the first two days would have been 30 and 31 July, while the third morning would have been that of 1 August.

Thus the case occurred from 30 July to 1 August 1888.

26. The Final Problem

First published November 1893

Watson mentions a 'lapse of two years' between the time of the events of this case and the time either of writing or of publication. If the case occurred in April 1891, as Watson indicates, November 1893 would be closer to three years, but we may reasonably suppose that Watson did not write the manuscript immediately before it was published. Probably he wrote it in spring or summer 1893, when it was about two years since the events.

Watson refers to his writings about Holmes's cases in such a manner as to suggest that their partnership began with *A Study in Scarlet* (as it did) and that the most recent case was *The Naval Treaty*. We know that of the recorded cases the most recent to have occurred was in fact *The Red-Headed League*, but as Watson was clearly referring back to his writings in the order in which they had been published, we need not concern ourselves further with this minor issue.

Holmes said that his most recent cases included 'assistance to the Royal Family of Scandinavia, and to the French Republic'. In *The Noble Bachelor*, four years earlier, Holmes mentioned that his most recent noble client was 'The King of Scandinavia'.[1] These

---

[1] Short, NOBL, 231.

cannot be the same case, so he must have helped this regal family on more than one occasion. The fact that one of these times was evidently during the year 1890—for Holmes was 'engaged by the French Government upon a matter of supreme importance' from winter 1890 until he suddenly appeared in Watson's consulting room on 24 April 1891—does not conflict with Watson's statement that 'in the year 1890 there were only three cases of which I retain any record', for he did not take part in or make notes of either of the cases of the Scandinavian royals, and the three published accounts were, as we have shown above and will show below, *The Valley of Fear*, *A Case of Identity*, and *The Red-Headed League*.

McQueen admits himself baffled by the fact that Holmes was apparently in two places at once in the first months of 1891, both solving a case 'of supreme importance' in France and actively pursuing Moriarty (who complained that Holmes frustrated his plans repeatedly in January, February, and March), for he believes that the French case was too demanding to have allowed Holmes to travel to London even occasionally for his encounters with Moriarty.[1] The very simple explanation we offer to this seemingly formidable conundrum is that Moriarty was the criminal mastermind behind the case which Holmes was solving in France.

We know that *The Final Problem* began 'upon the evening of the 24th of April', and repeated references to 1891 substantiate that as the year. Watson's wife, Mary, was still alive and well, though at this time she was 'away upon a visit'. When Holmes proposed to Watson that he join him for a week's sojourn on the Continent, Watson assured him that 'The practice is quiet' and

---

[1] McQueen, 118-121.

The Final Problem

that he had 'an accommodating neighbour', though this was no longer Anstruther, whose obliging services Watson had lost after moving to Kensington.

On the night that Holmes made his unexpected appearance at Watson's residence, he said that 'In three days, that is to say on Monday next', Moriarty and his gang would be captured. Holmes arrived at Watson's house on the night of Friday 24 April 1891, therefore, and the next day they departed for the Continent. Watson says that 'We made our way to Brussels that night and spent two days there, moving on upon the third day as far as Strasburg'. This would seem to indicate that they arrived in Strasburg on Tuesday 28 April, yet 'On the Monday morning [the 27th] Holmes had telegraphed to the London police, and in the evening we found a reply waiting for us at our hotel'. This was regarding the capture of the criminals—they learnt that Moriarty had escaped—but Watson clearly states that they were at the Strasburg hotel when they discussed this on the Monday evening.

Though it would seem at first from a computation of the days spent travelling that they should have arrived in Strasburg on the Tuesday, it is evident, therefore, that they had arrived by the evening of the Monday. Noting that Watson says that they left Brussels for Strasburg 'upon the third day', it becomes clear that he must have meant the third day of their journey, which, taken from their departure on Saturday, the 25th, would be Monday, the 27th. Two full days were not, then, spent at Brussels, but rather two calendar days, from Saturday night to Monday morning. Holmes must have sent his telegram from Brussels and indicated for the reply to be sent to a particular hotel in Strasburg where they received it upon their arrival that evening. They discussed

The Final Problem

matters 'in the Strasburg *salle-à-manger*...for half an hour' but continued their journey that same night.

In any case this is a minor point, and one of no great importance for determining the overall date of the case, for Watson tells us that 'It was upon the 3rd of May that we reached the little village of Meiringen', and on the 4th, a Monday, they made the fateful journey to the Reichenbach Falls. The momentous events of this case lasted from 24 April to 4 May 1891.

27. The Hound of the Baskervilles

First published from August 1901 to April 1902

Like *The Sign of Four*, this case contains volumes of contradictory evidence which have caused considerable disagreement amongst chronologists as to the date. In the first place it will be useful to determine the months and days of the case, thereby limiting the possible years.

The Month and the Day

The case began on the day that 'Dr.' Mortimer returned to Baker Street, having left his stick behind the day before.

On the second day, Mortimer called upon Holmes with Sir Henry Baskerville at 10 a.m. This day they also met for luncheon at 2 p.m. Sir Henry said that he intended to go to Baskerville Hall 'At the end of the week', and Holmes asked, 'I suppose that by Saturday all might be ready?' The second day cannot, therefore, be a Friday, or Holmes would have said 'tomorrow'.

On the Saturday morning, Holmes said that 'I have made some inquiries myself in the last few days', while Mortimer averred that he and Sir Henry had not been 'shadowed during the last two days'. This shows that two days had elapsed since they had last gathered on the day of the luncheon, the second day. Although Thursday afternoon to Saturday morning at 10:30

might conceivably have been referred to as two days, it is far more probable that the second day of the case was a Wednesday, that Thursday and Friday were the 'few days' and 'two days' which had intervened, and that Saturday was the fifth day of the case. Surely, if only Friday had elapsed, Mortimer and Holmes would both have said 'yesterday'.

Selden escaped on the Wednesday before the arrival of Sir Henry and Watson at Baskerville Hall; this Wednesday we have determined to be the second day of the case.

The case clearly occurred in autumn, as the moor showed signs of dying vegetation upon the day of their arrival (Saturday, the fifth day). Watson observed that night that 'A half moon broke through the rifts of racing clouds'.

On Sunday, the sixth day, Watson went to Grimpen to ask if the telegram sent by Holmes had been received by Barrymore personally. He met Mr Stapleton, who mentioned that the autumn rains rendered the Grimpen Mire especially dangerous. Stapleton further remarked that Cyclopides was 'seldom found in the late autumn'. Later this day Stapleton called upon Sir Henry at Baskerville Hall.

On 'the very next morning' (the seventh day, Monday), Stapleton showed the spot where the death of Sir Hugo Baskerville supposedly occurred in the legend, and Sir Henry met Mrs Stapleton for the first time.

On Thursday, apparently 11 October, the seventeenth day (see below concerning 13 October), Mortimer visited Baskerville Hall, and after the Stapletons arrived, Sir Henry showed everyone the yew alley. This was 'The other day—Thursday, to be more exact' relative to 13 October.

The 12 October was the night upon which Watson observed Barrymore at the window for the first time.

The 13 October was the morning when Watson wrote his first report. This would most likely have been a Saturday, given the reference to Thursday as 'the other day'. Watson also says in his first report that 'a fortnight has passed' since Selden escaped. This suggests that 13 October was the sixteenth day of the case, as Selden was said to have escaped on the second day, a Wednesday; but it must have been at least the nineteenth day, because it was a Saturday, so Watson must have been using the term fortnight loosely. The first report was written, then, on the weekend of the nineteenth and twentieth days. Presuming that it was the nineteenth, as that would be closer to a fortnight, we can assert that 13 October was a Saturday.

On this day Watson discussed with Sir Henry after breakfast what he had seen Barrymore doing (he wrote the first report early, before eating), and they determined to wait up for him that night. He never appeared. Earlier, after the conversation about Barrymore, the interview on the moor between Sir Henry and Mrs Stapleton, so rudely interrupted by her 'brother', had occurred. Sir Henry said on this day that he had only known Mrs Stapleton 'these few weeks'; this suggests that three weeks had passed since the seventh day, when Sir Henry met the lady. We know from the evidence of the first report, however, that he said this on the nineteenth day, so in fact less than two weeks had elapsed. Sir Henry's imprecision may be attributed to his infatuation with Mrs Stapleton: his strong sentiments would have made him feel exceptionally familiar with her and would have distorted his perception of time. Also on this day Sir Henry and Watson arranged to dine at Merripit House 'next Friday'.

The 14 October (a Sunday, the twentieth day) was the night upon which Watson and Sir Henry followed Barrymore, after which they went out upon the moor to capture Selden. There was a moon full enough to afford some light, but mostly covered by clouds, making for a night which was, at times at least, 'pitch-dark'. Of this peculiar moon, Watson referred to 'the lower curve of its silver disc'.

The 15 October (a Monday, the twenty-first day) was definitely the day that Watson wrote his second report. He composed it fairly early, as he said that 'To-day we mean to communicate to the Princetown people' about Selden. He referred to their pursuit of the convict 'last night', fixing it on the night of the 14th-15th. He also said, however, at the beginning of the report that 'To-day' was the day when Stapleton violently interrupted Sir Henry's interview with Mrs Stapleton; but he then declared that those events happened after his conversation with Sir Henry about Barrymore, as detailed above, which he plainly stated took place on the morning following his discovery of Barrymore at the window (on the 12th). Since that conversation and Sir Henry's meeting with Mrs Stapleton both occurred on 13 October, the 'To-day' regarding the latter was clearly an error.

Watson's journal entry for 'October 16th' described a 'dull and foggy day'. He suggested in his diary entry that it was the day after 'the excitements of the night', presumably the chase of Selden, which occurred on the night of the 14th-15th of October, not the 15th-16th, and he told of Barrymore confronting Sir Henry about pursuing Selden 'this morning after breakfast'. All of this shows that this entry actually addressed the events of 15 October and that Watson wrote his 'second report' before breakfast on that day to describe the events of the two previous days. We can only suppose that his hand-written '15th' for this day's journal entry was so illegible that when he returned to it later it looked to him more like a '16th'.

The Hound of the Baskervilles

Watson's entry for 17 October (a Wednesday, the twenty-third day) appears to actually refer to that day. He walked on the moor and met Mortimer, who told him about 'L.L.' He spoke with Barrymore about the other man whom Selden had seen on the moor. Barrymore said that he did not know if Selden was still at large, and that he had last taken food to him 'three days ago'. As Barrymore provided him with food 'every second night' if he replied to the signal, this would agree with the fact that Watson saw Barrymore at the window on the night of the 12th, that he did not appear on the night of the 13th, and that the last time Barrymore had tried to give Selden food was upon the night of the 14th, when he was caught in the act by Watson and Sir Henry.[1] Barrymore had no need to give him food on the night of the 16th because already on the morning of the 15th Barrymore had 'provided him with all that he can want' until 'in a very few days the necessary arrangements will have been made and he will be on his way to South America'.[2]

Watson said that 18 October (a Thursday, the twenty-fourth day) was the day after his discovery of 'L.L.' and conversation with Barrymore about the man on the tor living in a hut, so those events undoubtedly occurred on 17 October. On the 18th, he visited Mrs Lyons and went in search of the man amongst the stone huts whom he discovered to be Holmes. Together they found Selden's body after his encounter with the hound. Watson

---

[1] We suspect that Barrymore, after Watson and Sir Henry returned from their pursuit of Selden, slipped outside with the food and left it at whatever location had been predetermined, thus providing for the escapee in the event that he should dare to return. Watson would therefore have had good reason to ask him if he had seen Selden, whom they had chased rather far away, that night.
[2] Since, as of the morning of the 17th, Barrymore had last taken food to Selden three days ago (on the night of the 14th), whatever supplies he gave him on the morning of the 15th clearly did not include comestibles.

said that 'the shadows were thick upon the moor'. He later spoke of the moon rising and making the moor 'half silver and half gloom'. It was bright enough for him to distinguish Stapleton from a distance. All of this suggests that the moon was close to full at this time. As Holmes and Watson walked back to Baskerville Hall, Holmes remarked that Sir Henry was engaged to dine with the Stapletons 'to-morrow', which means 19 October must have been a Friday, and the 18th was certainly a Thursday.

This Friday was the twenty-fifth day of the case. Holmes and Watson pretended to abandon Sir Henry and to go to London, but in fact they did not leave Dartmoor. They visited Mrs Lyons, Lestrade arrived, and they hid themselves on the moor to watch as Sir Henry departed from Merripit House that night. Watson said 'a half-moon bathed the whole scene in a soft, uncertain light'. Thus the moon was waning from mid-October and was then about half full; on the 18th it was, consequently, not as close to full as we had supposed.

Saturday 20 October was the twenty-sixth and final day of the case. Mrs Stapleton showed Holmes, Watson, and Lestrade the path into the mire, and they discovered Stapleton's hideout.

The final tabulation of days is as follows:

- ❖ 25 September, a Tuesday, the first day: Mortimer introduces the case
- ❖ 26 September, a Wednesday, the second day: Sir Henry and Mortimer visit Baker Street and Selden escapes from prison
- ❖ 29 September, a Saturday, the fifth day: Sir Henry and Watson arrive at Baskerville Hall

- ❖ 30 September, a Sunday, the sixth day: Watson meets Stapleton while in Grimpen
- ❖ 1 October, a Monday, the seventh day: Sir Henry meets Mrs Stapleton
- ❖ 11 October, a Thursday, the seventeenth day: Mortimer and the Stapletons visit Sir Henry
- ❖ 12 October, a Friday, the eighteenth day: Watson sees Barrymore going to the window at night
- ❖ 13 October, a Saturday, the nineteenth day: Sir Henry and Mrs Stapleton meet on the moor
- ❖ 14 October, a Sunday, the twentieth day: Watson and Sir Henry chase Selden on the moor
- ❖ 15 October, a Monday, the twenty-first day: Barrymore speaks with Sir Henry about Selden
- ❖ 17 October, a Wednesday, the twenty-third day: Watson speaks with Barrymore about the man on the moor
- ❖ 18 October, a Thursday, the twenty-fourth day: Watson finds Holmes's retreat on the moor
- ❖ 19 October, a Friday, the twenty-fifth day: Sir Henry is attacked by the Hound of the Baskervilles
- ❖ 20 October, a Saturday, the twenty-sixth day: Holmes investigates Stapleton's hideout

The 19 October, which was without a doubt a Friday, was a Friday in 1883, in 1888, in 1894, and in 1900. These are the only tenable years for the case.

Evidence for an Earlier Case

Mortimer's stick was engraved with the year 1884. This clearly precludes the year 1883, as does Watson's Medical Directory's reference to Mortimer as a 'House-surgeon, from 1882–1884'. Holmes said that 'he [Mortimer] left five years ago—the date is on the stick', which would place the case in 1889, but we know that to be impossible, so some mistake must have occurred (see below).

When Mortimer arrived, Holmes said, 'Don't move, I beg you, Watson'. This is indicative of a very early date in the partnership, most likely within a few years of 1881, but we have already eliminated 1883 as a possible year. A similar remark was made at the time of *The Sign of Four* in September 1887, and we have already explained that this was a mere jest; the same may be true in this instance.

Watson says that he was flattered by Holmes's words of praise for him, which may suggest an earlier date, when he would have been keen to impress Holmes, though given Holmes's rather austere nature Watson would doubtless have been glad of any praise at any time.

'Congratulate me, my dear Holmes, and tell me that I have not disappointed you as an agent—that you do not regret the confidence which you showed in me when you sent me down.' This appeal was made by Watson in his second report, and it betrayed a lack of self-confidence and a hunger for approval more likely to characterise the earlier years. This supposition is supported by Watson thinking his discovery of the man on the tor would have been a triumph where his 'master had failed'.

Holmes said that the apparent death of the baronet was 'the greatest blow which has befallen me in my career'. Given that

Openshaw met his untimely demise in autumn 1887 through a definite lack of caution on Holmes's part, this statement would most logically have been made before then—but we already know 1883 to be an impossible year.

Holmes said that 'we have never had a foeman more worthy of our steel'. Even if we regard Stapleton as being more formidable, in a supremely cunning sort of way, than Milverton, Moran, and company, we can hardly credit him with being superior to Moriarty. It seems that this case occurred before January 1890, when Holmes encountered Moriarty's work first-hand in the affair of *The Valley of Fear*.

Evidence for a Later Case

Mortimer, in his first interview with Holmes, referred to him as 'the second highest expert in Europe', second only to Monsieur Bertillon. Zeisler argues conclusively that, because Alphonse Bertillon's system of criminal detection was not published until 1890, this comment could only have been made after that date.[1]

'He had never said as much before, and I must admit that his words gave me keen pleasure, for I had often been piqued by his indifference to my admiration and to the attempts which I had made to give publicity to his methods.' This statement by Watson indicates a later date, for he mentions his attempts to publicise Holmes's methods, obviously via his published accounts, and there were not enough to warrant the use of the plural 'attempts' before the publication of his second case in 1890. Again, Holmes said that 'in all the accounts which you have been so good as to give of my own small achievements you have

---

[1] Zeisler, 118.

habitually underrated your own abilities'. This second mention of multiple accounts presented to the public necessitates a date after 1890, probably after 1891.[1]

Sir Charles made his money in South African speculation, returning to Devonshire two years before his death. The only plausible gold or diamond rush by which Sir Charles might have made his fortune was the Witwatersrand Gold Rush of 1886; this fact eliminates 1888, for 'It is only two years since he took up his residence at Baskerville Hall', and he could not have heard of the discovery, which only occurred in July 1886, travelled to the Witwatersrand (even if he had already been elsewhere in South Africa for some reason), made his fortune through speculation, and returned to England all by the end of the year 1886, which date would even then be closer to a year and a half than two years from the date of his death (from late 1886 to May 1888). Thus this is strong evidence for 1894 or 1900, as his speculation most likely lasted some considerable time, and Sir Charles may not have gone directly to Baskerville Hall after making his fortune.

Watson spent all day at his club while Holmes familiarised himself with Dartmoor; Holmes remarked that Watson had no intimate friends, and he obviously had neither wife nor medical practice. Thus 1887–1891 becomes untenable, eliminating the possibility of an 1888 date. The year 1894 remains viable, as we know from *The Norwood Builder* that Watson had by July of that year sold his practice and moved back to 221B, and he was still there in 1900.

---

[1] We would note that these references to cases already published are not of the same type as the specific references to case names which we have in some instances discredited. These allusions are more general and therefore more absolute and cannot be discounted with such impunity.

Holmes referred to 'five hundred cases of capital importance'. According to Watson in *The Speckled Band*, he had notes for some seventy cases in the years 1881–1889, and although Holmes obviously handled many more, of course nowhere near all of these were of 'capital importance'. Indeed, it seems unlikely that a full five hundred of great importance would have been handled any time before 1900.

Watson agreed to go to Baskerville Hall with Sir Henry, saying, 'I do not know how I could employ my time better'. These are decidedly not the words of a married man, nor of a man with a practice, so this is additional evidence that the case must have occurred after the Return.

Sir Henry remarked that he wanted to install 'a row of electric lamps' on the drive leading to the Hall. Although the first electric lamps were installed commercially in the mid-1880s, they were not widely available for private use at that time. Indeed, electric lighting did not begin to be used on a large scale until after the Great War, and even amongst the wealthy it only started to become popular during the Edwardian Era. A later year is clearly more likely.

Stapleton said that he recognised Watson as Holmes's associate because 'The records of your detective have reached us here, and you could not celebrate him without being known yourself'. This additional reference to multiple published accounts corroborates a date no earlier than 1890.

Watson and Sir Henry ran after Selden for a considerable distance; they 'were both fair runners and in good condition'. This does not suggest an early case when Watson was younger, for his leg was decidedly a bother to him at the time of *A Study in Scarlet* and still during *The Sign of Four* (whether the latter is dated in '87, '88, or '89 being irrelevant); it indicates rather that an older Watson had finally healed and taken it upon himself to become more physically fit. This evidence does not, incidentally, support 1894 over 1900, for, although one might presume that Watson, being younger, would be also naturally fitter then than in 1900, the fact is that in 1895 Watson could not keep pace with Holmes's running due to his 'sedentary life'.[1] Ultimately, his endurance in *The Hound of the Baskervilles* favours 1900 (when he, being 48, could still have been an active runner), and we may infer from this that he sought to improve his stamina after the embarrassing episode in 1895 and was consequently more fit by 1900. Indeed, as early as 1897 he had so far improved himself that he was able to run across Hampstead Heath with Holmes.[2]

Mrs Laura Lyons's working with a typewriter is further evidence for a later date. Typewriting did not really emerge as a viable profession until the 1890s, so it is not likely that Sir Charles would have chosen it for her in 1888 or any other earlier year. Miss Sutherland was indeed earning some extra money through the use of a typewriter in June 1890, as we noted above, but this was not her profession, so the fact that Sir Charles thought typewriting the best *profession* in which to establish Mrs Lyons definitely suggests that this case occurred after the Return.

'We all three shook hands, and I saw at once from the reverential way in which Lestrade gazed at my companion that he had learned a good deal since the days when they had first worked together. I could well remember the scorn which the theories of the reasoner used then to excite in the practical man.' This statement suggests a date long after *A Study in Scarlet*, and also after *The Norwood Builder*, an 1894 case in which Lestrade had

---

[1] Short, SOLI, 652.
[2] See our discussion of *Charles Augustus Milverton* for the evidence for the date of this incident.

still much contempt for Holmes, saying to him that 'You are too many for me when you begin to get on your theories, Mr. Holmes',[1] and in which Watson commented upon 'Lestrade staring at my friend with amazement, expectation, and derision chasing each other across his features'.[2] The statement in *The Hound of the Baskervilles* is far more in consonance with Lestrade's attitude in *The Six Napoleons* of June 1900,[3] by which time Lestrade openly expressed his admiration for Holmes's abilities. This supports not only a later date, but also, more specifically, 1900 over 1894.

Earlier or Later?

As is clear from the facts discussed above, there is far more evidence for a later case than for an earlier one. The year 1883 is definitely too early, and there are multiple objections to this date in the text. As to 1888, it is impossible given the fact that Watson was married at that time, but even if he were not, there are a number of other objections. Even ignoring our dating of *The Sign of Four*, 1888 would still be untenable. How, then, do we explain the evidence suggesting an earlier case?

Regarding the 1884 date on Mortimer's stick and Holmes's comment that it was from five years ago, we know that when Watson wrote *The Hound of the Baskervilles* for publication he was still restrained by the prohibition from Holmes to reveal to the public that Holmes was alive. Thus, when he wrote this account, he had to make it seem to have occurred before Holmes's

---

[1] Short, NORW, 592. See our discussion of *The Norwood Builder* for the evidence for its date.
[2] Short, NORW, 605.
[3] See our discussion of *The Six Napoleons* for the evidence for its date.

supposed death in April 1891. What better way to do this than to obfuscate the real date with plainly stated false ones, early in the narrative? The probability of this theory is only increased by the fact that we are not the only chronologist to have proposed something like it. After formulating our theory independently, we learnt that the Rev. G. Basil Jones proposed a similar theory,[1] and although he failed to adhere to the evidence of the days and dates and opted for 1899 as the year, he still used the theory to show that the case occurred after the Return.

Holmes's remark to Watson to remain when Mortimer arrived definitely suggests an early date. This entire paragraph, and parts of the entire opening episode, have a feel of the early years. Obviously, Watson, when he began writing, had the intention of thoroughly disguising the case to make it seem to have occurred in the early 1880s. His efforts amounted to nought, however, for as he progressed into the later portions of his narrative he unconsciously strayed from this objective.

McQueen believes that Watson's surprise at being recommended by Holmes to accompany Sir Henry to Baskerville Hall indicates an early year, before he had been sent on other missions by Holmes,[2] but we think Watson's reaction was merely the result of the mission involving a considerable length of time at a great distance from London.[3] Furthermore, as McQueen himself notes as a counterpoint, Watson may have been surprised at a later date because Holmes's caustic remarks about his performance in *The Solitary Cyclist*, *The Disappearance of Lady*

---

[1] Dakin, 148-149.
[2] McQueen, 152-153.
[3] *The Disappearance of Lady Frances Carfax*, the only case in which Watson went on a mission even more demanding than this one on behalf of Holmes, did not occur until 1901 (as shown in our discussion of the case).

Frances Carfax, and *The Retired Colourman* had led him to believe that he would not again be entrusted with a serious mission.[1]

As noted above, Holmes was such an austere man, and so seldom gave compliments to anyone, that there is no reason why Watson should not have been pleased by one of the rare occasions on which his friend offered him praise, no matter what the year or how long the partnership. We do not doubt that this would have satisfied Watson in 1900 nearly as much as in 1888.

Watson's supplicatory Second Report to Holmes in which he pined for approval may be explained by the fact that this was the largest task with the greatest responsibility that Holmes had yet entrusted to him. Naturally, he was anxious not to disappoint the faith which his friend had placed in him by sending him.

Regarding Watson's remark that his discovery of the identity of the man on the tor would have been a triumph where Holmes had failed, the same reasons given for the point immediately above apply, as does the simple fact that Watson wished to make this statement supremely ironic in hindsight: he sought to triumph where he thought Holmes had failed, but in the end this was by discovering Holmes himself.

What are we to make of Holmes's statement that the death of Sir Henry was his greatest failure ever, given that he let Openshaw walk away to his death in 1887? It can, for several reasons, be explained without accusing Holmes of caring more about the titled baronet than the commoner Openshaw. Firstly, Openshaw had come to Holmes for advice, he had given it, and his client had died as a result of Holmes's not appreciating the immediacy of the danger. This was, to be sure, a grave mistake

---

[1] McQueen, 152-153, 163. He places the case of Lady Frances Carfax before *The Hound of the Baskervilles*.

that led to a tragedy. Sir Henry, meanwhile, was Holmes's client; Holmes had given him advice and, realising how dangerous the situation was, ordered Watson to watch over him; and when he thought that he had permitted the baronet to go out alone, fully aware of the danger and yet foolishly allowing it to materialise anyway, he really believed that he had suffered his greatest blow. Both men were thought to have died as a result of his own actions, and both supposed deaths were tragic, but evidently Holmes regarded the instance in which he *definitely knew* of the immediate danger, and failed to prevent it, as the more egregious.

Secondly, Holmes said that 'In order to have my case well-rounded and complete, I have thrown away the life of my client'. The circumstances were not the same with Openshaw, and he understandably felt even worse about not immediately warning Sir Henry for the sake of the completeness of his case.

Thirdly, if *The Hound of the Baskervilles* occurred in 1894 or 1900, the death of Openshaw had occurred either seven or thirteen years earlier, and while we may be sure that Holmes never forgot it, the immediacy and shock of the death of Sir Henry might very reasonably have resulted in his uttering the exclamation in question in the harrowing wake of his fresh defeat. This third observation favours 1900, more distant from Openshaw's death, over 1894.

Holmes's two statements—'I told you in London, Watson, and I tell you now again, that we have never had a foeman more worthy of our steel', and 'I said it in London, Watson, and I say it again now, that never yet have we helped to hunt down a more dangerous man'—suggest the impossible, namely that Stapleton was a more formidable criminal than Professor Moriarty. Perhaps he was more clever than Moran, and possibly Milverton, but not Moriarty. The only explanation of these alleged statements, which Watson quoted Holmes saying on both of these occasions, as well as, in slightly less superlative terms, a third time, is that Watson employed them as a means of convincing his readers that the case had occurred before Holmes's showdown with Moriarty in 1891.

1894 or 1900?

In deciding between 1894 and 1900, the first point to consider is the moon. In 1900, the moon was full on 8 October. It was at half on 14 October, the night of the convict chase, which is tenable; but it would then have been at precisely one quarter, waning, on the night of the crisis, when Watson specifically states that it was a half-moon. Meanwhile, in 1894, 14 October was the full moon, which is perfectly acceptable—if there were thick clouds, it would not have been too bright—and the 19th was only two days before the half-moon.

However, Watson stated that on the night of Saturday 29 September he saw a 'half moon'. In 1894, 29 September was a *new moon*. In 1900, 1 October was a half-moon; thus, two days earlier, on 29 September, the moon would have been close to half full. The moon, on overall balance, favours 1900, as it is a possible match for all three dates in this year, while 29 September is irreconcilable in 1894. Watson, we must suppose, wrongly remembered the precise stage of the moon on the night of the crisis.

Another point to consider is that in reply to Lestrade's question, 'Anything good?', Holmes said, 'The biggest thing for years'. This was a very significant and complicated case, and 1894 or 1900 could be possible, though overall it seems more probable that this statement would have been made in 1900, after six years of cases to compare its importance to, not in 1894, after only half of a year had passed since the Return.

We must also consider a second conflict regarding Holmes's comment about Sir Henry's apparent death being his greatest defeat. In 1898, Holmes's client Hilton Cubitt was murdered by Abe Slaney, arguably because, as in the case of Sir Henry, Holmes was too concerned about having a complete case and failed to take adequate precautions for his client's safety.[1] This obviously supports 1894 as the year, for Cubitt's death would then be in the future, thereby explaining why Holmes did not seem to consider it to be as serious as Sir Henry's apparent demise.

The rest of the evidence has already been presented above and appears in the following summary:

In favour of 1894:
   1. Cubitt's death in 1898
In favour of 1900:
   1. The electric lamps
   2. Watson's stamina as a runner
   3. Lestrade's reverence for Holmes
   4. The elapsed time since Openshaw's death
   5. The moon
   6. Holmes's comment to Lestrade

The electric lamps and time since Openshaw's death, while they favour 1900, do not categorically disqualify 1894, but the moon stages and especially Lestrade's attitude towards Holmes in this case, juxtaposed with his behaviour in *The Norwood Builder* and

---

[1] See our discussion of *The Dancing Men* for the evidence for the date of this incident, the year of which was unquestionably 1898.

The Six Napoleons in 1894 and 1900, respectively, definitely preclude 1894.

As to Cubitt's death, we would note that in that instance Holmes was not certain of the full magnitude of the danger which threatened his client, for though he suspected that the whole mystery revolved upon something criminal in Elsie's past, he had no reason to fear that it would end in murder until the evening when he received both the final set of dancing men drawings from Cubitt and the telegram from New York confirming that Slaney was 'The most dangerous crook in Chicago',[1] and by then it was too late for him to prevent the tragedy. Thus, though Holmes surely felt the loss of his client to be a serious blow, he could not blame himself to the same degree as in the case of Sir Henry, for whom he knew the danger was both lethal and imminent.

The Hound of the Baskervilles occurred from 25 September to 20 October 1900.

---

[1] Short, DANC, 633.

28. The Empty House

First published September 1903

'It was in the spring of the year 1894' that Ronald Adair was murdered. The inquest 'led up to a verdict of wilful murder', and Watson, having 'read the evidence at the inquest', says that 'All day as I drove upon my round I turned over the case in my mind, and found no explanation which appeared to me to be adequate'. He was, then, still in practice at this time, and in fact he still owned the same practice as at the time of Holmes's disappearance, for he states that, after visiting the scene of the murder in the evening following his professional round, 'I retraced my steps to Kensington' and 'had not been in my study five minutes when the maid entered to say that a person desired to see me'. This person was, of course, Sherlock Holmes.

Watson says that Adair was killed 'on the night of March 30, 1894'. Holmes was already preparing to return to England when he heard of Adair's death, whereupon he 'came over at once to London'. Watson says that Holmes revealed himself on an 'April evening'; this was upon the same day that Holmes arrived in London. This day, the day of the case, was apparently the day after the inquest into the death of Ronald Adair, since the results would have appeared on the following morning in the papers and been available for Watson to read and spend 'All day' mulling over.

The Empty House

The French papers would have published the death of Adair on 31 March or 1 April, and Holmes would have arrived a couple of days later, after concluding his affairs in France. The inquest, which probably began on 2 April, the Monday following the tragedy, would not have taken long to reach its unenlightened conclusion, so it was evidently upon Tuesday 3 April that Watson spent the day doing his professional round and thinking about the inquest, and upon which Holmes arrived in London and revealed himself.

The case, then, occurred on the evening of Tuesday 3 April in the year 1894.

29. The Norwood Builder

First published October 1903

Watson states that 'At the time of which I speak, Holmes had been back for some months, and I, at his request, had sold my practice and returned to share the old quarters in Baker Street'. This case evidently occurred in mid-1894. Holmes said that 'The weather has been so very warm these last few days', suggesting a summer date, and his subsequent statement that he 'crawled about the lawn with an August sun on my back' suggests that that is the month, though an intense sun in any summer month might conceivably be thus denominated.

Some chronologists cite Watson's statement that 'this period includes the case of the papers of ex-President Murillo'—which, they aver, refers to the same man who was involved in the events of *Wisteria Lodge*—as proof of this case occurring after *Wisteria Lodge*, and they accordingly either move *The Empty House* several months earlier and place *Wisteria Lodge* in March 1894,[1] or they date this case after *Wisteria Lodge* in 1895.[2] None of this manipulation is, however, necessary, for two reasons: there were no papers involved in the *Wisteria Lodge* case, and the Murillo of *Wisteria Lodge* was repeatedly referred to as a dictator but never as a president. Thus, far from there being any proof that these

---

[1] Dakin, 162-163.
[2] Bell, 86.

The Norwood Builder

two cases actually involved the same man, there is rather evidence to the contrary. Bell further argues that Watson's failure to list *The Norwood Builder* amongst 'our work for the year 1894'[1] at the beginning of *The Golden Pince-Nez*, a November 1894 case,[2] is proof that the former did not occur in 1894,[3] but this is a baseless claim, for the list provided by Watson not only is far from exhaustive, but also contains unpublished cases exclusively, of which *The Norwood Builder* is not one.

On the day that John Hector McFarlane appeared at the Baker Street rooms to tell his tale, Holmes went to Blackheath and afterwards to Oldacre's house in Norwood. The next morning Watson awoke to find that Holmes had received a telegram from Lestrade, and this prompted the two men to return to Norwood, the upshot of which visit was that Holmes solved the case, to Lestrade's ineffable shock and chagrin.

With no better evidence to rely upon, we turn to Zeisler's meteorological data for some guidance. Holmes remarked that it had 'not rained for a month' and that 'this drought has made everything as hard as iron', in addition to commenting, as noted above, that it 'has been so very warm'. Zeisler, by showing that July and August 1894 were quite rainy, whereas from 11 June to 2 July it rained only once, and by further noting that it was above eighty degrees Fahrenheit during the week prior to 2 July, presents a strong argument that the case began on Monday 2 July 1894 and ended the following day.[4] As there is no evidence that would contradict or supersede the meteorological data, we concur with him that the case occurred from 2 to 3 July 1894.

---

[1] Short, GOLD, 782. See page 783 for a full list of the cases referred to here.
[2] See our discussion of *The Golden Pince-Nez* for the evidence for its date.
[3] Bell, 86.
[4] Zeisler, 102.

30. The Dancing Men

First published December 1903

Mr Hilton Cubitt said that 'Last year I came up to London for the Jubilee', and he was married to his wife shortly thereafter. He also referred to 'my marriage last year', which places this case definitely in a year succeeding a Jubilee. The Golden one was in 1887 and the Diamond one in 1897, so the case was in either '88 or '98. Watson's presence at Baker Street seems to have been permanent, as he watched Holmes working with his chemicals for hours upon hours, which fact eliminates 1888, when he was married and living away from Baker Street.

Cubitt said that 'about a month ago, at the end of June', his troubles began, so the case apparently occurred in late July. He found the first scribble of dancing men 'About a week ago—it was the Tuesday of last week'. After this, 'None did come for a week, and then yesterday morning I found this paper lying on the sun-dial in the garden'. Presumably he discovered that the following Tuesday, and the day upon which he first consulted Holmes was therefore a Wednesday at the end of July, probably Wednesday 27 July 1898.

Watson indicated that a fresh development arose 'one afternoon a fortnight or so later'. Some dates which Cubitt supplied can be used to help compute when precisely this was. The 'next morning' after his interview with Holmes—that is, on

The Dancing Men

28 July—he saw more dancing men. 'Two mornings later', on 30 July, more appeared. 'Three days later a message was left scrawled upon paper'; this was on 2 August. On this night the moon was apparently quite full, as Cubitt mentioned that he 'was seated by the window, all being dark save for the moonlight outside', and that his wife's face grew 'whiter yet in the moonlight'. Further, he mentioned 'the shadow of the toolhouse'. Incidentally, 2 August in 1898 *was* a full moon, thus supporting this scheme of days.

Cubitt mentioned no other dates, however, and as Watson claims that 'a fortnight or so' had passed, an inconsistency arises. Cubitt, upon returning to Holmes, remarked eagerly that 'I have several fresh dancing men pictures for you to examine, and, what is more important, I have seen the fellow'. The most recent of these developments was on the night of 2 August, as explained above, and there can be no doubt that Cubitt came the very next day, 3 August, to see Holmes again, furnish him with the additional clues, and ask for his advice. As he was contemplating putting 'half a dozen of my farm lads in the shrubbery' to surprise the perpetrator, it is clear that he had not yet taken any action, and there is no conceivable reason why he would have waited an entire week after these events before consulting Holmes, especially since he did nothing of his own accord in the interim.

Watson, then, apparently committed an error in stating that a fortnight had elapsed between the two visits of Hilton Cubitt, for he very clearly returned to Baker Street on 3 August. The cause of this inaccuracy is unclear, and we can only speculate. Perhaps he was thinking about the fact that the case spanned a total of eleven days when writing the manuscript and, carelessly forgetting that the phrase was meant to be a reference not to the total duration of the case but rather to the time between Cubitt's two visits, decided to artistically but erroneously say 'a fortnight or so'. In any case, it was 'two days' later, on 5 August, that Cubitt sent Holmes one more sheet of dancing men, whereupon Holmes and Watson went to Ridling Thorpe manor as early as possible on 6 August. They were, regrettably, too late to save their client.

The case occurred intermittently from 27 July to 6 August 1898.

31. The Solitary Cyclist

First published December 1903

Watson says that 'On referring to my notebook for the year 1895, I find that it was upon Saturday, April 23, that we first heard of Miss Violet Smith'. Unfortunately for Watson's credibility, 23 April was a Tuesday in 1895. Miss Smith did, however, comment that 'Last December—[was] four months ago', which serves to confirm that the case did occur sometime in April in some year. We know, too, that the case certainly began on a Saturday, for Miss Smith stated that she went home to visit her mother every Saturday morning and returned to Farnham on each succeeding Monday, and it was en route to her mother's that she stopped to consult Holmes. The explanation for all of this apparent confusion is rather simple: 13 April was a Saturday in 1895, suggesting that Watson's note of the date was so illegibly scribbled that he mistook the '13' for a '23' when composing the manuscript.

Watson went to Farnham on the following Monday, the 15th. Holmes visited the place the next day, Tuesday the 16th. The following Saturday, the 20th, was the day that they both went back with the intention of making sure that Miss Smith arrived safely at the train that was to take her home. The case, then, occurred from Saturday 13 April through Saturday 20 April in the year 1895.

32. The Priory School

First published January 1904

Watson says that 'We have had some dramatic entrances and exits upon our small stage at Baker Street, but I cannot recollect anything more sudden and startling than the first appearance of Dr. Thorneycroft Huxtable'. The implication that there were many previous clients to compare this one to suggests a later date. Holmes, meanwhile, called Watson 'My colleague' and said that 'we are very busy at present', so this case occurred at a time when Watson was living with Holmes and had no practice of his own.

The 'H' volume of Holmes's encyclopaedia of reference stated that the Duke of Holdernesse had been 'Lord-Lieutenant of Hallamshire since 1900'. This suggests that the year was 1901 or later, as it would not otherwise have said 'since 1900'. It could not be later than summer 1902, as Watson married and left Baker Street once again at that time,[1] obviating any consideration of 1903. Zeisler interprets the reference to the encyclopaedia to allow the case to be placed in 1900 by claiming that Holmes might have updated his encyclopaedia with current events

---

[1] See our discussions of *The Dying Detective*, *The Three Garridebs*, *The Illustrious Client*, and *The Blanched Soldier* for more about Watson's second marriage.

throughout the year.[1] His argument, however, would only make sense if a month were indicated. As only the year is stated, it falls apart upon that one word 'since': if the year were still 1900, the Duke could not have been Lord-Lieutenant *since* 1900.

'He [Lord Saltire] was last seen on the night of May 13—that is, the night of last Monday', and Huxtable, when he called upon Holmes, declared that 'now on Thursday morning we are as ignorant as we were on Tuesday'. In 1901, 13 May was a Monday. The case must, therefore, have occurred in 1901, in May, beginning on Thursday the 16th. The investigation continued on Friday 17 May when Holmes and Watson found the body of the German master and followed the tyre tracks, and it concluded on Saturday 18 May when they visited the Duke of Holdernesse.

Holmes stated that 'the moon was at the full' on the night of the 13th. However, the full moon was actually on 3 May in 1901, and as it was at half on the 11th, it was already moving towards a quarter moon on the 13th. Watson apparently either made an error in his notes or failed to take note of the moon at all and, when he tried to remember what Holmes had said, his memory failed him. This supposition is corroborated by the fact that in 1902, the only other possible year, the full moon was on 22 May, scarcely closer to the 13th. In 1900 the moon was full on 14 May, but dating the case in that year would require us to believe that Huxtable was wrong in saying that the 13th was a Monday, and it is, in any case, impossible given the encyclopaedia extract. Both of these points are far more cogent indicators of the date than is the description of the moon.

---

[1] Zeisler, 123-124. He does this for the sake of the full moon on 14 May 1900, as mentioned below.

The Priory School

Holmes's comment about being a poor man must be regarded as mere bluffing on his part, not as an indication of a case in the early 1880s. He was obviously comparing his own comparatively miniscule riches to those of the affluent Duke of Holdernesse in saying this, and therefore we should not allow it to affect the dating of the case.

The case occurred from Thursday 16 May to Saturday 18 May 1901.

33. Black Peter

First published February 1904

There are few cases whose dates Watson makes as clear as this one. 'I have never known my friend to be in better form, both mental and physical, than in the year '95', Watson begins; 'In this memorable year '95 a curious and incongruous succession of cases had engaged his attention', including 'the death of Captain Peter Carey', Watson continues; and 'He [Carey] was born in '45—fifty years of age', Watson concludes. The case definitely occurred in 1895.

Watson remarks that 'save in the case of the Duke of Holdernesse, I have seldom known him claim any large reward for his inestimable services'. *The Priory School* occurred in 1901, of course, but this need pose no difficulty. Watson evidently inserted this comment because he knew that *The Priory School* would be published immediately before this case in *The Return of Sherlock Holmes* series and naturally wished to refer back to the one glaring and recent instance of Holmes accepting a large reward since, even though it occurred after this case, it would be read by the public before it. This preface was, in any case, obviously an added afterthought, written by Watson solely for the publication, and did not constitute a part of his original notes for the case.

Black Peter

'During the first week of July' Watson noted that Holmes was frequently absent from their rooms, and Watson was not aware of the nature of his activities. This confirms that Watson was living at Baker Street, which fact agrees with 1895. On the first day of the case, Inspector Hopkins stated that 'he [Carey] died just a week ago to-day', and 'the crime was done upon the Wednesday' in the early hours of the morning. The first day of the case was, then, the Wednesday of the second week of July in the year 1895—that is, Wednesday 10 July. Holmes and Watson returned to London the next morning (11 July) having spent the night at the Brambletye Hotel after apprehending Neligan. Holmes invited Hopkins to breakfast on Friday morning (12 July) at which time they caught Patrick Cairns and the case concluded.

The case lasted, then, from Wednesday 10 July to Friday 12 July 1895.

34. Charles Augustus Milverton

First published March 1904

Watson says that 'It is years since the incidents of which I speak took place'. As the account was published in 1904, this suggests very strongly that the actual events occurred in the previous century. Holmes's comment that Milverton was 'the worst man in London' does not necessitate that the death of Moriarty had already occurred, since he said 'worst', not 'most formidable' or some other modifier indicating puissance. Holmes made it quite obvious that he regarded blackmail as the most dastardly form of crime.

Holmes remarked to Watson that 'We have shared the same room for some years, and it would be amusing if we ended by sharing the same cell'. Holmes's use of the present perfect tense, as opposed to the simple past, indicates that Watson was living at Baker Street when this case occurred. It could not have been before 1885, as they would otherwise not have spent sufficient years living together to have warranted such a remark, and it could not have been between the winter of 1887–1888, immediately prior to which Watson was married, and the winter of 1893–1894, when Holmes had not yet returned to London. It appears, then, to have been between 1885 and 1887, or between 1895 and 1900, but the former timeframe is most unlikely given the presence of an electric light in Milverton's study, mentioned no less than four times. Even amongst rich men like Milverton electric lights were uncommon before the Edwardian Era, so we may consider this a post-Return case.

Brend believes that this case must have occurred before *The Speckled Band* of April 1883 because Holmes and Watson were rather hesitant to burgle Milverton's house but seemingly had no qualms about infiltrating Dr Roylott's abode.[1] These two situations were, however, quite different, for in the former they were, for the sake of a client but entirely on their own initiative and without assistance, breaking into and entering Milverton's house, while in the latter they had specifically arranged with their client, who lived in the house and invited them to enter, to have a window unlocked to facilitate their entry. Again, in the case of Milverton their goal was to steal documents while their cause was to preserve a reputation, but with regard to Dr Roylott their intention was only to investigate while their cause was to potentially save a life. It is quite understandable, then, that Holmes and Watson would have had more reservations about burgling Milverton's house, and they doubtless would have debated it at length even if it were years after the incidents of *The Speckled Band*.

Bell, meanwhile, argues for 1884 by declaring that Holmes and Watson would have been too old to climb a six-foot wall and run for two miles in any year after the Return,[2] but Dakin soundly dispels this reasoning by observing that at the time of *The Sign of Four* Watson was still suffering from his wounded leg, and it was a question of whether he could withstand a long walk, let alone the rapid flight and run across Hampstead Heath that was the

---

[1] Brend, 62-64.
[2] Bell, 27.

sequel to the burgling of Milverton's house.¹ Our own observations concerning Watson's leg and stamina in our discussion of *The Hound of the Baskervilles* support a date after not only the Return, but also *The Solitary Cyclist* of 1895.

A comment made by Lestrade helps to further refine the year. At the end of the case, he called upon Holmes and said that 'I thought that, perhaps, if you had nothing particular on hand, you might care to assist us in a most remarkable case which occurred only last night at Hampstead'. He then continued that 'I know how keen you are upon these things, and I would take it as a great favour if you would step down to Appledore Towers and give us the benefit of your advice'. This is far more in consonance with Lestrade's demeanour in *The Six Napoleons*—deferent towards Holmes and fully admitting his ingenuity—than with his disdain for Holmes in *The Norwood Builder* and earlier cases.² Any year before the Return can therefore be eliminated, as can any time immediately after *The Norwood Builder* which, we have shown, occurred in July 1894.

The case, Watson tells us, began on 'a cold, frosty winter's evening'. Holmes, disguised as Escott, the plumber, spent 'some days' learning the layout of Milverton's house and the inclinations of its household. As he became engaged to the servant Agatha at the end of this period, we must prefer the longest possible timeframe; this, however, is not very long, for Holmes remarked on the first day of the case that Lady Eva Brackwell 'is to be married in a fortnight to the Earl of Dovercourt', and we learn from Milverton that the wedding was set for the 18th of the month. On the day that Holmes and

---

[1] Dakin, 177.
[2] See our discussions of *The Hound of the Baskervilles* and *The Six Napoleons* for more on the development of Lestrade's attitude towards Holmes.

Watson intended to burgle Milverton's house, Holmes commented that 'To-morrow is the last day of grace', and as Milverton had earlier declared that 'if the money is not paid on the 14th there certainly will be no marriage on the 18th', it is clear that 'To-morrow' was the 14th. The first day of the case, when Milverton came to Baker Street, was, then, the 4th of the month; Holmes courted Agatha from that very day until the 13th, a period of only eight days; and the case concluded the following morning with Lestrade's visit to Baker Street.

If one considers the statements in *The Devil's Foot* which indicate that Holmes was having a breakdown due to 'constant hard work of a most exacting kind',[1] it seems likely that the case of Milverton occurred in 1897 sometime shortly before *The Devil's Foot*. It was a very demanding case that required Holmes to assume a role which, being so dissimilar from his own personality, must have been a great strain, especially considering that he even went so far as to engage himself to be married. This might very well have caused a physical or mental breakdown. Bell would object to February of this year, for he states that no year in which the 14th of the month was a Sunday is possible since Holmes showed Watson a photograph in a shop window, which would have been shuttered on a Sunday, and the 14 February was a Sunday in 1897.[2] Christ forbids the 13th, when Holmes and Watson dressed as theatregoers, and the 18th, when the wedding was to take place, to be Sundays as well.[3] We gratefully accept this sound guidance and place the case from 4 to 14 January 1897, in which month neither the 13th, nor the 14th, nor the 18th was a Sunday.

---

[1] Short, DEVI, 1,041.
[2] Bell, 27.
[3] Christ, 49.

35. The Six Napoleons

First published April 1904

'It was no very unusual thing for Mr. Lestrade, of Scotland Yard, to look in upon us of an evening, and his visits were welcome to Sherlock Holmes, for they enabled him to keep in touch with all that was going on at the police head-quarters.' This statement places the case at least a few years after *The Norwood Builder*, at which time Lestrade still had considerable contempt for Holmes and was obviously not in the habit of visiting him on a regular basis. As it had become not unusual for him to visit by this time, clearly enough time had elapsed since July 1894 that Lestrade had come to admire Holmes without affecting otherwise and had done so for some time. Indeed, at the end of this account, Lestrade professed that 'I've seen you handle a good many cases, Mr. Holmes, but I don't know that I ever knew a more workmanlike one than that. We're not jealous of you at Scotland Yard. No, sir, we are very proud of you'. As noted above, Lestrade's attitude had already changed considerably by 1897, as demonstrated at the time of the case of Milverton[1]; *The Six Napoleons* could, therefore, reasonably be assigned to any year from 1897 onwards.

---

[1] Short, CHAS, 737-738.

The Six Napoleons

The sequence of events relating to the case is as follows. The busts were sold by Gelder & Co. on 3 June of the year previous to the current one. Beppo 'was paid last on May 20' of that year. He 'got off with a year', and the manager of Gelder & Co. had 'no doubt he is out now'. Thus the case might have occurred in June of the current year at the earliest, though it may have been as late as December.

The first bust was broken 'four days ago' from the evening when Lestrade visited Baker Street. The second and third were broken 'only last night'. 'Dr. Barnicot was due at his surgery at twelve o'clock' on this first day of the case, which could thus not have been a Sunday. Lestrade returned to Baker Street at 6 p.m. on the second day of the case. Holmes predicted that they would not 'be back before morning'. This day was not a Sunday because all of the shops were open and the factories running, which means that the first day could not have been a Saturday. Horace Harker's bust was broken on the night before this day (the night of the first day). Lestrade visited Baker Street once again at 6 p.m. on the third day of the case, when Holmes secured the last of the busts from 'Mr. Sandeford, of Reading'.

As Beppo 'was paid last on May 20', that day must have been a Saturday. The only year between 1894 and 1903 when 20 May was a Saturday is 1899. This date refers to the year before the case, which must, then, have occurred in 1900. Christ selects 1902 as the year, but his claim that a terraced stand that fell down at Glasgow ought to be identified as the very same stand that fell at Doncaster,[1] as related by Horace Harker, is improbable and unsubstantiated, and it is by no means a stronger argument than the fact that the 20 May must be a Saturday.

---

[1] Christ, 50.

The Six Napoleons

The six Napoleon busts were sold, then, on 3 June 1899. Beppo hid the pearl in one while they were drying. He was arrested sometime between 23 May—he collected his wages on 20 May and was arrested two days after the pearl was stolen, and he would have had neither the time, nor the safety, nor the need to collect his wages after stealing it—and 27 May (the next payday when he did not collect wages), the pearl being stolen between 21 and 26 May. In all likelihood the busts were not sold immediately after drying, so we may suppose that it was the earliest date possible that Beppo was arrested—23 May 1899. He would thus have been released after one year on 23 May 1900.

Beppo would have gone immediately to see his cousin who worked at the factory, who would on the next day—24 May—have discovered and told him who the purchasers of the busts were. He would have applied to work at Morse Hudson's shop the following day and would have begun working within a few days. He was apparently there for some time, for Hudson described him as 'a kind of Italian piecework man, who made himself useful in the shop', saying that 'He could carve a bit, and gild a frame, and do odd jobs'. Hudson could only have been able to find this out, and describe him as such, after Beppo had worked there for a couple of weeks. Presumably Beppo would have found his opportunity to search the ledgers and find the addresses of the buyers of the two busts within a fortnight, so that is a reasonable timeframe to suppose for his employment with Hudson.

It would, then, have been about 8 June, a Friday, that Beppo left Morse Hudson. We know, however, that Beppo 'was gone two days before the bust was smashed' at Hudson's shop, and he could not have destroyed the bust on Sunday 10 June, when the shop would have been closed. Beppo must, therefore, have

The Six Napoleons

left on Saturday 9 June, after collecting his wages (Hudson does not, after all, mention anything about him leaving suddenly and suspiciously, without collecting his wages). He accordingly smashed the first bust on Monday 11 June. Four days later, Lestrade visited Holmes; this was a Friday. The previous Thursday night the second and third busts had been destroyed. The second day of the case would then have been a Saturday, 16 June, exactly seven days after Beppo had quit his job—and, indeed, Hudson said that 'the fellow left me last week'. The last day of the case would have been Sunday 17 June, and the fact that 'Mr. Sandeford, of Reading' stated that 'the trains were awkward' strongly corroborates this as the correct day of the week.

Watson mentions that 'The wooden fence which separated the grounds from the road threw a dense black shadow upon the inner side', and that Beppo disappeared in 'the black shadow of the house'. He also says that 'all was dark save for a fanlight over the hall door'. The moon must have been well-nigh full if it were capable of casting shadows in such a fashion. In 1900, the full moon occurred on 13 June. This was only three days before the night when they captured Beppo, so the moon would still have been quite bright. Holmes said that 'We may thank our stars that it is not raining', so we may presume that the moon was not blocked by thick clouds.

The case occurred in 1900, beginning on Friday 15 June and ending on Sunday 17 June.

36. The Three Students

First published June 1904

Watson states that 'It was in the year '95 that a combination of events, into which I need not enter, caused Mr. Sherlock Holmes and myself to spend some weeks in one of our great University towns, and it was during this time that the small but instructive adventure which I am about to relate befell us'.

Holmes examined the black putty substance in Hilton Soames's bedroom 'in the glare of the electric light'. While electric lights were not common even in wealthy homes until the turn of the century, it is not unlikely that the University of Oxford,[1] like some other large institutions, would have installed at least some electric lighting by 1895; this statement does not, therefore, preclude Watson's declaration of the year of the case.

Dakin concludes that the case was in April or October based on the sunset, but he disregards the latter time because it conflicts with the long vacation which lasts until early October.[2] Christ, too, opts for spring, believing that the competitive examination for the scholarship would have been most likely to have occurred then.[3] Soames, however, said that Miles McLaren

---

[1] Dakin, 189-190. Dakin, who provides an excellent summary of the evidence for both Oxford and Cambridge, demonstrates that the former was clearly the location of this case.
[2] Dakin, 190.
[3] Christ, 51.

The Three Students

'was nearly expelled over a card scandal in his first year' and 'has been idling all this term'. The current term would have to be the Michaelmas Term of early October to early December, as McLaren—who no doubt, like most students, started his studies in the autumn of a given year—would not yet have been in his second year if it were only April, while if it were April of his second year, Soames surely would have said that he had been idling 'all this year'.

Holmes spent the first evening of the case investigating. The following morning, he returned to see Soames, and Gilchrist confessed and stated that 'I have been offered a commission in the Rhodesian Police, and I am going out to South Africa at once'. The first police force in Rhodesia, the North-Eastern Rhodesia Police, was not formed until July 1895.[1] This is further proof that the case could not have been during the Hilary or Trinity Terms of winter and spring 1895.

As McLaren 'has been idling all this term', the date could not have been too early in the term—November seems likely. Zeisler believes that the examination for the scholarship would have occurred after the close of the term as was customary,[2] but this may have been an exceptional case, and there is no way to know for certain when it was. The most we can venture to say is that the case spanned two days in November 1895, and that these were during a stay of several weeks in Oxford by Holmes and Watson.

---

[1] Newspapers began to refer to the colony by the title of Rhodesia in 1891, the South African government officially adopted it in 1895, and the British government followed suit in 1898.
[2] Zeisler, 103.

37. The Golden Pince-Nez

First published July 1904

Watson had 'three massive manuscript volumes which contain our work for the year 1894'. This is impressive given the fact that Holmes only returned from supposed death in April 1894, and thus had only had two thirds of a year to perform this copious amount of work. Watson explains that, out of all of the cases in these volumes, 'the episode of Yoxley Old Place' is the one which is conspicuous for its exceptional interest. This case, therefore, occurred in 1894.

Watson tells us that 'It was a wild, tempestuous night towards the close of November' upon which Stanley Hopkins came to Baker Street to relate the events of the case, and the following day they took a train 'at six in the morning' and arrived at their destination 'between eight and nine'. They saw 'the cold winter sun rise over the dreary marshes of the Thames and the long, sullen reaches of the river' during their train journey. As they left from Charing Cross at 6 a.m., and would only have been near enough to the river to see it for the first segment of the journey, the sun must have risen by 7. This, however, does not precisely agree with Watson's claim that the case was in late November, for even on 1 November the sun does not rise until 6:53. We are forced to surmise that the sun actually rose about 7:30 and that the discrepancy is the result of either the train's departure being delayed or Watson's utilising a bit of artistic license in his description of the sun. The latter would not be surprising as he refers to a 'winter sun' even though he clearly states that it was not winter proper but rather November. Possibly it was the breaking dawn, rather than the rising sun, that they saw.

The case began late one night when Hopkins visited and concluded on the following day at Yoxley Old Place. Due to a lack of further evidence, we cannot venture to say more than that the case occurred in late November 1894.

38. The Missing Three-Quarter

First published August 1904

Watson was living with Holmes, for he said 'we' and 'us' when referring to receiving telegrams at Baker Street. The case began 'on a gloomy February morning some seven or eight years ago'. From the date of publication, this would place it in either 1896 or 1897, presuming of course that Watson wrote this statement shortly before publication. He said that 'I had lost touch with my profession' because he did not know who Dr Leslie Armstrong was, and this agrees with a date in the later '90s since Watson stopped practicing in mid-1894. Holmes, meanwhile, referred to 'the gap left by the illustrious Moriarty', who was then dead; this again corroborates a date after the Return.

There is, however, an issue with Watson's claim that the case was in February. As Dakin notes, December was the month when the rugby matches between universities were played,[1] so this case must have occurred in December of '96 or '97. Christ further tells us that it was on the second Wednesday of December that the Oxford-Cambridge game was customarily held in any given year,[2] and we know that it was on the second day of the case that Watson read an excerpt from 'the local evening paper' about the match. Holmes confessed that 'Even

---

[1] Dakin, 197.
[2] Christ, 53.

the most insignificant problem would be welcome in these stagnant days', but there are no recorded cases in late autumn of 1896 or 1897, so either one is possible. Watson's claim of 'seven or eight years' noted above, however, definitely confirms that the year was 1896, as December 1897 would be significantly less than seven years.

The second Wednesday in December 1896 was the 9th of the month, so the three days of the case were 8–10 December 1896.

39. The Abbey Grange

First published September 1904

'It was on a bitterly cold and frosty morning during the winter of '97 that I was wakened by a tugging at my shoulder.'[1] This opening statement by Watson suggests that this case occurred in January or February 1897. Theresa Wright, Lady Brackenstall's maid, said that she and her mistress had met Sir Eustace Brackenstall in July, which was 'only eighteen months ago'. Furthermore, Lady Brackenstall was 'married in January of last year' and has 'been married about a year'. All of this confirms January as the month, and in connection with this it is worth noting that Holmes's initial failure to detect the true nature of the events of the case may be attributable to his exhaustion following the case of Charles Augustus Milverton, which occupied the first half of January 1897 and, we believe, ultimately resulted in Holmes's constitutional breakdown that led him to seek solitude and rest in Cornwall at the time of *The Devil's Foot*.

Theresa Wright claimed that she was able to see the three supposed burglars 'in the moonlight down by the lodge gate

---

[1] The American text reads: 'It was on a bitterly cold night and frosty morning, *towards the end of* [emphasis added] the winter of '97, that I was awakened by a tugging at my shoulder' (Arthur Conan Doyle, *The Complete Sherlock Holmes*, vol. 2 [New York: Doubleday & Company, Inc., 1930], 635). This is an excellent example of how the meddling of the American editors seriously compromised the validity of the American texts.

The Abbey Grange

yonder'. While there were not, in fact, any burglars to be seen, we may be sure that if there had not been sufficient moonlight that night for someone to have perceived figures at that distance, Holmes would have noted the discrepancy and immediately known the maid to be lying. If, then, Wright could believably claim to have seen three men across the lawn at night, the moon must have been very nearly full. In January 1897, the full moon was on the 18th.

The case occurred over the course of a single day. The night of the murder was most likely the 17th-18th, so Holmes became involved and solved the case on the 18th, a Monday in the year 1897.

40. The Second Stain

First published December 1904

This account contains some information which is useful in determining the time at which Holmes retired from active practice as a private consulting detective. We will begin by briefly discussing this before proceeding into what is necessarily a lengthy and complex analysis of the date of the case itself.

Watson informs us in the introduction to this case, presumably written shortly before the time of publication, that 'I had intended the "Adventure of the Abbey Grange" to be the last of those exploits of my friend, Mr. Sherlock Holmes, which I should ever communicate to the public'. His reason for this decision was 'the reluctance which Mr. Holmes has shown to the continued publication of his experiences' because 'he has definitely retired from London and betaken himself to study and bee-farming on the Sussex Downs, [and] notoriety has become hateful to him'. This series of statements serves to inform us that by the latter half of 1904 Holmes had finally retired from practice.

As to the case itself, Watson induced Holmes to permit him to publish this account by reminding him that he had 'given a promise that "The Adventure of the Second Stain" should be published when the time was ripe'. Watson mentioned in *The Naval Treaty* that 'The Adventure of the Second Stain' occurred

The Second Stain

in the same month (July 1888) as *The Naval Treaty*, yet he was no longer living at Baker Street and was married and in practice at that time, whereas at the time of this case he clearly was living at Baker Street. The explanation of this conundrum, which has to some extent already been addressed above, is that there are in fact three different cases which Watson in his notes entitled 'The Second Stain', and that neither the one referred to in *The Naval Treaty*, nor the one referenced in *The Yellow Face*, is the same as the one which is presented to the public here. This conclusion is substantiated by the fact that, as Dakin notes, Watson did not actually promise his readers an account on either of the previous occasions when he mentioned a 'Second Stain'.[1]

'It was, then, in a year, and even in a decade, that shall be nameless, that upon one Tuesday morning in autumn we found two visitors of European fame within the walls of our humble room in Baker Street.' Watson makes this statement and later corroborates it by remarking that it was an 'autumn morning' when the case began, seemingly clarifying the time of year.

There are four quotations which establish the political context of the case:

1. Watson refers to 'The illustrious Lord Bellinger, twice Premier of Britain'. He says this, however, in a paragraph which has no dialogue and in which he simply describes the two men who graced Baker Street with their presence on this day; it is possible, therefore, that in saying 'twice Premier of Britain' he was referring either to a man who was already by the date of the case serving his second term (and may or may not have served again later), or to one who served two terms as

---

[1] Dakin, 203.

Prime Minister during his entire career (before December 1904) and who might have been at the time of the case in either his first or his second term.
2. The publication of the missing letter could 'lead to European complications of the utmost moment. It is not too much to say that peace or war may hang upon the issue.'
3. 'The letter, then, is from a certain foreign potentate who has been ruffled by some recent colonial developments of this country.'
4. 'The whole of Europe is an armed camp. There is a double league which makes a fair balance of military power. Great Britain holds the scales.'

Another useful piece of quasi-political information is that Oberstein was mentioned by Holmes as being one of three active international agents. As he was arrested at the end of the case of *The Bruce-Partington Plans*, and thus could not be considered an active agent after that time, this case must have occurred before November 1895.[1] This dating is substantiated by the attitude of Lestrade towards Holmes. Lestrade summoned Holmes for assistance with the case, but he was neither friendly nor admiring. He 'chuckled with delight at having puzzled the famous expert', and he grumbled that 'The official police don't need you, Mr. Holmes, to tell them that the carpet must have been turned round'. As already discussed, this is behaviour that Lestrade would have exhibited only until 1896 at the latest.

This is, then, a case which occurred before November 1895, apparently in a September or October given the references to autumn. Watson was living at Baker Street, so it could have been

---

[1] See our discussion of *The Bruce-Partington Plans* for the evidence for its date.

The Second Stain

1894 or 1895, or it could have been some date between 1881 and 1886. The challenge is to find the year in which a man who had been (as of December 1904) twice Prime Minister was serving in either his first or, preferably, his second term, and under whose leadership an important colonial development likely to upset one of the great powers of Europe occurred. It could have been during the second Gladstone Cabinet of April 1880 to July 1885, or during the second Salisbury Cabinet of August 1886 to August 1892. It could not have been between July 1885 and January 1886 because this was Salisbury's first term (and he served more than twice) or between February and August of 1886 because this was Gladstone's third term. We may also tentatively eliminate 1894 and 1895, which were covered by the ministry of Rosebery (who only served once) and the third ministry of Salisbury. We remove 1881 from consideration due to the recency of Holmes and Watson's partnership, leaving us with 1882–1886.

Dakin argues that the Prime Minister in question must have been Gladstone, citing the description in the text and the illustrations drawn by Paget as proof.[1] The description is, in truth, sufficiently vague to be applicable to many aging gentlemen, while the illustrations are entirely useless as evidence since Paget knew even less than we do about the true identity of the man and the events and therefore might have chosen to make the 'Premier' resemble whichever contemporary Prime Minister he fancied. Baring-Gould, meanwhile, selects Salisbury, claiming that the year must have been 1886 because that is the only plausible year during which the Prime Minister was not also the Foreign Secretary (which post he believes to be the real equivalent of Watson's fictitious 'Secretary for European

---

[1] Dakin, 204.

Affairs').[1] We, however, believe that the man whom Watson refers to as 'Mr. Trelawney Hope' may just as likely have been either the Under-Secretary of State for Foreign Affairs or the Secretary of State for the Colonies—either of which posts Watson might have disguised with the intentionally misleading title of 'Secretary for European Affairs'. The fact that Baring-Gould and Dakin both fail to identify the colonial incident greatly compromises their arguments, and we feel that too little importance has been placed upon this fundamental aspect of the dating of this case by virtually every other chronologist. The colonial incident and the foreign potentate are far more integral to the case than the identity and description of the prime minister, and as such ought to be given more weight in determining the date. We must now turn to these aspects to complete our analysis.

We have thus far tentatively isolated the date to sometime between 1882 and 1886, but as we examine the political context of these years, they become increasingly improbable. The Anglo-Egyptian War of 1882 is an appealing candidate for the colonial incident, as it began about 12 August and concluded on 15 September. The British occupation of Egypt antagonised France, whose president might have sent the indiscreet message. The early year of this incident is an objection, however, for there are no indications that the case occurred so soon after Holmes and Watson met.

The Gordon Relief Expedition led by Wolseley in the autumn of 1884, to which France also objected, is another potential incident. If the French president had sent the indiscreet letter, then Bismarck would have been eager to have it published, as it

---

[1] Baring-Gould, 70.

might very well have caused a war between Britain and France, thereby driving France into an alliance with him against Britain—an eventuality which was most attractive to him, as his great object at this time was to prevent France from turning towards Russia and to make her dependent upon German support.[1] Holmes, however, called the sender of the letter an 'indiscreet Sovereign', and he would hardly have used such a title when referring to the French president. This is a point against both of these colonial developments.

There is a further major issue which disqualifies both incidents. 'Lord Bellinger' said the following: 'But if you consider the European situation you will have no difficulty in perceiving the motive. The whole of Europe is an armed camp. There is a double league which makes a fair balance of military power. Great Britain holds the scales. If Britain were driven into war with one confederacy, it would assure the supremacy of the other confederacy, whether they joined in the war or not.' This is problematic, for, although on 20 May 1882 Germany concluded the Triple Alliance with Austria-Hungary and Italy (which agreement was renewed on 20 February 1887), no second allied camp formed until 4 January 1894, when France and Russia, following several years of increasingly cordial relations, signed the Dual-Alliance. It was only after this second alliance was formed that the 'Balance of Power' between the continental powers of Europe was such that the entrance of the increasingly isolated Great Britain into either alliance—or, by deduction, the commencement of a war between Great Britain and either one of the alliances—would have gravely upset the balance of

---

[1] A.J.P. Taylor, *The Struggle for Mastery in Europe, 1848–1918* (Oxford: The Clarendon Press, 1954), 291-292.

power.[1] Thus both of the colonial developments that we have considered are invalidated by the fact that in 1882 and 1884 there was no second confederacy which might profit from the threatened war.

Having attempted to treat all of Watson's statements as entirely true and reliable, we have found that there is no arrangement of years, colonial developments, and the international political context which will satisfy the apparent requirements. This is not, in fact, surprising when we consider Watson's statement that 'If in telling the story I seem to be somewhat vague in certain details the public will readily understand that there is an excellent reason for my reticence'. Furthermore, he tells us that Holmes only permitted him to publish 'a carefully guarded account of the incident'. We must, therefore, treat Watson's account with a degree of scepticism as to its factual accuracy and consider which of the conflicting pieces of evidence are more likely true.

There are some facts whose veracity cannot be doubted. We can be certain that the case occurred before November 1895 given the mention of Oberstein, for *The Bruce-Partington Plans*, in which Watson mentions Oberstein to the reader for the second time, was not published until four years after *The Second Stain*, and Watson's readers could not, therefore, have derived any useful information regarding the date of this case from his mention of Oberstein here, giving him no reason whatsoever to falsify this information. It is clear, too, that Watson was living at Baker Street, so we may confidently eliminate 1887–1891 from consideration, and Holmes was presumed dead from April 1891 to April 1894, disqualifying 1892 and 1893 as well. The

---

[1] Taylor, 346.

The Second Stain

statements about the two confederacies in Europe and the probability of war with Britain resulting in the ascendancy of one alliance over the other are objectively factual—and integral to the events of the case—so we must certainly take this political context into account. This eliminates 1882–1886 as explained above, leaving 1894 and 1895 as the only two potential years during which there were two confederacies in Europe.

We must, therefore, seek an explanation for Watson's comment that the Prime Minister served twice, for this is not true of any Prime Minister in 1894 or 1895. It seems probable that the statement itself was a ruse to prevent identification of the actual Prime Minister, for this would have been one of the major identifying facts that Watson would have wished to conceal. It is, furthermore, a detail which he might have easily altered without compromising the logic or coherence of the rest of the account; the same cannot be said of the political context, any falsification of which would have completely distorted the importance of the lost document. By the same logic, Watson may have sought to further disguise the true events of the case by falsely indicating that it occurred in autumn. Although the season would have been less imperative to obfuscate than the identity of the Prime Minister, we should consider colonial events from any time of year from April 1894 to November 1895.

Due research reveals that the Chitral Campaign of 1895 is the most eminently well-suited candidate for the colonial development mentioned in this case. In early March 1895 the British sent a force to occupy Chitral, on the Anglo-Russian border in Central Asia, to ensure that it would remain a stable border ally against the Russians. After a protracted siege and the advance of two separate relief forces, the British were victorious on 20 April. A debate ensued within the British government as to whether to permanently occupy and possibly annex Chitral to prevent the Russians from seizing it. Initially, Rosebery's first (and only) ministry decided to evacuate Chitral, reasoning that garrisoning and building roads to it would be too costly. An agreement had recently been made with the Russians, too, that demarcated the border along the frontier of Afghanistan and awarded to the Russians most of the large region of mountains in Central Asia known as the Pamirs. When Rosebery resigned after suffering a defeat in Parliament regarding army estimates on 21 June 1895, Salisbury came back into power for his third term, and he promptly determined to retain Chitral and maintain a garrison there. Several years later it was discovered from the evidence of a Russian officer that if the British had withdrawn, the Russians would very likely have invaded Chitral and had in fact formed elaborate plans for the purpose. They never invaded, though, probably because Holmes succeeded in recovering the lost letter.

When one considers this scenario at length, every aspect of it fits seamlessly into the parameters of the case. The Russian Tsar, Nicholas II, sent the indiscreet letter, of which his ministers knew nothing, after hearing that the British had suddenly changed their minds about annexing Chitral. The letter was probably addressed to the Secretary of State for the Colonies, since it was by a colonial matter that the Tsar was perturbed; this means that Mr Trelawney Hope was in fact none other than The Right Honourable Joseph Chamberlain.[1] The Tsar was surely

---

[1] It is also possible, as mentioned above, that Hope's position was that of Under-Secretary of State for Foreign Affairs, which would mean that his name was an alias for George Nathanial Curzon. Nevertheless, we believe that Chamberlain is the correct identification, and mention this only to show those who insist upon a role in the Foreign Office that such a role is readily available

incensed further than he would have been otherwise as a result of being suddenly disabused of his belief that British expansion in the region would cease following the aforementioned agreement regarding the border between the Russian and British empires. In his immediate exasperation with being frustrated in his clandestine plan to occupy Chitral himself, he rashly sent a hastily composed, indiscreet message without fully reflecting upon the ramifications—namely that it would, if made public, drive his country, and therefore France, with whom he had been in an alliance since January 1894, into war with Britain, which would in turn make him far too vulnerable to the encroachments of Germany upon his western territories and of Austria-Hungary upon his Balkan domains. He therefore regretted sending it. The Germans, the Austro-Hungarians, or possibly even the Italians, meanwhile, were the ones interested in acquiring and publishing this document, as they could thereby ignite war between Britain and Russia. The Germans would have benefitted by ensuring that Britain did not incline towards the Franco-Russian alliance, the Austrians by seizing territory in the Balkans with little opposition from an otherwise-occupied Russia, and the Italians by potentially receiving British assistance in their faltering war with Abyssinia which the Franco-Russian alliance opposed.

Further support for this hypothesis comes from the fact that the 'excellent reason for my reticence' which Watson was compelled to uphold, even in 1904, was that as of 1904 the British and Russian governments were still contending for power in Tibet and struggling for supremacy in Central Asia. It was not until they finally reached an agreement with the signing of the

---

without eliminating the years in which the Prime Minister served also as the Secretary of State for Foreign Affairs.

The Second Stain

Anglo-Russian Convention of August 1907 that they were able to settle their differences and form a tripartite alliance with France. Thus in December 1904 Holmes had good reason to insist that Watson heavily disguise the details of this case in order to make them sufficiently vague as to be apparently unrelated to the actual events in Chitral, as an overt reference to them would only have further soured the already unamicable relations with Russia. Yet more evidence lies in the fact that *The Bruce-Partington Plans*—Watson's account of which, by revealing that Oberstein was no longer an active agent after November 1895, made it easier for readers to identify the date of *The Second Stain*—was not published until December 1908, more than a year after the Convention was signed.

Oberstein's very existence is another point in favour of 1895. At the time of this case, he was an active agent, just as he still was in November 1895 at the time of *The Bruce-Partington Plans*; it is possible that he was an active agent a decade earlier, in the mid-1880s, but it is far more likely that he did not pursue his nefarious career for so long with impunity. Thus it is more than probable that these two cases occurred within a fairly short time of one another. We would add that Brend's argument—that *The Second Stain* must have occurred a long time before *The Bruce-Partington Plans* because in the former case Holmes knew all of the international agents in London but in the latter he had to ask Mycroft for a list[1]—is negated by our explanation that Holmes very reasonably wished to know from his omniscient brother whether any new agent had filled the vacancy left by the late Eduardo Lucas—as in fact one had done.

---

[1] Brend, 74-75.

The Second Stain

The days of the case were as follows. For the whole of the first day—a Tuesday—'and the next and the next Holmes was in a mood which his friends would call taciturn, and others morose'. This covers the first three days of the case. Then, 'Upon the fourth day there appeared a long telegram from Paris'. This was the Friday. Holmes and Watson were summoned by Lestrade to the scene of the crime; they then called upon Lady Hilda Trelawney Hope and the case concluded. Thus the case began on a Tuesday, and, given the course of events in Chitral, it was probably in July or August of 1895. Only two of Watson's indications were found to be intentionally deceptive: his references to autumn and his statement that 'Bellinger' was 'twice Premier' (Lord Salisbury, whom we identify as 'Lord Bellinger', being in his third term at the time of the case, as noted above).

As for the precise date, the following data serve to definitely fix it. According to the *London Standard* of 12 August 1895, from a report from Simla of 10 August, 'The proposals of the Indian Government for holding Chitral have now been sanctioned'.[1] The *Lloyd's Weekly Newspaper* of 11 August 1895, a day earlier, contains the same report, namely that as of Saturday night (10 August) in Simla, 'The proposals of the Indian Government for holding Chitral have now been sanctioned'.[2] Before this date, the newspapers had little to say on the subject save that the British force in Chitral could not be removed before September for climatic reasons.

The debate on the decision of Salisbury's ministry to retain Chitral continued throughout August, and in early September (the 3rd or 4th) the British representative oversaw the durbar at

---

[1] 'The Future of Chitral', *The Standard*, 12 August 1895, No. 22,187, page 5.
[2] 'The Future of Chitral', *Lloyd's Weekly Newspaper*, 11 August 1895, No. 2,751, page 11.

The Second Stain

which the new pro-British ruler was instated.[1] The Russian Tsar, however, would have heard of, and overreacted to, the news that the British government had sanctioned the retention of Chitral, and would not have waited to see how the debates or the durbar went. This is obvious given his rash action and subsequent hasty regret at having sent the message in the first place.

The 10 August was a Saturday in 1895. The Simla report, via Reuter's Agency, was not published in the London papers until the 11th and 12th. Trelawney Hope said that 'The letter…was received six days ago'. Watson indicates that the case began on a Tuesday for them. If this was Tuesday the 20th, then the missive arrived six days earlier, on Wednesday 14 August. The Tsar doubtless wrote and despatched it on the very day that he learnt of the incident; as it would have taken about four days to arrive in England, it would appear that his agents in Simla or London had apprised him of the events a day or two before they appeared in the London newspapers.

This most complex and deceptively written case began on Tuesday 20 August and concluded on Friday 23 August in the year 1895.

---

[1] 'The Position of Chitral', *The Standard*, 3 September 1895, No. 22,206, page 5.

41. Wisteria Lodge

First published August 1908

With regard to the commencement of this case, Watson says that 'I find it recorded in my notebook that it was a bleak and windy day towards the end of March in the year 1892'. This is a patent falsehood—Holmes was presumed dead and far from Baker Street in 1892—so we must attempt to pierce the mendacious veil which Watson has thrown over the date of this case.

Watson apparently lived with Holmes at this time, for he mentioned that they sat at lunch together at Baker Street. Watson knew Holmes's mannerisms quite thoroughly; he comments that he 'could tell by numerous subtle signs, which might have been lost upon anyone but myself, that Holmes was on a hot scent'. All of this suggests a date shortly before Watson's marriage—1886 or 1887—or after the Return.

The case began on the day that Mr John Scott Eccles awoke to an empty house and subsequently called upon Holmes. Eccles said that 'It is late in March, so quarter-day is at hand'. The first quarter-day of any year is 25 March. As Eccles supposed that the intention of abandoning the house was to avoid paying rent (which was, as the sequel showed, actually paid in advance), the first day must have been shortly before rent was due on 25 March. Watson later affirms that 'It was a cold, dark March evening' when at 'nearly six o'clock' he and Holmes, accompanied by Baynes, arrived in Esher. This was still the first day of the case. Then, however, 'Day succeeded day' of inactivity, Holmes filling the time with 'solitary walks', until finally 'some five days after the crime', which occurred the night before Holmes began his investigation, Watson read an article in a paper about the arrest of the cook. This was the fifth day of the case, upon the night of which it concluded.

It definitely occurred in March. Watson was living with Holmes, but it could not be before 1887, because Murillo only arrived in Europe in 1886. He was traced by Baynes back from 'Paris and Rome and Madrid to Barcelona, where his ship came in '86', and Garcia and company 'discovered him a year ago'. All of this travel and searching could scarcely have been completed by 1887. By 1888 Watson was married; thus this case must have occurred after the Return.

It could not have been in 1894, because Holmes had not yet returned to London in March of that year. As noted above, Dakin insists that the reference to 'the case of the papers of ex-President Murillo'[1] in *The Norwood Builder* signifies that this case must have occurred in early 1894, before *The Norwood Builder*, but to make this date work he resorts to the unjustifiable expedient of moving *The Empty House* to February 1894.[2] This is a far more doubtful proposition than the alternative, namely that the Murillo referred to in *The Norwood Builder* was not the same one as the man in this case who, as we have already had occasion to observe, neither bore the title of president nor had any papers of exceptional significance.

---

[1] Short, NORW, 584.
[2] Dakin, 218.

Wisteria Lodge

Wisteria Lodge could not have been in 1896 either, for on 27–28 February of that year Holmes was engaged in solving the affair of the Red Circle,[1] and thus he could not have lamented, as he does in this case, to Watson only a few weeks later in March that 'you know how bored I have been since we locked up Colonel Carruthers'. No more probable is 1897, because Holmes had a physical breakdown in that March, and no mention is made, nor indication given, of that in this case. He was, besides, busy solving *The Devil's Foot* in Cornwall in mid-March, and thus could not reasonably have complained of protracted boredom a week later. It seems unlikely that it would be much later than 1897, because Murillo arrived in 1886, and it can hardly be supposed that he would have succeeded in roaming Europe for upwards of ten years with impunity. This leaves 1895 as the most likely year. Evidently, the '1892' which Watson gives us is either a misprint or an intentional deception due to the political nature of the case.

In 1895, 25 March was a Monday. The case definitely occurred sometime in the week preceding this. Eccles intended to visit Garcia for 'a few days at his house', and the weekend seems the most natural time for such a visit. Bell is surely correct in stating that the day Eccles called upon Holmes could not have been a Sunday since earlier that same day he had gone to 'the chief land agents', whose office would not have been open on a Sunday.[2] We know that Eccles's visit was cut short on its second day by the death of Garcia, so there is no objection to supposing that Eccles arrived on Friday, having intended to stay until Sunday. This puts the murder of Garcia on the night of Friday

---

[1] See our discussion of *The Red Circle* for the evidence for its date.
[2] Bell, 81.

Wisteria Lodge

22 March. Eccles, then, awoke to find his host missing on Saturday 23 March, and he called upon Holmes later that day, the first day of the case. The conclusion came four days later, on Wednesday 27 March 1895.

42. The Bruce-Partington Plans

First published December 1908

'In the third week of November, in the year 1895', this case began. 'From the Monday to the Thursday' nothing worthy of note occurred, and Holmes became frustrated at the lack of cases on the fourth day, Thursday. Cadogan West was found dead on the Tuesday morning, and it was on the Thursday morning that Mycroft and Lestrade called upon Holmes, who began investigating that same day. The next morning Mycroft and Lestrade returned to Baker Street, and that night they all went to Oberstein's lodgings in Caulfield Gardens.

Watson recalled hearing of Mycroft at the time of the affair of the Greek interpreter; this case thus occurred after July 1886. Holmes said that 'I did not know you quite so well in those days', which confirms that this case occurred many years later. Watson, meanwhile, says that 'for a moment I saw something in his eyes which was nearer to tenderness than I had ever seen', showing that this case must have been before *The Devil's Foot* of March 1897, at which time Holmes betrayed more real emotion than at any other recorded time.[1] There can be no doubt that 1895 was the year of this case.

---

[1] Short, DEVI, 1,060.

Mycroft said that 'In the present state of Siam it is most awkward that I should be away from the office'. While summer 1893 was the time when the dispute between Britain and France over Siam was at its height, Holmes was not in London then; evidently it was a later incident which occupied Mycroft, which is not surprising given that the conflict was not settled in 1893. Indeed, there can be no doubt that what Mycroft was referring to was in fact the negotiations preceding the Anglo-French agreement concerning Siam which was reached in late December 1895, and actually published on 15 January in the following year.[1] These negotiations would have been at their height in November 1895.

Watson's statement of the date is, then, clearly accurate. The third full week of November in 1895 began on Monday the 18th, on which night West died. The case began for Holmes on Thursday the 21st and ended with the capture of Oberstein at 'the Charing Cross Hotel at noon on Saturday'. This was clearly Saturday the 23rd, not the 30th, for Oberstein had already (presumably on Tuesday the 19th) 'put up for auction' the Bruce-Partington plans, and while it is a wonder that they had not already sold within those four days, it is inconceivable that they would not have sold during the week and a half that would have preceded Saturday the 30th.

---

[1] Taylor, 366.

43. The Devil's Foot

First published December 1910

Watson says that it was 'in the spring of the year 1897 that Holmes' iron constitution showed some symptoms of giving way in the face of constant hard work of a most exacting kind, aggravated, perhaps, by occasional indiscretions of his own'. As we have already proposed, it was probably his tireless crusade against Milverton which largely caused this breakdown. In any case, 'In March of that year [1897] Dr. Moore Agar, of Harley Street', told Holmes that he must rest, and it was 'in the early spring of that year' that Holmes and Watson went to Cornwall. Watson also says—in 1910—that 'Now, after thirteen years, I will give the true details of this inconceivable affair to the public'. This makes the 1897 date definite.

Watson states that the case was brought to them on 'Tuesday, March the 16th', and the 16 March was indeed a Tuesday in 1897. Zeisler pedantically objects that Watson must have been wrong about both the day and the month because spring had technically not yet begun on 16 March, so he places the case in April.[1] This wilful rejection of a patent date for the mere sake of explaining a technicality does Zeisler no credit; Watson was clearly thinking of March as the month when spring begins, and was trying to

---

[1] Zeisler, 109-110.

avoid the misleading mental picture that would have been conveyed had he used the word winter instead. After all, it is but few of the reading public who would be more likely to picture winter weather, rather than that of spring, when presented with the phrase 'March the 16th'. It was, then, on Tuesday the 16th that Holmes investigated the death of Brenda Tregennis and the insanity of her two brothers, and on Wednesday the 17th that Vicar Roundhay appeared in the morning to tell Holmes and Watson that Mortimer Tregennis had died from the same symptoms as his sister. They heard nothing from the police 'for the next two days', and it was on the second of these days that the case concluded with the interview with Dr Leon Sterndale.

The case occurred, then, from Tuesday 16 March to Friday 19 March 1897.

44. The Red Circle

First published March 1911

Mrs Warren brought this case to Holmes's attention one day, and the next morning she returned to tell him of the abduction of her husband. Holmes and Watson then paid her a visit and caught a glimpse of Emilia Lucca in her room, after which they repaired to Baker Street. Later that day they returned to Mrs Warren's lodgings and the case concluded. All of this was on a 'winter evening', so the case occurred sometime in January or February of a given year.

Watson was living with Holmes, which means the case occurred in a winter between 1882 and 1887 or between 1895 and 1902. There are two points in favour of the latter timeframe. Firstly, Inspector Gregson, who was still with Scotland Yard, evinced some degree of respect for Holmes: 'I'll do you this justice, Mr. Holmes, that I was never in a case yet that I didn't feel stronger for having you on my side'. Given that Gregson was with Scotland Yard in 1881 (and had been for some time since he was already an inspector at that time), it may seem unlikely that he would still have been working as late as 1900, but it is certainly possible that he was, and the fact that he acknowledged Holmes's expertise precludes any early, pre-Return date. Secondly, Holmes's willingness to solve the case without any pay—'It is Art for Art's sake'—also suggests a later

180

date, when he would have been sufficiently wealthy to afford the luxury of working for free.

An argument made by Rolfe Boswell in favour of 1901 or 1902 is that Holmes's supposition that there was 'some mark, some thumb-print, something which might give a clue to the person's identity' on one of the notes written by Emilia Lucca would only make sense after 1901, when Scotland Yard began formally assessing fingerprints using the Galton-Henry system.[1] But as Hall notes, Lestrade and Holmes were both aware of fingerprinting already in 1894 at the time of *The Norwood Builder*, so this observation proves nothing.[2] Holmes was, besides, generally ahead of Scotland Yard in such forensic matters, so we would not be surprised if he spoke of fingerprints considerably before 1901.

Mr Warren, who was abducted, 'has to be out of the house before seven' to work as a timekeeper, and Holmes told Mrs Warren that the abductors 'mistook your husband for him [the elusive lodger] in the foggy morning light'. Civil twilight, the time before sunrise when there is sufficient light to distinguish objects, begins at 6:50 a.m., shortly 'before seven', on 9 February. The 'foggy morning light' would be the twilight, which would last for the next half hour. Sunrise, as opposed to civil twilight, is at 6:50 on 27 February. The case, then, occurred roughly between 9 February and 27 February.

Although Holmes declared that 'I really have other things to engage me' when Mrs Warren asked him to take her case, it is apparent that he did not actually have any serious cases on hand at the moment because he turned to his 'great scrap-book in

---

[1] Hall, 48.
[2] Hall, 48.

The Red Circle

which he was arranging and indexing some of his recent material', a task to which he would not have devoted his time if he had had any demanding cases to occupy him. Nevertheless, since he had records to file, it appears that he did handle some cases sometime in the last few months. The year, therefore, was most likely not 1895, when in February and March he was suffering from inactivity, for if it were then he would have had nothing to index.[1] It also could not have been 1897, because in January and February of that year Holmes was very busy with cases which led to his breakdown in March, while at the time of this case he had nothing more important to deal with than a scrapbook.

There are a number of possible years that remain: 1896, 1898, 1899, 1900, 1901, and 1902. Holmes remarked to Watson at the end of the second day of the case that 'it is not eight o'clock, and a Wagner night at Covent Garden! If we hurry, we might be in time for the second act.' In winter 1898, 1899, 1901, and 1902, there were no such performances. There was on 22 February 1900 a performance at the Royal Opera House, Covent Garden, which included a couple of pieces by Wagner,[2] but as there was only one piece by him in each of the two lengthy parts it would have been odd for Holmes to have described it as a 'Wagner night'. Furthermore, the first of the two parts of the concert did not begin until 8:30 p.m., which would render Holmes's remark—that it was not yet 8, giving them time to arrive before the second part—absurd, for they could have walked from Mrs Warren's place 'at the north-east side of the British Museum' to

---

[1] Short, WIST, 892.
[2] 'Concerts', *Daily Mail,* 21 February 1900, No. 1,197, page 1.

The Red Circle

the Royal Opera House in less than a quarter of an hour and would have arrived well before the first part had begun.

A more fitting concert was the Wagner performance on Friday 28 February 1896. The *Standard* of London for that date describes a concert which began at 7:30 that evening at the Olympia London venue and consisted of a three-part orchestral programme, the second act of which was composed entirely of pieces by Wagner.[1] This fits quite nicely with Holmes's description of a Wagner night, and he and Watson should have been able to arrive in time for the second act, the Wagner portion, since the concert began at 7:30, and it was shortly before 8 when Holmes proposed to Watson that they should attend. The only issue is that the location of this concert was the Olympia London, not the Royal Opera House, Covent Garden, specified by Holmes. This is evidently the result of Watson not making note of the location of this concert and failing to accurately remember it when writing the manuscript. Since it would have taken about thirty-eight minutes for them to travel (at the average carriage pace of eight miles per hour) the five miles of roads that separate the British Museum from the Olympia London, we can only hope that the driver complied with Holmes's request to hurry, for if not they may not have arrived in time for the Wagner portion after all.

The events of the case occurred from Thursday 27 to Friday 28 February 1896.

---

[1] 'Olympia', *The Standard*, 28 February 1896, No. 22,359, page 4.

45. The Disappearance of Lady Frances Carfax

First published December 1911

Watson had been 'feeling rheumatic and old' and took a Turkish bath; it would seem that he had reached the advanced years of his life by this time. Additional evidence for a later date is that Holmes entrusted Watson with travelling to Lausanne to investigate without him and that Holmes boasted that 'Scotland Yard feels lonely without me'. Additionally, Holy Peters (alias Schlessinger) was bitten on the ear 'in a saloon-fight at Adelaide in '89', and the fact that Holmes said the precise year, rather than 'a year ago' or 'a few years ago', definitely makes this a post-Return case.

Holmes remarked that Watson had a companion in his hansom cab; while this might possibly have been his second wife,[1] this seems quite improbable. As Watson agreed happily to go to Lausanne, saying 'Splendid!', and made no mention of either asking or telling his wife, it is not likely that he had one. Furthermore, he mentions hearing Holmes 'prowling about the house' during the night, so he was apparently living at Baker Street.

---

[1] See our discussions of *The Dying Detective*, *The Three Garridebs*, *The Illustrious Client*, and *The Blanched Soldier* for more about Watson's second marriage.

The Disappearance of Lady Frances Carfax

As to the sequence of days, Holmes asked Watson to go to Lausanne on the first day. Two days later Watson arrived there. He then spent several days travelling to Baden and to Montpellier, interviewing the maid, meeting Holmes, and returning to London. More than a week passed before they discovered the sale of the jewels at the pawnbroker's shop. Then several more days passed while 'the Hon. Philip Green' watched for another sale at the shop.

The evidence suggests that this was a post-Return case which occurred before Watson's second marriage and before he had returned to practice. The fact that no great surprise was expressed by either Watson or Holmes when Holmes suggested that Watson go to the Continent for him indicates that this case occurred after *The Hound of the Baskervilles*, as Watson was at that time still somewhat surprised at being asked by Holmes to go to Dartmoor. Presumably after that prolonged sojourn in Holmes's service he finally accepted his usefulness and did not demur again in the future.

As *The Hound of the Baskervilles* occurred in October 1900, this case was probably in 1901. Holmes intended to tell Mrs Hudson that they would both be dining the following evening at Baker Street, so it must have been sometime before October 1901, by which time Mrs Hudson was no longer cooking for them.[1] Furthermore, *The Problem of Thor Bridge* of early October 1901 followed 'a month of trivialities and stagnation'.[2] Thus the case of Lady Frances Carfax must have been in 1901 sometime before September. Dakin points to the fact that Holy Peters sat all day 'upon a lounge-chair on the verandah [sic]' as evidence that the

---

[1] Short, THOR, 1,216.
[2] Short, THOR, 1,216.

case took place in the summer.[1] His reasoning is sound and, as there is nothing to contradict it, we concur that this case, one of the most difficult to place, occurred in summer 1901. Watson has, unfortunately, given us no further evidence which would enable us to determine the month and the day.

---

[1] Dakin, 237.

46. The Dying Detective

First published December 1913

Watson states that Holmes's payments to Mrs Hudson 'were princely' and that 'I have no doubt that the house might have been purchased at the price which Holmes paid for his rooms during the years that I was with him'. This most probably refers to the years after the Return, not the early years of the partnership before Watson's first marriage, for at that time Holmes had not yet achieved the incredible renown which Watson's accounts later helped him to attain and which secured him wealthy clients, domestic and international, who in turn made him quite affluent.

Further evidence which precludes any date before the Return is that there was a 'tinted electric light' at Smith's house in Lower Burke Street. This would be highly unlikely before 1891, as already noted. Smith, being moderately wealthy, might have had it installed somewhat before Edwardian times, so we must consider any post-Return date.

Watson says that Mrs Hudson came to tell him of Holmes's illness 'in the second year of my married life'. This cannot be a reference to his marriage with Mary Morstan, so it must be referring to his second marriage, an event which warrants a brief discussion. Watson could not have been remarried before July 1902, for he was not married at the time of *The Three Garridebs* in late June 1902.¹ Holmes, however, retired in late 1903.² In order, therefore, for Watson to be in the second year of his second marriage before Holmes's retirement, Watson must have remarried in summer 1902; his second year would therefore have begun in summer 1903. Watson says, in fact, that Mrs Hudson came to him on 'a foggy November day'. This would, then, be November 1903, probably mere weeks before Holmes retired. Indeed, it is possible that the extreme deprivations to which Holmes was compelled to subject himself for this case caused him to expedite his retirement.

Mrs Hudson said that Holmes became ill 'on Wednesday afternoon' and 'For three days' had not eaten or drunk, indicating that the case began on a Saturday. The most we can assert, then, is that it was on a Saturday in November 1903. In selecting this date, rather than a date in the late 1880s, we are alone amongst the chronologists, none of whom—not even those who believe Watson to have had a second (or third) wife somewhere around 1902—seems to have appreciated the impossibility of an electric light and the improbability of Holmes's 'princely' payments in such early years. Only Zeisler offers any meaningful argument against 1903—that if this were indeed Holmes's last case, Watson would have mentioned the fact³—but this alleged omission is fully explained by the supposition that Watson did not at the time of publication have either the intention or the permission to inform the public of Holmes's retirement. He only mentioned it four years later when he published *His Last Bow*, and even then he did not refer to the year of Holmes's retirement.

---

[1] See our discussion of *The Three Garridebs*.
[2] See our discussion of *The Creeping Man*.
[3] Zeisler, 86.

47. The Valley of Fear

First published from September 1914 to May 1915

At the beginning of this account Holmes asked Watson if he had ever heard him speak of Moriarty, and Watson answered by identifying the professor as 'the famous scientific criminal'. This shows that Moriarty was very much alive at this time, and would seem to place the case before his death in May 1891. This, however, is problematic because Watson also told Holmes in April 1891, at the time of *The Final Problem*, that he had never heard of Moriarty, suggesting contrarily that *The Valley of Fear* occurred at a later date. In seeking an explanation, we must remember that while Moriarty was referred to as a professor at the time of this case, he had become an ex-professor by the time of *The Final Problem*. Possibly this was the result of his being denounced, if not legally convicted, following nefarious events such as those of this case, but whatever the cause, this clearly demonstrates that this case occurred before *The Final Problem*, and we are left to explain why Watson denied having ever heard of Moriarty in 1891.

It is most likely that the 'never' of Watson in *The Final Problem* was another instance of literary license. Because *The Final Problem* was published more than twenty years before *The Valley of Fear* (at which time Watson quite probably had no intention of publishing *The Valley of Fear*), in his account of the former he needed to include, for the benefit of the reader, a description of Moriarty, a description which would not have fit smoothly into the narrative of the case if Watson had published his actual reply that Holmes had previously mentioned Moriarty at the time of the events at Birlstone. Though it is possible that editorial decisions led to this incongruity, we feel that the significant extent of the apparent alterations to the text make it far more likely that Watson made the changes himself.

Certain chronologists, like McQueen[1] and Brend,[2] refuse to believe that Watson was guilty of any subversion in *The Final Problem*, and they have accordingly suggested that the Moriarty of *The Valley of Fear* was not the same Moriarty as the one from *The Final Problem*, but rather his brother. To discount such a theory, one need only look to the opening pages of *The Valley of Fear* in which Holmes mentioned that Moriarty was the author of *Dynamics of an Asteroid*, obviously a book that a professor, not a colonel or a station-master, would have written. (Moriarty's 'younger brother [who] is a station-master in the West of England' may have been a third brother, or he may have been the same brother who was a colonel at the time of *The Final Problem*.) Furthermore, in *The Valley of Fear* Moriarty is given such superlative epithets as 'this king-devil', and there is no chance that this could refer to the famous professor's brother. *The* Moriarty was, then, alive at this time, which fact necessitates a date before May 1891. Likewise, Colonel Sebastian Moran was still at large, placing the case prior to *The Empty House* of April 1894 and thus prior to *The Final Problem*.

---

[1] McQueen, 203-204.
[2] Brend, 114.

We have thus proven that this case occurred before April 1891. Watson says that 'Those were the early days at the end of the 'eighties, when Alec MacDonald was far from having attained the national fame which he has now achieved'. The implication of this is that the case occurred during the last few years of the 1880s, and this agrees nicely with our observations thus far. On the first day of the case, Holmes said that it was 'the seventh of January'. Watson later indicated that the murder occurred on 'the night of January 6th'. On the second day, 8 January, they solved the case, so we may tentatively place this case on 7–8 January of a year in the late '80s.

This hypothesis is corroborated—and further refined—by the fact that Watson describes Holmes as 'one who already stood alone in Europe, both in his gifts and in his experience'. This indicates a later date, after Holmes had attained international fame, following at least his cases for such clients as the King of Scandinavia and the French government. Any year from 1888 onwards would be consonant with this.

Further evidence comes from the local inspector, White Mason, who said, 'Come along, Dr. Watson, and when the time comes we'll all hope for a place in your book'. This clearly suggests a date sometime after the publication of at least *A Study in Scarlet*, but more likely after the publication of a number of cases, as the inspector evidently had the opportunity to read some of Watson's works and had reason to expect the publication of more. The earliest possible date after which at least two cases had been published was February 1890, when *The Sign of Four* was first published. Additional confirmation of Watson's literary endeavours having progressed significantly lies in the fact that Edwards handed Watson his account of the Valley of Fear and called him 'the historian of this bunch'. He also referred to Watson's readers as 'your public'. All of this implies that Edwards had read, or at least heard of, several cases published by Watson.

This case definitely occurred, then, after December 1887, when Watson's first case was published. It could not, however, have occurred after February 1890, when the second one was published, because as of January 1891 Holmes had been working for the French government for several weeks already and did not conclude his investigation until spring 1891.[1] As to 1888, Watson was newly married as of the previous November, and he remarked that he had been absorbed by the interests of his new life with Mary and had not seen much of Holmes in the first half of 1888, though he read of at least three international cases, in Odessa, Trincomalee, and Holland.[2] Thus 1888 may be eliminated.

The years 1889 and 1890 remain. The latter is more likely, for Watson published his second book in February 1890, and it is quite probable that its imminent publication had been advertised, in which case it would not be surprising that both the inspector and Douglas had Watson's writings on their minds and made comments about them. Furthermore, Holmes would have had sufficient illustrious clients by this time to have gained international repute. Watson says quite clearly that it was in the late '80s, but January 1890 is technically at the end of the '80s, and this statement, in any case, is not as important as the multiple references to Watson's writings, which remarks would not have been made if his second publication were not forthcoming.

---

[1] Short, FINA, 537.
[2] Short, SCAN, 3-4.

Having shown that this case occurred in 1890, we must address two objections: the dating of Edwards's manuscript, and Watson's presence at Baker Street and complete disregard for his wife. As to the former, Watson informs us that the events in the actual Valley of Fear, as recorded by Edwards, happened 'some twenty years' ago. Counting backwards from our selected year of 1890 places these events in 1870, yet the narrative written by Edwards opens by stating that 'It was the fourth of February in the year 1875'. Counting forwards from this would incongruously place the case in 1895, so we must consider either the date of 1875 or the span of twenty years to be patently false, for they are far less cogent factors than those used above in determining 1890 to be the year. The proof of this is manifestly demonstrated by the many improbabilities of the hypothesis of McQueen, who dates the case in 1899. In attempting to explain the many issues to which his choice gives rise, he unconvincingly asserts, among other things, that the Moriarty gang reformed after the professor's death under the leadership of his brother.[1] We think it far more likely that the 1875 or the twenty years was intentionally misstated by Edwards or Watson due to the sensitive nature of the events concerned, but even if this is not the case, there are other theories, also more probable than McQueen's, that have been propounded in defence of a pre-Return date.[2]

The other objection to 1890 lies in the fact that Watson seemed to be living at Baker Street and had no consideration whatsoever for his wife. He did not mention her, did not inform her that he was going to Birlstone Manor (to our knowledge),

---

[1] McQueen, 194-206.
[2] See the lengthy and learned evaluations of Dakin (211-213) and Hall (23-24) for further possible explanations of this particular issue.

and appeared to be visiting Holmes for at least one day but possibly more, as he observes that Holmes had not touched his breakfast. To further complicate matters, Watson informs us in his epilogue that 'Two months had gone by' when 'one morning there came an enigmatic note slipped into *our* [emphasis added] letter-box', and he refers to Mrs Hudson as '*our* [emphasis added] landlady'. Thus it appears that Watson was visiting or living with Holmes on 7 January and that in early March he considered himself to be a resident of Baker Street.

We might explain the visit in January easily enough, but Watson's residence at 221B in March suggests something more serious. Quite possibly his continued neglect of his professional practice throughout 1889 led to an estrangement with Mary. She had done her best to humour his penchant for solving cases with Holmes during the past two years, but he had doubtless gone too far when he had disappeared without a word of explanation on the night of 21 June 1889 and gone with Holmes to spend the night at the St Clair residence. If the situation continued to deteriorate throughout the rest of the year, Watson would have spent more and more time at Baker Street and by the New Year would have been sleeping there more than at his home. We may be sure that he deplored this rupture with his wife, and it may have been in an effort to heal it that he added details of his courtship with Mary to his account of *The Sign of Four*, published in February 1890. In early March he would still have been spending most of his time at Baker Street and might have regarded the letterbox and the landlady as his own as well as Holmes's. It was probably about this time that he acquired the new practice in Kensington, hoping thereby to prove to Mary that he was dedicated to his medical work. This, together with the novella, would seem to have won him a second chance, leading him to leave Baker Street once again.

There is no doubt that this case occurred in 1890 and that Watson had a wife, and we feel that the above theory plausibly explains the attendant conflicts. It can never be entirely proven, of course, but it is more credible and better supported by fact than the theories propounded by those who place the case either after the Return, like McQueen, or before Watson's marriage, like Dakin.[1] In any case, even if the explanation of Watson's living at Baker Street in early 1890 is not as we have supposed, and the truth lies in some other direction, the facts which favour 1890 remain, so the case definitely occurred from 7 to 8 January 1890. It was one of the only three recorded cases for that year, the other two being *A Case of Identity* and *The Red-Headed League*.

---

[1] Dakin, 210.

48. His Last Bow

First published September 1917

We learn a number of important facts from the details of this case. Watson said: 'But you had retired, Holmes. We heard of you as living the life of a hermit among your bees and your books in a small farm upon the South Downs.' Evidently, Holmes had been retired for some years (apparently since the end of 1903) before agreeing to perform this final case, which Holmes said 'has cost me two years'. When Watson said 'We heard of you', he was surely including his second wife and himself in the 'we'; this, then, is further proof of a second marriage.

A noteworthy feature of this case is that it was written in the third person. Watson states in *The Problem of Thor Bridge* that 'In some [cases] I was myself concerned and can speak as an eye-witness, while in others I was either not present or played so small a part that they could only be told as by a third person'.[1] This is one of only two published cases from the latter category.

Few cases are easier to date than this one. It began 'upon the second of August', according to Watson. This was manifestly in the year 1914, as he called it 'the most terrible August in the history of the world'. It took place, then, on Sunday 2 August 1914, and happily no one disputes this.

---

[1] Short, THOR, 1,216.

49. The Mazarin Stone

First published October 1921

At the beginning of this account—the second to be written in the third-person point of view—Watson found 'himself once more in the untidy room of the first floor in Baker Street'. He remarked to Billy, the page boy, that everything in the room 'seems very unchanged'. Clearly Watson did not live at Baker Street and had not for some time, and he was also evidently in medical practice, for Holmes deduced that he was a 'busy medical man, with calls on him every hour'.

When he saw the 'facsimile' figure of Holmes, Watson remarked to Billy that 'We used something of the sort once before', obviously referring to the figure used in the affair of *The Empty House*. Billy stated that this was before his time, yet Billy was mentioned as having been at Baker Street in 1890, at the time of *The Valley of Fear*. This case could not have been that early, however, not only due to Billy's statement, but also because Count Sylvius's involvement in 'the robbery in the train-de-luxe to the Riviera on February 13, 1892' was mentioned as a past event. Another objection to a date before the Return is that Holmes had a gramophone. As this device first became popular only about 1894, we may conclude that this case occurred in some later year.

The date of the case, therefore, cannot be before, and is likely long after, 1894, and since we know that Watson was in practice and had been living away from Baker Street for a while, we can further deduce that it was not before or immediately after Watson's second marriage in summer 1902, until which time he was living at Baker Street and was not in practice. The narrator (who may or may not be Watson) says that 'It was seven in the evening of a lovely summer's day', which leaves summer 1903, shortly before Holmes's retirement, as the only possible time.

With regard to Billy, who was the page at this time and at the time of *The Valley of Fear*, the only reasonable conclusion which can be made is that there were two different pages named Billy throughout the years at Baker Street. This is an entirely reasonable supposition given both the ubiquity of the name Billy and the fact that the two times he is mentioned are some thirteen years apart according to our dates, leaving ample time for other pages with different names to have served between the departure of the first 'Billy' and the arrival of the second one.

An issue arises, however, with the description of the rooms at Baker Street given by the narrator. There was a 'waiting-room' and a 'second exit' from the bedroom, neither of which was ever previously mentioned. Holmes said that this 'second door from my bedroom leads behind that curtain' that covered 'the alcove of the bow window'. This second door, so integral to the events of the case, is not a familiar feature of the rooms.

The authorship of this case, which apparently occurred in summer 1903, must ultimately be regarded as spurious, given the irregular description of the rooms at Baker Street, as well as the odd if explicable conflict with regard to Billy. Quite possibly Watson, nearing seventy at this time and no longer feeling inclined to write, decided for some reason to give to his literary agent, Doyle, the notes for this case, as well as the permission to publish an account of it based upon them. The alternative, more doleful to consider, is that Watson was deceased by this time, and that he had bequeathed to Doyle some of his notes and manuscripts with the request that they be published.

50. The Problem of Thor Bridge

First published February 1922

Watson remarks on the first day of the case that 'It was a wild morning in October'. He mentions looking at 'the yard behind our house', then talks of descending to breakfast with Holmes. He evidently lived at Baker Street at this time.

The date of the letter from Gibson was 3 October, and the letter stated that Gibson would call at 11 a.m. the next day. The case began on that morning, 4 October. They spent the night at Winchester, and on the morning of the 5th they visited Grace Dunbar. That same day they returned to Thor Bridge, performed the experiment with the revolver, then went to the local inn. Holmes said that he would see Gibson the next morning and arrange for Miss Dunbar's release, so the final day was the 6th.

As to the year, Watson speaks of his case notes stored in the 'travel-worn and battered tin dispatch-box' in such a way as to indicate that they had been sitting 'in the vaults of the bank of Cox and Co., at Charing Cross', for a long while as of the date of publication. He says that 'There remain [sic] a considerable residue of cases of greater or less interest which I might have edited before had I not feared to give the public a surfeit which might react upon the reputation of the man whom above all others I revere'. Watson had, then, been withholding these cases for some time, though the fact that the year of publication is 1922 makes any date before Holmes's retirement plausible.

'Billy' was mentioned opening the door for a visitor, so it would seem that this case occurred either when the first 'Billy' was present at the time of *The Valley of Fear*, around 1890, or when the second one was present, in the early 1900s. This later 'Billy' is only mentioned in *The Mazarin Stone*, which we have concluded was written by Doyle, not Watson; the notes for it, however, were Watson's, so there is no reason to doubt that there was in fact at this time a 'Billy' at Baker Street. The earlier timeframe is in any case impossible, for we know that during this case Watson was living with Holmes, whereas from November 1887 until mid-1894 he was living elsewhere and in practice.

Knowing that the case occurred in October enables us to eliminate some years from consideration. Watson was no longer at Baker Street in October 1902, so 1901 is the latest possible year. Brend prefers 1900 to 1901, arguing that Holmes would not have told Gibson that 'My professional charges are upon a fixed scale' if he had earlier in the year accepted £6,000 from the Duke of Holdernesse.[1] Watson was in Devonshire with Sir Henry Baskerville in October 1900, however, so this year is impossible. Brend's claim is, in any case, hollow, for Holmes's remark was disingenuous and was intended to snub Gibson, and he might have made it under any pecuniary circumstances. Bell confines the case to a year in which 3 October was a Wednesday because on the first day of the case (4 October) Holmes remarks that there is a 'copy of the *Family Herald* which I observed yesterday upon the hall-table', and the *Family Herald* was published weekly

---

[1] Brend, 163.

The Problem of Thor Bridge

on Wednesdays.[1] His argument is flawed, however, for he overlooks the simple fact that the *Family Herald* may have been lying on the hall-table not because it was just delivered but simply because someone, perhaps the new cook, was reading the previous week's issue and had set it there.

The final piece of evidence which must be accounted for is the fact that Holmes referred derisively to 'our new cook'. Mrs Hudson was definitely still at Baker Street at the time of *The Dying Detective* in November 1903, mere weeks before Holmes retired. Therefore, the new cook who is mentioned must have been hired as a result of Mrs Hudson's growing weary of Holmes's irregular dining habits and no longer wishing to do the cooking herself. This favours 1901, not least because earlier in that same year Holmes had asked Mrs Hudson, who was evidently still cooking, 'to make one of her best efforts for two hungry travellers at seven-thirty to-morrow'.[2]

A later date is also favoured by the presence of Billy, for he would not have been working at Baker Street for more than a few years, and since he was apparently still there in summer 1903, it is unlikely that he would have started any earlier than 1901. We must, therefore, choose the latest possible date for this case, and assert that it occurred from 4 to 6 October 1901.

---

[1] Bell, 107.
[2] Short, LADY, 1,027.

51. The Creeping Man

First published March 1923

'It was one Sunday evening early in September of the year 1903' that the case began with a telegram from Holmes to Watson. Many details support this date. Watson refers to 'the ugly rumours which some twenty years ago agitated the university'. This lapse of time agrees perfectly with the date of publication. It must be a late case, because Watson says that 'The relations between us in those latter days were peculiar'. He also refers to Baker Street as 'what had once been my home', indicating that the case occurred after his second marriage. Watson mentions being called away from his work by Holmes, so he was in practice again, and when Watson goes to 'Camford' with Holmes, he says that it 'involved frantic planning and hurrying on my part, as my practice was by this time not inconsiderable'. The latest possible date is most probable, given that it would have taken time for his practice—which he had only acquired about the time of his second marriage in summer 1902—to grow. The fact that this was 'one of the very last cases handled by Holmes before his retirement from practice' confirms later 1903.

More precisely, Bennett said that it was 'the night before last—that is, September 4'—that the professor most recently exhibited his strange behaviour. We know that it was a Sunday evening—obviously Sunday the 6th—when he said this. It was 2

The Creeping Man

a.m., technically 5 September, a Saturday, when the events occurred, but Bennett, in saying the 4th, was clearly referring to the date when that night began. On Monday the 7th, Holmes and Watson went to Camford and visited the professor. On the morning of the 8th, they were at a local inn and Bennett visited them. They then returned to London, having agreed to meet at the inn on the morning of 'next Tuesday', the 15th—although in the event Bennett did not visit them until that evening. Holmes sent Watson a message on the 14th, a Monday, asking him to meet him the next day at the railway station. That day they travelled together to Camford and that night they solved the case.

It was 'on July 2' that Roy first attacked the professor. The dog attacked 'Again on July 11' and yet again 'upon July 20'. In August the dog attacked him on the 26th. On 5 September the same thing happened. Holmes predicted that it would happen again 'next Tuesday', which would be the 15th, as it was the 7th, a Monday, when he said this. Holmes explained that the 'trouble' with the professor happened apparently 'at nine-day intervals, with, so far as I remember, only one exception. Thus the last outbreak upon Friday was on September 3, which also falls into the series, as did August 26, which preceded it.' Holmes later reasserted that 'every nine days the professor takes some strong drug'.

The issue which arises is that Holmes said four or five times that the professor took his drug at nine-day intervals, yet the dates given in the account do not appear to agree with this. First of all, the statement by Holmes that an incident occurred on 'Friday…September 3' is clearly a typographical error, for the 3rd was a Thursday in 1903, and it is obviously supposed to read 'September 4', as this is what Bennett said. Furthermore, while the dates in July were in fact all nine days apart, nine-day intervals do not count forwards to 26 August, but rather to the 25th. Nine days from 26 August would be 4 September, but the 15th, the 'next Tuesday' when Holmes expected 'fresh developments', was eleven days later. He was certain that it would be on that Tuesday, but this would break the nine-day cycle. We cannot hope to explain this by supposing that when Holmes so categorically declared that events would transpire 'next Tuesday', he meant in the small hours of the morning of Tuesday—practically speaking, Monday night—because we know that Holmes and Watson did not even travel to Camford until the Tuesday. To explain these inconsistencies, therefore, we must enter into a more intricate analysis of the dates given by Bennett.

On 2 July, 'it was on that very day' that Roy attacked the professor, suggesting that the encounter was during the daytime. The incidents of the 11th and 20th would presumably have been during the day too, as would the 'period of excitement upon August 26' mentioned by Holmes. But when another attack occurred in the small hours of the morning of the 5th (referred to as the 4th by Bennett), the professor continued in his ape-like state throughout the next day and into the night, for Miss Presbury saw her father's face at the window on 'September 5th', as Holmes referred to it (and if it was after midnight it was technically the 6th). Let us suppose that when the professor injected himself on a given night, the effects of the drug kept him moody and morose throughout the following day, and, later in his course of taking the drug, he remained in his ape-like state into the next night as well. This would explain how he was seen to be acting like an ape on the nights of both 4 and 5 September.

With regard to 2 July, the professor apparently took the drug late on the 1st—it seems that he habitually administered the drug late at night, and it was on the following day that his strange behaviour was apparent—and the effects lasted most of the next day. The same sequence of events occurred on the 11th, 20th, 29th, and so on, until he came to mid-August, when it appears that his dose of the 15th/16th left him feeling the effects longer than ever before, probably into the night of the 16th/17th. He thus elected to postpone his next dose until nine days from that night, so he did not take it until the night of the 25th/26th, and felt the effects on the 26th—'a period of excitement'. The drug once again lasting into the following night as on the 16th, he accordingly continued with his nine-day scheme from the night of the 26th, not the 25th, and took his next dose late on the 4th. This agrees with the fact that Bennett saw him under the drug's influence at 2 a.m. on the 5th. His body was now replete with the drug, and the effects of this dose lasted not only into the night of the 5th but also into the morning of the 6th, when the professor 'was sharp and fierce in manner'. As he had now reached the point at which he was fully affected for two nights and part of a second day by each dose, he counted his next nine days from the night of the 6th, not the 4th or 5th. This means that he would have planned to take his drug again on the night of the 15th, the Tuesday night that Holmes had predicted.

On that Tuesday, Holmes repeatedly insisted that 'If the cycle of nine days holds good, then we shall have the Professor at his worst to-night'. What Holmes had observed was that the 'cycle of nine days' now meant taking the drug nine days after its effects had worn off, not after last taking it. So Presbury administered it nine days after the 26 August, as the effects had lingered into that night, meaning he took it late on the 4 September or perhaps even in the first hours of the 5th. Since the effects lasted into the 6th, he then had to adjust his cycle and take the most recent dose nine days from the 6th. He was in correspondence with his

The Creeping Man

provider, Dorak—on the 7 September Bennett told Holmes that 'He seems to have written this morning'[1]—regarding his progress, and this man, following the guidance of Lowenstein, did not send him another packet of the drug until Tuesday the 15th, to be administered that night. Holmes evidently perceived this pattern, being aware that the effects had lasted into the morning of the 6th, and that is why he confidently did not expect anything until 'next Tuesday'.

The 'one exception' to the nine-day rule which Holmes mentioned apparently occurred sometime between 20 July and 26 August, the period for which Watson does not provide us with any of Bennett's dates. Perhaps it was this exception, and not lingering effects from the dose of the 15th/16th, which delayed the professor's cycle by a day, resulting in his dose of the 25th/26th being apparently a day late. Alternatively, he may have had a gap of ten days followed by one of eight, or vice versa, for unknown reasons; the two deviations taken together would only really constitute one exception from the cycle, as the latter would have merely been a measure to remedy the discord occasioned by the former.

The case began for Holmes on Sunday 6 September and ended on Tuesday 15 September in the year 1903. This scheme of days is supported by the fact that Miss Presbury described 'bright moonlight outside' on the night of the 6th and that the 7th was the full moon in September 1903. Watson, furthermore, noted 'the half-moon' on the night of the 15th, and the moon was in fact at half, waning, on the 14th.

---

[1] Doubtless with regard to his dose of the 4th having lasted into the 6th.

52. The Sussex Vampire

First published January 1924

The note that Holmes tossed to Watson at the beginning of the account was dated '*Nov. 19th*'. The next morning, the 20th, Ferguson called at Baker Street, and Holmes sent his return letter to Morrison, Morrison, and Dodd on '*Nov. 21st*' after solving the case. This establishes the month and the days, leaving us to find the year.

It is clear that Watson was still living with Holmes for several reasons: Holmes said, 'what do we know about vampires?', emphasising 'we'; he referred to 'This Agency' to indicate his and Watson's collaborative work; and he stated that 'Watson, of course, comes with us'. Knowing that November was the month, we may, therefore, exclude all years from 1887 to 1893 and from 1902 onwards.

Holmes, referring to the events concerning the *Gloria Scott,* said that 'I have some recollection that you made a record of it, Watson'. *The Sussex Vampire* apparently occurred after February 1893, then, when *The "Gloria Scott"* was first published, leaving the years from 1894 to 1901 inclusive as possibilities. Christ eliminates 1901 by showing that in this case Holmes made Watson send a wire, a task which ought to have been performed by the page who was at Baker Street in October 1901[1] if that were the year.[2] November 1900 is equally impossible, for during that month Holmes and Watson handled several cases of the greatest importance,[3] of which this could not possibly be considered one. We also remove 1899 and 1897 from consideration because, as Christ,[4] Hall,[5] and Bell[6] each explains, the letter of the 19th would not have been delivered on a Sunday, and the letter of the 21st would not have been posted on one. We eliminate 1895 because from Monday 18 November to Thursday 21 November Holmes suffered from a lack of cases prior to *The Bruce-Partington Plans*.[7]

Of the remaining possible years for the case—1894, 1896, and 1898—the most likely for several reasons is 1894. Holmes's remarks, such as saying that Watson would naturally come with him and referring to his partnership with Watson as an Agency, seem to suggest that he and Watson had recently begun to work together again, and it was in summer 1894 that Watson sold his practice and returned to Baker Street. Apparently, Holmes regarded his resurrected consulting practice as Watson's new occupation and decided to refer to their revived partnership as an Agency. Happy to have his friend and biographer back with him, Holmes announced that Watson would naturally be joining him for the investigation.

Additionally, as Watson's account entitled *The "Gloria Scott"* was published in February 1893, it would have been recent

---

[1] Billy is mentioned in *The Problem of Thor Bridge*.
[2] Christ, 67.
[3] Long, HOUN, 442-443.
[4] Christ, 67.
[5] Hall, 59.
[6] Bell, 103.
[7] Short, BRUC, 968.

The Sussex Vampire

enough in Holmes's mind in November 1894 that he would have still had occasion to refer to it. Dakin excludes 1894 because *The Golden Pince-Nez* occurred in late November of that year,[1] but this reasoning is unsound. Holmes said during *The Sussex Vampire* that 'There is a lull at present', showing only that *The Golden Pince-Nez* began after 21 November, when this case concluded.

The Sussex Vampire occurred, then, from 19 to 21 November 1894.

---

[1] Dakin, 267.

53. The Three Garridebs

First published October 1924

Watson says that the case occurred at 'the latter end of June, 1902, shortly after the conclusion of the South African War'. This agrees with the facts that 'Holmes refused a knighthood'— doubtless for services rendered in the war effort—earlier in June of the same year, and that there was a telephone at Baker Street. Watson commented about Holmes spending 'several days in bed, as was his habit from time to time'; obviously these are the words of a Watson who lived at Baker Street. He could not, then, have been remarried before July 1902.

John Garrideb came to Baker Street on the first day of the case, and Holmes and Watson visited Nathan Garrideb that evening. John first called upon Nathan 'last Tuesday'. According to both John and Nathan, John found and called upon Nathan 'two days ago', making the first day of the case a Thursday. On the Friday Holmes and Watson repaired to Nathan's house and apprehended John.

The case, being at 'the latter end of June, 1902', must have been in the last week of the month; this means that it lasted from Thursday the 26th to Friday the 27th.

54. The Illustrious Client

First published November 1924

The case began 'upon September 3, 1902', according to Watson. He said that he was 'living in my own rooms in Queen Anne Street at the time', confirming that between *The Three Garridebs* in June 1902 and this case he had married for the second time and left Baker Street. Holmes and Watson visited a Turkish bath together on the first day. Watson joined Holmes at Baker Street in the afternoon, then took care of 'some pressing professional business' before meeting Holmes 'at Simpson's'. On 4 September, Watson met Holmes at Simpson's, their 'Strand restaurant', once again, and Holmes told him about the interview between Kitty Winter and Violet de Merville. Two days later, on Saturday 6 September, Watson read of the murderous attack upon Holmes.

'For six days the public were under the impression that Holmes was at the door of death' following this, and 'On the seventh day', Watson tells us, Holmes's stitches were taken out and Watson brought him the news of Gruner's impending departure. This day, when Holmes charged Watson with studying Chinese pottery, was apparently Saturday 13 September. Holmes said, however, that Gruner's intention to leave on the following Friday allowed them 'Only three clear days' to conclude the case, which would seem to suggest that Gruner should actually have been departing on the Wednesday. In explanation of this, we would direct attention to the fact that Gruner's boat was scheduled to leave from Liverpool—early in the morning, for all we know—so it is not unreasonable to suppose that he would have left by train for Liverpool on the Thursday, a fact which Watson neglected to record himself saying. This would leave Monday, Tuesday, and Wednesday as the three clear days.

The question, then, is why Holmes did not consider Sunday the 14th to be a 'clear day'. Given that on the Saturday he was already planning to have Watson spend a day studying pottery when he made this remark, it seems that he removed the Sunday from his calculation of days because it was only from the Monday that he and Watson would be prepared to act against Gruner. As Holmes had a lot of variables to consider—how quickly Watson could memorise facts about pottery, when Sir James Damery could bring him 'the real egg-shell pottery of the Ming dynasty', and how likely Gruner was to be at home and disengaged when Holmes predicted—it was only reasonable that Holmes should wish to have a few different days upon which he could execute his plan. For him, the 'clear days' were days upon which he might act against Gruner, not simply days until Gruner was leaving.

Dakin, to reconcile the issue of the 'clear days', offers the explanation that Holmes and Watson did not immediately announce to the public that Holmes's wounds might prove to be mortal, instead conveying merely that his condition was worsening for the first day or two following the attack.[1] This explanation would put Holmes's seventh day of suffering on

---

[1] Dakin, 258.

either Sunday 14 or Monday 15 September, but neither of these days is in fact possible. The former leads to the impossibility of Watson visiting 'the London Library in St. James' Square' to study pottery on a Sunday, when it would have been closed, while the latter results in him doing this on a Monday, improbable because the Thursday would then be the third clear day and Gruner could not then have left a day early, as we think is more likely than not. Furthermore, and even more importantly, it would have been most odd for Holmes to have delayed exaggerating his injuries for even one day, let alone two, since already on the day of the attack he told Watson that 'I have my plans. The first thing is to exaggerate my injuries.' Bell's theory is not much more attractive, for he simply resorts to the expedient of ascribing the fault to Watson, claiming that the case actually began on the 13th and that Watson accidentally dropped a '1' from his manuscript.[1] This hypothesis also allows only three days until the departure, thereby failing to account for the probability that Gruner would have left London on the Thursday.

Watson, having received his orders on the 13th and dutifully studied Chinese pottery for twenty-four hours, returned to Baker Street on the evening of the 14th. Holmes, who had already acquired the egg-shell pottery, had no reason to delay any longer, so he sent Watson to call upon Gruner that same evening. The plan succeeded, Watson returned to Holmes, and the case concluded. It lasted, then, from 3 to 14 September 1902.

---

[1] Bell, 115.

55. The Three Gables

First published September 1926

Watson says that 'I had not seen Holmes for some days, and had no idea of the new channel into which his activities had been directed'. Furthermore, Holmes 'had just settled me into the well-worn arm-chair on one side of the fire'. These statements imply that Watson was no longer living at Baker Street. Isadora Klein's drawing-room had 'an occasional pink electric light'. Klein almost certainly would not have had electric lighting before the Return, and the only timeframe after 1894 during which Watson was not living at Baker Street and Holmes was still in active practice was summer 1902 to the end of 1903.

Further speculation about the date becomes irrelevant when we consider a few facts which demonstrate that Watson was very likely not the author of this account. First of all, Holmes committed the highly unorthodox and uncharacteristic impropriety of referring to Steve Dixie by first name only. Secondly, Holmes made a number of derisive comments about Susan, the maid at the Three Gables. This behaviour contrasts glaringly with his conduct towards women throughout the rest of the recorded cases: he was consistently gentlemanly and respectful, in spite of his sceptical attitude towards them. Lastly, Holmes, in referring to why someone should wish to buy Mrs Maberley's entire house and all of its contents, remarked that 'Dr.

The Three Gables

Watson agrees, so that settles it'. Holmes never at any other time needed Watson's opinion to substantiate or validate his own, rendering this statement not only odd but also inconsistent with Holmes's very nature and customary aplomb.

Holmes's behaviour is, in fact, so out of character that we cannot doubt that this account is spurious, written by someone who did not know Holmes personally. As with *The Mazarin Stone*, Watson probably sold or bequeathed the notes for the case to Doyle, who attempted to the best of his ability to recreate the actual events of the case—with what degree of success has been shown above.

In any case, for what it is worth, Bell is doubtless right in believing that the date must be in the latter half of May since geraniums would not be bedded any earlier,[1] and we accept Baring-Gould's date of Tuesday 26 May to Wednesday 27 May 1903[2] for the events which inspired this story.

---

[1] Bell, 117.
[2] Baring-Gould, 316.

56. The Blanched Soldier

First published October 1926

This narrative is unique in being the first published account written by Holmes himself. Watson had at this time 'deserted me for a wife', Holmes says; this was after Watson's second marriage, for Holmes states that it was 'in January, 1903', that James Dodd visited him. Dodd first went in search of his friend Godfrey Emsworth at his home 'on Monday'. On that night there was 'a bright half-moon'. In 1903, there was a half-moon in January on both Tuesday the 6th and Tuesday the 20th, so this day was either Monday the 5th or Monday the 19th. Dodd sent the letter announcing his intention to call upon Holmes 'in the afternoon, and a good deal has happened since then', namely that Colonel Emsworth threw him out of his house. This happened on the night of the second day that he was visiting, Tuesday the 6th or 20th. He evidently came to Holmes the next morning, Wednesday the 7th or 21st. Holmes, however, could not attend to Dodd's matter 'until the beginning of the next week'. This was probably the next Monday, the 12th or 26th.

At the time of this case, Holmes also had 'a commission from the Sultan of Turkey which called for immediate action, as political consequences of the gravest kind might arise from its neglect'. There are a number of contemporaneous newspaper articles which serve to elucidate what precisely this commission

217

was. The *Standard* of London of 7 January 1903 states that the Sultan of Turkey authorised on 18 September 1902 the passage of four Russian torpedo-boat destroyers—disarmed, flying merchant flags—through the Dardanelles. This allegedly contravened the treaty of Berlin and other agreements.[1] The British embassy in Constantinople had issued on 5 January 1903 a protest against this action. According to the *Standard* of London of 13 January 1903, Ali Haydar Midhat, writing from Folkestone on 11 January, said that 'The Note presented by Sir Nicholas O'Conor, his Britannic Majesty's Ambassador at Constantinople, demanding from the Porte the same privileges as those accorded to Russia for the passage of torpedo-boats through the Dardanelles and the Bosphorus, has just provoked a very lively discontent in political circles in St. Petersburg'.[2]

Up to this point the situation was escalating, but the *Daily Mail* of London of 16 January 1903, quoting an article from their correspondent from 15 January, claimed the following: 'The [Dardanelles] incident has been greatly exaggerated. England felt in duty bound not to protest, but merely to draw the Porte's attention to a contravention of the treaty, not a violation. Neither the Porte nor England nor any other Power attributes importance to the incident, and Turkey will not answer the British communication.'[3] The *Standard* of London of 19 January noted that, as of 18 January in Constantinople, Turkey had not yet responded to the British protest, and that another Russian torpedo-boat was still scheduled to pass through 'early this

---

[1] 'Russia and the Dardanelles', *The Standard*, 7 January 1903, No. 24,505, page 5.
[2] 'The Dardanelles Question', *The Standard*, 13 January 1903, No. 24,510, page 7.
[3] 'Dardanelles Incident', *Daily Mail*, 16 January 1903, No. 2,105, page 5.

week'.[1] Furthermore, 'the departure of the British Ambassador [at Constantinople] on leave without an answer' confirmed that no response was expected.[2]

Obviously, Holmes became involved in some capacity in the Dardanelles Incident, as this minor international political event was called, probably being consulted by the Turkish ambassador in London. The matter commenced with the lodging of the British protest on 5 January and escalated from that point until the British demanded the same privileges as the Russians on the 11th. By the 15th, however, the importance of the incident to both the British and the Turks had apparently become minimal, given the suddenly apathetic attitude of the former to the lack of compensatory action by the latter.

Holmes was evidently consulted by James Dodd on Wednesday 7 January, before which time he had already been consulted by the Turkish ambassador, who of course would have had information about the Dardanelles Incident before the London newspapers received reports of it. Holmes had to defer investigating Dodd's case because during the rest of that week he was completing his work for the Sultan, the result of which was a de-escalation of the crisis sometime before the 15th. It seems probable that Holmes settled the disagreement on the 12 January, the day after Ali Haydar Midhat wrote his article which is the latest written news suggesting that the incident was serious. If this were the case, Holmes, having just helped to avert 'political consequences of the gravest kind', could have investigated the far less important affair of Godfrey Emsworth's disappearance on the 13th, which, being a Tuesday, was still at

---

[1] 'The Near East', *The Standard,* 19 January 1903, No. 24,515, page 5.
[2] 'The Near East', page 5.

'the beginning of the next week'. Perhaps the most definitive evidence in support of the Dardanelles Incident being the object of Holmes's commission from the Turkish Sultan is that the minor incident appears only in the densest of history books; it is not unlikely that if Holmes had not been called in to settle the matter, it would have become one of the major incidents of early twentieth-century European history.

The only potential objection to our dating is that Holmes says that 'at the moment I was clearing up the case which my friend Watson has described as that of the Abbey School, in which the Duke of Greyminster was so deeply involved', a statement which some chronologists believe refers to *The Priory School*. Holmes does not, however, say that Watson had published the case, and since *The Priory School* occurred in May 1901, it would make no sense for Holmes to say that he was solving it in January 1903. Blakeney suggests that *The Priory School* may have had such serious repercussions that Holmes was still settling them two years later,[1] but that is hardly credible, and we conclude rather that the cases of the dukes of Greyminster and Holdernesse were two separate affairs. As it was Watson, not Holmes, who described the Abbey School[2] and the Duke of Greyminster, just as he had earlier described the Priory School and the Duke of Holdernesse, this is evidently not a matter of aliases but of two different cases. This is a far more agreeable conclusion than that the whole account of *The Blanched Soldier* is spurious, as Dakin, who is a little too willing to discard cases, believes.[3]

The case occurred on Wednesday 7 January and on Tuesday 13 January 1903.

---

[1] Blakeney, 107-108.
[2] Note that this is a proper noun, the name of a specific institution.
[3] Dakin, 261.

57. The Lion's Mane

First published November 1926

When this case, which was also written by Holmes, began, he was at last living at 'my little Sussex home, when I had given myself up entirely to that soothing life of Nature for which I had so often yearned during the long years spent amid the gloom of London'. Watson had 'passed almost beyond my ken', Holmes says; 'An occasional week-end visit was the most that I ever saw of him'. This is clearly after Holmes retired at the end of 1903, which agrees with the fact that, as Holmes relates, the case began on a morning 'Towards the end of July, 1907'.

It was a week day, not a week-end, for Ian Murdoch 'insist[ed] upon some algebraic demonstration before breakfast'. This corroborates the fact that Maud Bellamy said that 'Tuesday was to-day, and I had meant to meet him to-night'. It was probably Tuesday the 23rd, not the 30th, for if it had been the last Tuesday of the month, Holmes would have very likely said '*at* the end', rather than '*towards* the end', of July.

From this date, the case was temporarily suspended. 'A week passed' according to Holmes, and his housekeeper said that the dog ate 'nothing for a week', suggesting that exactly seven days later the case continued—on Tuesday the 30th. Holmes visited the site of the tragedy after hearing of the death of McPherson's dog, and he retired for the night after consulting a book. The next day, Wednesday, a local inspector called upon Holmes, Ian Murdoch was attacked by *Cyanea Capillata*, and the case was solved.

The case thus occurred on 23, 30, and 31 July 1907. Zeisler, who dates it in July 1909, leads Dakin, Baring-Gould, and Folsom all astray with his insistence that 1907 could not be the year because there was no 'severe gale', as recorded by Holmes, in later July of that year.[1] Zeisler, in making this argument, seems to have forgotten that it was not Watson—whom we have seen to be occasionally indifferent to the accuracy of his dates—but rather Holmes, a man of the most meticulous mental exactitude, who wrote this narrative. We cannot conceive, nor will we do him the injustice to believe, that he permitted an incorrect date to be printed in one of the only two narratives that he ever published. Doubtless, as Hall very astutely observes, the gale in question was simply brief in duration and only affected the limited area of Fulworth and its environs,[2] and such a localised storm is not likely to have been recorded in the weather records upon which Zeisler places such great reliance.

---

[1] Zeisler, 135-136.
[2] Hall, 9.

58. The Retired Colourman

First published December 1926

On the first morning of the case, Holmes told Watson that Amberley 'Retired in 1896'. 'Early in 1897 he married a woman twenty years younger than himself', Holmes continued, 'And yet within two years he is, as you have seen, as broken and miserable a creature as crawls beneath the sun'. This statement suggests that the case began in late 1898 or early 1899, but Watson tells us that 'on a summer afternoon I set forth to Lewisham'. He also said that 'the weather was hot'. This shows that the case actually occurred during the summer. It could not have been summer 1899, as that would contradict the statement 'within two years', so it must have been summer 1898, a year and a half after Amberley's retirement and marriage. This fits with Holmes's specification 'within two years', which remark also suggests that August was the month, as it would be closer to two years than June or July would.

Watson, having gone to Lewisham to investigate for Holmes (who was occupied with the case of the Coptic Patriarchs), returned to Baker Street late in the evening of the first day. He spent the following morning waiting for Holmes, then went to Little Purlington with Amberley to see the vicar. Watson and Amberley were obliged to spend the night there, and when they returned to Baker Street the next morning, they found a note

The Retired Colourman

from Holmes requesting that they go to Amberley's house, where Amberley was soon arrested. 'A couple of days later' Holmes and Watson read about the case in a paper.

No fewer than three different telephones were mentioned, one of them at the Railway Arms at the small village of Little Purlington and another at Baker Street. The presence of telephones in so many locations in 1898 is surprising, but it is, nevertheless, possible.

Ultimately, the most we can be sure of is that this case spanned five days in August 1898. Which five days remains a mystery.

59. The Veiled Lodger

First published January 1927

Watson makes the significant statement that 'Mr. Sherlock Holmes was in active practice for twenty-three years, and that during seventeen of these I was allowed to co-operate with him and to keep notes of his doings'. Watson and Holmes began their partnership in March 1881, and it lasted until Holmes apparently died in April 1891; this constitutes ten of seventeen years. From 1894 to 1903 the partnership continued; this is nine more years, making a total of nineteen. Holmes began his career in 1877, then, four years before Watson joined him. Presumably it was in this year that Holmes received the first of those three cases from former fellow students which he mentioned to Watson when recounting the affair of *The Musgrave Ritual*.[1]

Watson claims that he spent seventeen years working with Holmes, but, as we have computed above, it was actually nineteen years. This discrepancy may be the result of a typographical error, the 'seventeen' being printed because the '19' on the manuscript was not legible and strongly resembled a '17' with a crossed seven. Alternatively, given that there are no recorded cases from August 1898 to June 1900, a span of nearly two years, it could be that, for reasons beyond our ken, Watson

---

[1] Short, MUSG, 399.

was not permitted to take notes—or perhaps even to participate in cases—during that time. We cannot be certain which of these hypotheses is the true one, but either one would make the 'seventeen' accurate.

As to the date of this case, Watson tells us that it began 'One forenoon—it was late in 1896'. At the beginning of the case, however, he received a note from Holmes 'asking for my attendance' at Baker Street, suggesting that he did not live there at the time of this case. This means that the case could not have been in 1896. Watson later mentions that he 'called upon my friend [Holmes]', substantiating the conclusion that this case could not possibly have occurred between mid-1894 and mid-1902, during which years Watson lived at Baker Street. Yet more definitively, Holmes told Watson that 'you were with me then' when referring to the Abbas Parva tragedy of seven years ago, implying that he was no longer living with him in the present. From 1896 seven years back would be 1889, and Watson was not living with Holmes then. It is all wrong; the date given by Watson is surely false. This is not, in fact, altogether surprising, for Watson says that 'In telling it [the case], I have made a slight change of name and place, but otherwise the facts are as stated'. Clearly, he also made a change of date which the foregoing statement was intended to belie.

Dakin adheres to the date given by Watson by arguing, in explanation of his absence from Baker Street, that he may have been temporarily living at and running a colleague's practice, or simply visiting friends.[1] The former is quite unlikely since Watson was, without difficulty or a thought as to the patients he was supposedly committed to caring for, able to go to Baker

---

[1] Dakin, 280.

The Veiled Lodger

Street and remain with Holmes for the rest of the day to discuss the case and call upon Mrs Ronder, and, however inattentive he may have been to his own patients at times, we must do him the justice to believe that he would not have so lightly abandoned a fellow doctor's patients. The latter theory, meanwhile, fails to explain satisfactorily why Watson was still living away 'Two days later'. In any case, these absences would have been only temporary, and Holmes rather clearly implies that Watson was no longer living at 221B. Even more implausibly, Bell claims that Watson married for the second time in 1896 and was thus living away from Baker Street until early 1897,[1] but this theory requires us to believe that Watson lost his second wife after no more than a year and is simply not credible, not least because there is no actual evidence for a marriage at this time in his life. Lastly, and perhaps most gravely, Brend, who leaves this case in 1896, opines that Holmes and Watson's friendship was temporarily compromised and that Watson left Baker Street in the year 1896 as a result of Holmes criticising Watson for his gambling on horse races and of Watson reprimanding Holmes for his drug usage.[2] This theory bears mentioning only as an example of unsound reasoning: there is no evidence anywhere to suggest that Holmes and Watson harboured serious resentment about any of the criticisms mentioned in the published accounts, nor is it consonant with their personalities that they would allow mere chiding to result in such an estrangement.

When might the case have occurred, then? The years 1888, 1889, and 1890, when in the later part of the year Watson was living away from Holmes but when seven years earlier he was

---

[1] Bell, 91-95.
[2] Brend, 142.

living with him, are all plausible. It could also conceivably have happened in 1894 between May and July, during the short time frame between Holmes's return to London and Watson's return to Baker Street, but this would ignore Watson's claim that it was in the later part of a year. It may also have occurred in 1902 or 1903.

Christ offers a strong argument in favour of 1890, supported by the fact that in 1883 Holmes was relatively young and new to his profession and would therefore have been more likely than at a later time to be 'worried' by the Abbas Parva tragedy of which he 'could make nothing'.[1] Holmes may, however, have been distracted by other cases at any time in his career and thus been unable to solve this tragedy, and we prefer the year 1903 for several reasons. In the first place, there are two pieces of evidence which strongly suggest a late year rather than an early one. Holmes said that 'Edmunds, of the Berkshire Constabulary', called upon him seven years ago at the time of the Abbas Parva tragedy to ask for advice, and it is unlikely that Holmes's reputation, limited as it was in 1881, 1882, and 1883, would have brought a provincial official to London to consult him. Furthermore, Mrs Ronder tells Holmes that 'I know your character and methods too well, for I have followed your work for some years. Reading is the only pleasure which Fate has left me'. This clearly shows that she had been reading numerous cases published by Watson over the years, something which would not have been possible prior to the Return. Thirdly, the fact that most of the other cases presented in the collection entitled *The Case Book of Sherlock Holmes* are from after the Return favours a later year for this case, though this is admittedly only a

---

[1] Christ, 73.

The Veiled Lodger

matter of probability. Lastly, it is possible that Watson chose to use 1896 as his false date for the case because it was in fact another date associated with the case—the date, seven years earlier, when the Abbas Parva tragedy had occurred.

Thus Holmes and Watson went to see Mrs Ronder in 1903, when Watson was not living with Holmes. We may suppose that it was in the later part of the year, as Watson said, for he had no reason to disguise the time of year. As *The Creeping Man* of 6–15 September was one of Holmes's last cases, this one probably occurred shortly before it, in the first week of September. It began on a given day and concluded two days later; the precise days cannot be determined from what scant evidence Watson provides.

60. Shoscombe Old Place

First published March 1927

Watson notes that Holmes 'had been bending for a long time over a low-power microscope', and when Holmes decided to go to Shoscombe, there was no question of Watson not joining him, no mention of patients or practices or wives. This case occurred, then, between 1881 and 1887 or between 1894 and 1902, during a time when Watson was living at Baker Street. Considering that all of the other cases published by Watson in the collection entitled *The Case Book of Sherlock Holmes* occurred after the Return, as noted previously, the latter timeframe seems more likely, though this is not definite.

Regarding the time of year, it was 'on a bright May evening' that Holmes and Watson went to Shoscombe; that morning the case had begun with a visit from Mr John Mason. The next day they performed the test of the dog approaching the carriage, then investigated the crypt at night when 'It was pitch-dark and without a moon'. On this second night of the case, Sir Robert admitted that 'my sister *did* die just a week ago'. John Mason, conversely, asserted during his visit to Holmes and Watson on the first day of the case that 'For a week now' Lady Beatrice had not stopped to see the horses or even say 'hello', implying that she had been dead for a week. As the language of Sir Robert was more precise, we think that the lady died seven days before the second day of the case, not the first, and that Mason used the word *week* more loosely.

Sir Robert, in recounting his thoughts on the night of his sister's death, stated that he had believed that 'If I could stave things off for three weeks all would be well', as he would thus have been able to run his horse in the Derby at Epsom and pay his debtors. As of the second night of the case, a week had passed since Lady Beatrice's death; two weeks therefore remained before the Derby. This second night of the case was near the new moon, indicating that the Derby occurred about two weeks after the new moon in May of the year of the case. There was 'a bit of moon' on the night that Mason followed Sir Robert to the old crypt for the second time (apparently the third night after Lady Beatrice's death) which would make sense if the new moon occurred during the following week.

The scheme of all of these events, then, is as follows: there was a series of four weeks in which Lady Beatrice died sometime during the first week, when there was some moon showing; in which—during the second week, precisely seven days after Lady Beatrice's death—Sir Robert revealed everything (on the second day of the case) and there was a new moon; and in which, during the fourth week, the Derby at Epsom occurred.

There are sixteen years, as stated above, in which the case could have occurred. It could not have been in 1896 or 1900, because in both of those years the horse that won the Derby was owned by the Prince of Wales, and we may be sure that this illustrious royal was not the man whose name Watson chose to disguise as Sir Robert Norberton. Similarly, 1882 and 1886 may be eliminated since the duke of Westminster owned the winning horse in those years, and 1894 and 1895 are not plausible because the winning horse was owned by Lord Rosebery in both of those years. Pierre J. Lorillard IV, an American tobacco magnate, owned the winning horse in 1881, and he could not have been Sir Robert Norberton because he neither lived in England nor suffered from financial difficulties. Yet another year—1901—is discounted by the fact that the 'owner' of the winning horse was not its owner at all: William Collins Whitney, an American, leased the steed from Lady Valerie Meux, another American who was married to a British baronet. Finally, the Derby in 1884 ended in a dead heat, and since Shoscombe Prince was the clear winner of his race, this year is equally implausible, leaving us with seven possible years.

When we consider the calendars and moon phases for these years, and compare them with the date of the Derby at Epsom in each of the years, it quickly becomes apparent that the only year which matches such a scheme of weeks as delineated above is 1883:

Year	Day of New Moon	Day of Derby
1883	6 May	23 May
1885	14 May	3 June
1887	22 May	25 May
1897	1 May and 31 May	2 June
1898	20 May	25 May
1899	9 May	31 May
1902	7 May	4 June

In 1883, there was a space of two weeks and three days between the new moon and the Derby. Holmes and Watson's second night on the case, when there was no moon, would have to have been within a day on either side of the new moon, as the moon still has the appearance of a new moon on those two days. The latest date is most probable, so 7 May, a Monday, was the second

Shoscombe Old Place

day of the case. Exactly seven days before this, on Monday 30 April, Lady Beatrice had died. Holmes was called in six days later—on Sunday 6 May (the actual day of the new moon) and the case concluded on the 7th. Sir Robert said that he had to prevent his sister's death from becoming known 'for three weeks' as of 30 April, which date would have been precisely Monday 21 May. This is two days before the Derby, but we may reasonably presume that Sir Robert did not literally mean three weeks to the day, and as two days beyond is less than half of a week, he naturally said three, not four, weeks. This would also provide for the 'bit of moon' which was mentioned on the third night after Beatrice's death, the night of 3 May.

The case for Holmes, then, lasted from Sunday 6 to Monday 7 May 1883. Sir Frederick Johnstone, for whom Sir Robert Norberton was an alias, was the owner of the winning horse in this year. Though we initially favoured a year between 1895 and 1902, there is simply no year in that range that can fit the facts. Zeisler[1] and Baring-Gould[2] select 1902, but this conflicts with the fact that the new moon was on 7 May and the Derby on 4 June in that year. Besides, as Hall notes, Watson would hardly have been so irresponsible as to spend 'about half my wound pension' on horse racing with his second marriage imminent in summer 1902.[3] Christ places the events in 1883, but he selects an early year for reasons entirely different from our own: he doubts that Holmes would have had anything left to learn from Watson

---

[1] Zeisler, 128. Zeisler was under the erroneous impression that the Derby in 1902 was run on 21 May, having assumed that it was always held on the first Wednesday after Whitsunday; had he verified this assumption he would have found that the race was actually on 4 June in 1902, making that year impossible.
[2] Baring-Gould, 314.
[3] Hall, 40.

about horse racing if they had lived together for a long time and had also already solved the case of Silver Blaze together.[1] We must admit that this argument, though it would support our own, loses its cogency when one recalls that Holmes was not a man to store such information for very long after it had ceased to be useful, and thus, if he even had sounded Watson for facts about the turf during the case of Silver Blaze, he very likely would have suppressed them by the time of the Return, allowing for a later date for *Shoscombe Old Place*. Besides, Holmes asked Watson about specific people currently involved in horse racing, not about the racing itself, and, as this is information that would change fairly regularly, Holmes would have needed Watson, who read about such matters in the papers, to update him. The validity, or lack thereof, of Christ's argument does not compromise our own conclusions, however, and we trust that we have shown 1883 to be indubitably the correct year.

---

[1] Christ, 74.

PART II: A BIOGRAPHY

The Lives of Mr Sherlock Holmes and Dr John H. Watson

John Watson was born sometime in the year 1852, followed two years later by the man whom he was destined to immortalise through his writings, Sherlock Holmes. Virtually nothing definite is known of the childhood of either man, and it is only with their further education that we obtain our first real glimpse into their lives. Watson decided to pursue a career as a military doctor, while Holmes, unsure what path to follow in life, began attending the University of Oxford in 1872. In July of the following year, he became fortuitously involved in his first case when he visited his friend, Victor Trevor, at Donnithorpe during the summer holiday. Victor's father was the man who gave Holmes the idea to put his remarkable faculty for deduction to practical use, and he was not slow in acting upon the suggestion. Indeed, having left the Trevors', he spent seven weeks in London performing chemical experiments and only stopped when Victor sent him a telegram in September urging him to return to Donnithorpe, where he was present for the dramatic revelation of the senior Trevor's involvement with the lost ship the *Gloria Scott* many years earlier.

At the end of the spring term in 1874 Holmes left Oxford without graduating, convinced that he had already learnt all that could be useful to him there. He installed himself on Montague Street in London, apparently having received a small allowance or inheritance from his parents, and spent his time studying everything and anything that might prove useful for detective work. In 1877 he received his first formal client—one of his acquaintances from Oxford who had seen his powers first-hand—marking the beginning of his career as a consulting detective. Other such former fellow students subsequently came with their problems; the third to do so was Reginald Musgrave, who on the morning of 18 July 1878 called upon him at his rooms in London. The same afternoon Holmes accompanied him to Hurlstone and was able to solve the mystery of the Musgrave Ritual and locate the corpse of the brilliant but unfortunate butler, Brunton. This is the case which made Holmes's name, presumably because Musgrave trumpeted his brilliance, and following it he saw an appreciable increase in clients.

In the two and a half years between this case and his meeting Watson, Holmes handled at least eight cases: the Tarleton murders, Vamberry the wine merchant, the old Russian woman, the affair of the aluminium crutch, Ricoletti the club-foot and his wife, Mrs Farintosh, Mortimer Maberley, and a forgery case. Watson, meanwhile, had completed his medical studies and had become an army doctor, and he found himself shipped off to Afghanistan after the outbreak of the Second Afghan War in 1878. At the battle of Maiwand on 27 July 1880 he was wounded, not once but twice: he was hit by a Jezail bullet in the leg, and he also injured his shoulder. He was sent back to Peshawar to recover, but fell victim to enteric fever. After two perilous months his health improved, and he boarded the troopship *Orontes* which arrived in England in November. He drifted irresistibly to the capital and spent far more money than his pension provided staying at a private hotel. Then, on 1 January

1881, he ran into his old acquaintance Stamford, who introduced him to Mr Sherlock Holmes.

Both men were seeking a flatmate, and they settled happily upon a flat to share at 221B Baker Street. Watson spent his first two months there observing Holmes, whose profession was a mystery to him. Then, on 4 March, Holmes asked him to accompany him to a crime scene, and Watson at last learnt that Holmes was a private consulting detective. The next day Watson witnessed his first arrest—that of Jefferson Hope—and the case he would one day publish as *A Study in Scarlet* concluded. Holmes and Watson spent some time discussing the case the following day, Watson doubtless taking notes of Holmes's explanations.

Watson spent the next eight months observing Holmes and his methods, presumably accompanying him on some of the cases that he solved, and by the time Percy Trevelyan came to 221B in late November 1881, he was familiar enough with Holmes's thought processes to follow his deductions concerning Trevelyan. This client told them of the peculiar manner in which a Mr Blessington had paid to establish him as a doctor on the condition that his mysterious benefactor be permitted to live at the practice as a resident patient. The three men repaired to the practice that night, and Holmes promptly determined that Mr Blessington was a liar and, to Watson's astonishment, left the premises abruptly. The next morning Trevelyan called them back, and Holmes, after studying Blessington's room and making some inquiries elsewhere, proved that Blessington, whose real name was Sutton, had not committed suicide but rather had been hanged. His three executioners escaped British justice, but they received their deserts when they were lost at sea with the foundered ship *Norah Creina* some time later.

A Biography

A few months after this, Alexander Holder brought the affair of the beryl coronet to Holmes's attention on the bright and snowy morning of Friday 24 February 1882. Watson, though he was not yet in the habit of joining Holmes for all of his cases, listened to Holder's story at Baker Street, and Holmes insisted upon his accompanying them to Holder's house. Holmes spent the day investigating at this house, then at Burnwell's, then at Holder's again, before finally visiting the unfortunate Arthur Holder in prison. The next morning, Alexander Holder returned to Baker Street, and Holmes explained to him the whole sequence of events, demonstrating the worthiness of his son and the lack thereof of his niece, and returned the missing portion of the beryl coronet to him.

The following year, on 4 April 1883, Miss Helen Stoner came to Baker Street and explained to Holmes and Watson the strange circumstances of her sister's death, and how she had begun to fear for her own life. After she left, her step-father, Dr Grimesby Roylott, burst into their rooms and warned them to keep out of his business. Holmes, whose interest was only piqued by this unfriendly intrusion, paid a visit to Doctors' Commons to look at a will before he and Watson both met Miss Stoner at Stoke Moran and searched the rooms there. They repaired to the Crown Inn for a few hours, then at 9 p.m. entered Miss Stoner's room, which she had vacated, and prevented her being murdered by a snake, which creature took instead the life of the nefarious step-father.

A month later, on 6 May, John Mason came to Baker Street to seek the assistance of Holmes with regard to the strange behaviour of his employer, Lady Beatrice Falder. Holmes, joined by Watson—who now habitually accompanied him—went to Shoscombe that same evening and stayed at the Green Dragon

A Biography

Inn. With the help of a Shoscombe spaniel, they discovered that Sir Robert Norberton had kept the death of his sister, Lady Beatrice, secret for the past week in order to prevent his creditors from seizing the estate. Holmes warned him that his sister's death must be reported, but the police were not overly concerned by what had happened, and the creditors bided their time until the race. Two weeks later, on 23 May, Sir Robert's horse, Shoscombe Prince, won the Derby at Epsom; very probably Holmes and Watson were there to see it happen.

By early 1884, Watson had begun to formally keep records of the cases he solved with Holmes and had written a few complete accounts, though Holmes was not very impressed with the ones which Watson showed him. It may be Holmes's criticism that dissuaded Watson from attempting to have any of his writings published until he finally overcame his diffidence three years later. In any event, the first three months of 1884 were bereft of any noteworthy cases, and it was not until Miss Violet Hunter presented her conundrum on 7 April that Holmes had a problem worthy of him. A fortnight after their initial interview, Miss Hunter sent Holmes a telegram begging his assistance, and the next morning, on the 22nd, Holmes and Watson met her at the Black Swan Hotel in Winchester at 11:30. At 7:30 that evening they joined her at the Copper Beeches, where the whole affair was concluded satisfactorily. Miss Hunter lost her position with the Rucastles, but she went on to achieve greater things as the head of a private school at Walsall. Much to Watson's disappointment, Holmes, who had seemed impressed by her, took no further interest.

Discouraged by Holmes's unfavourable opinion, Watson had in 1884 given up writing accounts of their cases, contenting himself with merely taking more or less vague notes. Holmes, having noticed this and the fact that Watson was no longer so eager to join him for cases, made an effort to atone for the harsh criticism he had given earlier when, the grotesque affair of the severed ears and the cardboard box having come to his attention in August 1885, he asked Watson to accompany him and add the case to his annals. Watson, who was in financial straits and had been constrained to cancel his holiday, could not resist this distraction and readily agreed. He no doubt thanked himself for having taken thorough notes when some eight years later he wrote a full account of this singular incident for publication. Holmes and Watson met Lestrade in Croydon and visited Susan Cushing, who had received two severed ears in the post. They learnt that Sarah Cushing was too ill to receive visitors, then lunched at a hotel, and finally stopped at the local police station, where Holmes told Lestrade that he ought to arrest Jim Browner for murder. Two days later they received from Lestrade a typewritten copy of Browner's confession.

On Saturday 3 April 1886 Holmes and Watson returned late in the afternoon from a walk in the park and were disappointed to find that they had missed a client, for they had been without a case for some weeks. Mr Grant Munro soon returned to Baker Street, however, and explained at length the strange behaviour of his wife and the unsettling yellow face he had seen in the neighbouring cottage's window. Holmes supposed that Effie Munro's first husband was living in the cottage and blackmailing her, but after he and Watson arrived in Norbury at 7 that evening and with Munro entered the cottage, he learnt that he had been quite wrong in his surmises and had to concede that a woman had outwitted him for the first time in his career. Fully admitting his error, he asked Watson to use the incident to remind him of

A Biography

his fallibility should he ever become overly confident in the future.

At the beginning of July 1886 Holmes solved the Manor House case. A week later, on the 7th, Watson was shocked to learn that Holmes, who had never in all of their years together spoken of his family, had a brother. Holmes took Watson to meet Mycroft at the Diogenes Club that same evening, and Mr Melas, a Greek interpreter, presently arrived, at Mycroft's behest, to recount his bizarre experience of two nights before. They all parted ways, but Holmes and Watson found Mycroft in their sitting room not long after, and they, having collected Inspector Gregson, set out for The Myrtles, Beckenham, where they arrived shortly before 11 p.m., only just in time to save Mr Melas from death by charcoal, but too late to save the unfortunate Paul Kratides. The criminals escaped in spite of Holmes's best efforts, though they were later found murdered, supposedly by the deceased man's sister, in Budapest.

By 1887 Holmes's repute had extended beyond the borders of Britain, and in early February of that year he travelled to the Continent to look into the problem of Baron Maupertuis and the Netherland-Sumatra Company, which had baffled the police of three countries. After two months of incessant and exacting work, Holmes brought the affair to a successful conclusion, but he immediately suffered a constitutional breakdown, and on 15 April Watson found him lying ill at the Hotel Dulong in Lyons and took him back to Baker Street. Then, on 25 April, Watson decided to take Holmes to visit his old friend Colonel Hayter, and the next day, following the news of the burgling of the Cunninghams' house, Holmes, in spite of his convalescent state, became involved in solving another crime. He handily showed that the Cunninghams were in fact the criminals, and he felt all the healthier for it—so much so, in fact, that he and Watson returned to Baker Street the next day.

Having recovered from his ailment, Holmes spent the next couple of months busily solving cases. The Paradol Chamber, the Amateur Mendicant Society, the lost British barque *Sophie Anderson,* the Grice Patersons in the island of Uffa, and the Camberwell poisoning all rank amongst the problems that Holmes investigated in the first half of this memorable year of 1887. When summer came, however, the clients disappeared, and Holmes was irritated by a lack of work. All through the season he waited in vain for the bell to ring and a client to bring him a case, and as a result he relied increasingly upon drugs to stimulate himself, a dangerous habit of which Watson became ever more critical. Watson, for his part, was dealing with lingering discomfort in his wounded leg, apparently due to complications in his Achilles tendon, though his shoulder had completely healed by this time. During this summer of inactivity, he began writing a complete account of the first case he had ever taken part in, more for personal fulfilment than from any hopes of profit, but he happened to discuss it with a fellow doctor, one Arthur Conan Doyle, who convinced him that it was worthy of publication and offered to serve as his literary agent. Holmes, although he feared that such publicity would make it harder for him to mingle incognito amongst the criminal classes, reluctantly permitted Watson to proceed with the project, doubtless hoping that it would bring some new clients to put an end to his ennui.

Finally, on Tuesday 6 September Miss Mary Morstan came to 221B. Watson was instantly enamoured of her and sought to excuse himself from the room out of embarrassment, but Holmes insisted upon his remaining. She asked Holmes and Watson to accompany her that night to her meeting with

A Biography

Thaddeus Sholto, who led them all to Pondicherry Lodge, where they found his brother dead and the Agra treasure missing. Holmes and Watson immediately began their investigation, which did not conclude until Friday the 9th when they apprehended Jonathan Small, the man who had taken the treasure. That same night Watson—upon finding that Miss Morstan was not, after all, one of the wealthiest heiresses in England—proposed marriage. He then returned to Baker Street where he, Holmes, and Inspector Jones heard Small's story, and Watson rather naively remarked that, as he was soon to be married, this would surely be his last case.

Immediately after becoming engaged, Watson, who had been struggling financially for some years and could hardly support a wife with his pension income alone, began searching for a job in the medical field, and within a couple of weeks he had secured a part-time position. On Thursday 22 September Holmes, after entreaties from Colonel Ross and Inspector Gregory, decided that he must go to Dartmoor to look into the affair of the missing racehorse, Silver Blaze. He did not expect Watson, busy as he was with his new job and *fiancée*, to join him, but Watson was not working that day and had no obligations to Mary, for she was visiting her aunt on the Continent, so he offered to accompany Holmes, who was only too glad to accept. They spent the day investigating at the stables and on the moor, but Holmes explained nothing, simply telling Colonel Ross to keep Silver Blaze enlisted to run in the Wessex Cup on the following Tuesday.

The next evening Holmes and Watson received a call from young John Openshaw, who related to them the terrible history of his family and the fear he had for his own life. Holmes, in a grave miscalculation that would haunt him for the rest of his days, underestimated the danger that surrounded the man and sent him away after having done nothing more than give him some advice and promise to look into his problem the next day. Walking alone on this stormy night through the streets of London, Openshaw was murdered. Holmes, who learnt of his client's fate the next morning, spent the day tracking down the three murderers only to discover that they had already fled on a ship bound for America. He explained to Watson, who had been busy performing his new medical duties, that he had arranged for them to be apprehended by the police upon their arrival; but their ship ultimately foundered at sea, and they received the same sort of justice as the murderers of Mr Blessington. A few days later, on 27 September, Watson again accompanied Holmes to Winchester, where the dramatic conclusion of the affair of Silver Blaze unfolded. After the horse, which Holmes had found and ensured would be present, won the race, Colonel Ross accompanied Holmes and Watson on the train back to London and to Baker Street as Holmes explained everything.

Not very many days later, on 7 October, Watson, still plagued by a dull pain in his wounded leg, did not go to work, and, as Mary was still at her aunt's, he spent the day lying listlessly in the sitting room of 221B. This ultimately gave him the opportunity to be present for what would be his last case for quite some time: the singular visit of Lord St Simon, who came to see Holmes about his missing bride, Miss Doran, at 4 in the afternoon. Lestrade arrived to discuss the case with Holmes just after Lord St Simon left, after which Holmes went out to search for Miss Doran's real husband, Francis Moulton. At 9 that evening, Lord St Simon, Moulton, and his wife all appeared at Baker Street, and the lord learnt that Miss Doran was in fact Miss Moulton and thus that he was still a noble bachelor. Watson spent the following weeks preparing for his nuptials, which took place in November. On Mary's side were her aunt who came from abroad, Mrs Forrester, and her close friends; John was pleased to see that Sherlock Holmes had accepted his invitation.

This was the last time that the two men saw each other for many months. While Watson settled into married life, sought better employment, and supplemented his income with his first publication, *A Study in Scarlet,* Holmes was busy handling a series of demanding international cases, including the Trepoff murder in Odessa, the Atkinson brothers' tragedy in Trincomalee, and the delicate affair of the royal family of Holland. During these months Watson heard little of and saw none of Holmes, for he was fully preoccupied by the need to establish himself in full-time medical practice. Finally, in March 1888, he purchased the foundering practice of the ailing and aging Mr Farquhar, in the Paddington district. Fortunately, the practice was situated in a house well-equipped to double as a residence for him and Mary.

It was just after this, on 20 March, that Watson happened to pass along Baker Street and stop in to see Holmes, quite possibly to share the news that he had acquired his own practice. Holmes, who was delighted to see his old friend, deduced this fact before he could share it and also took advantage of Watson's fortuitous visit to draw him into the affair of the Bohemian crown-prince's scandalous photograph. Watson dutifully returned to his wife that night, but at 3 the next afternoon he was back at Baker Street to assist Holmes with the case, and that night he slept at 221B. The case concluded the next morning with Holmes suffering his second defeat at the hands of a woman, though his client ultimately came out of it all unscathed in spite of Holmes's failure.

A Biography

For the next three months Watson's time was fully occupied by his new practice, and, with the exception of a single visit when Holmes showed him the golden snuffbox which the king of Bohemia had given him, he did not see Holmes again until the morning of Saturday 16 June, when Holmes made his first appearance at Watson's house. Watson, who had only the night before been reviewing some of his old case notes as he worked on some new manuscripts for eventual publication, was only too glad to join Holmes for another investigation, assuring him that his neighbour Jackson would take care of any patients who called in his absence. With their client, a stock-broker's clerk by the name of Hall Pycroft, the two men made their way to Birmingham where they prevented the suicide of a dastardly criminal.

Holmes, encouraged by his friend's readiness to join him for the case of Pycroft, returned to Watson's house just before midnight on Wednesday 20 June to offer him the chance to accompany him for another adventure. He found Watson preparing to retire for the night, but Watson was more than ready to stay awake to discuss the death of Colonel Barclay, and he was sure that Jackson would watch his practice again while they were in Aldershot the next day. During their conversation, Holmes (to whom Watson had shown the manuscripts of past cases that he had completed) likened his present lack of information concerning the death of Barclay to the situation of a reader of Watson's accounts, from whom important details were withheld in order to produce an effect of surprise. This time Watson fortunately did not let this criticism deter him from continuing his writings, which soon included the account of their visit the next day to Aldershot. There they met with Henry Wood, whose crooked back only made his tale more miserable, and they learnt that Barclay had not been murdered but had died of apoplexy.

Following this case, the partnership was largely revived, with Watson visiting Baker Street frequently and Holmes calling upon Watson at his residence in Paddington on occasion. July 1888 was a very busy month in which Watson, finding that summer was the slowest time of the year at his practice, was able to join Holmes for four cases, two of which Watson penned and entitled 'The Adventure of the Second Stain' and 'The Adventure of the Tired Captain', though he never published them. The third of the July cases occurred on 23rd of the month; it was a case brought by Watson to Holmes when an engineer showed up at his practice early on that Monday morning with his thumb missing and a strange tale to tell. The three men, along with Inspector Bradstreet of Scotland Yard, soon arrived in Eyford and found that the house where the engineer had lost his thumb was in flames, and that the perpetrators of that heinous attack had already disappeared, never to be apprehended.

The fourth and final of the July 1888 cases was that of Percy Phelps and the naval treaty. Early on the morning of the 30th Watson received a letter from his old schoolfellow Phelps asking for Holmes's assistance, and with the full concurrence of his wife he decided to take the letter to Holmes. The two men visited Phelps at Briarbrae, then returned to London in the afternoon to see Inspector Forbes at Scotland Yard before finally calling upon Lord Holdhurst at Downing Street. Watson, his practice slower than ever, returned to Briarbrae with Holmes the next morning. Holmes then sent Watson and Phelps back to Baker Street (Watson presumably sending a telegram along the way to inform his wife that he would not be returning home that night) to await his return the next morning, when he very dramatically presented his client with the missing naval treaty.

As summer drew to a close, so did Watson's respite, and he soon found himself constrained to devote most of his time and energy to caring for his increasing number of patients. Indeed, he was so inundated with work that it was not until the second day after Christmas that he found time, between professional calls, to stop at Baker Street and wish Holmes the compliments of the season. When he arrived on this Thursday morning, Holmes was in the process of studying a hat which had been brought to him by Peterson, the commissionaire, following his encounter with a drunkard two days previously. Not long after, Peterson himself burst into the room, a blue carbuncle in his hand; Holmes sent Peterson away to put an advertisement for the hat in the papers and told Watson that he would inform the countess of Morcar that they had her missing carbuncle. Watson left to finish his work for the day, but returned in time to see Mr Henry Baker reclaim his lost hat. Holmes and Watson then set about tracking down the provenance of the goose which had temporarily housed the carbuncle, going from the Alpha Inn to Covent Garden Market. It was there that they found James Ryder, who, after returning to Baker Street with them, soon admitted to having stolen the gem. Holmes let him flee, believing he would thereby save him from future crime. The countess reclaimed her lost carbuncle the next morning, Holmes passing the £1,000 reward on to Peterson, and Watson had another case for his annals after a long drought.

The winter and spring of 1889 were no less demanding upon Watson's time than the second half of 1888 had been, and he did not have the chance to accompany Holmes for a case again until June. On the morning of the 7th, Holmes sent a telegram asking

A Biography

Watson to join him in going to the Boscombe Valley; Watson was hesitant to abandon the many patients he had on his schedule, but Mary could see that he was in need of a brief holiday and reassured him that Anstruther (who had recently bought Jackson's practice) would doubtless take care of his patients for the day. They arrived in Ross late in the afternoon and began their investigation, then spent the night at the Hereford Arms as they had not yet finished. The next day Holmes solved the case and let the murderer, John Turner, walk free—though his shattered health only permitted him seven months more of life.

Not many weeks later, on 21 June, Watson, who was still very busy with his professional work, fortuitously became involved in another mystery with Holmes. It began with a visit from his wife's friend Kate Whitney, who sent Watson to fetch her husband from an opium den. He found not only the husband but also Sherlock Holmes, to whose invitation to travel to Kent to pursue an investigation he was only too eager to assent. They spent the night at the residence of Mrs Neville St Clair, Holmes smoking instead of sleeping, then returned at first light to London, where Holmes showed that Mr Neville St Clair was illegally incarcerated upon the absurd charge of having murdered himself. The upshot was not so harmless for Watson, whose wife was not at all pleased with him for having run off with Holmes without even a word of warning or explanation. Hitherto she had not objected to his continued friendship and occasional cooperation with Holmes, but she could not condone his behaviour this time, especially so soon after a previous exploit.

The summer of 1889 was not slack for Watson as that of the previous year had been, nor was the remainder of the year any less busy—but he nevertheless devoted considerable time to writing the manuscript of the case of his wife and the Agra treasure, which he entitled *The Sign of Four*. Holmes was occupied with cases for most of the year, but he finished it with a long succession of weeks without work. He was only too happy, therefore, to welcome the increasingly frequent visits of Watson, who was now openly quarrelling with his wife and sought solace in his old armchair at 221B. She disapproved of his putting his writing before his professional work, and as one disagreement inevitably led to another, she also began criticising him for the times he had abandoned his patients to solve crimes. Watson was understandably perplexed, for she had herself encouraged him to join Holmes in the past, but she assured him that this had been solely in the hope that he would finally satisfy his lust for adventure, leave his bachelor ways behind him, and settle down to serious work.

By the end of the year, Watson was in the habit of spending more nights at Baker Street than at home. On the morning of 7 January 1890 Inspector Alec MacDonald came to ask Holmes to accompany him to Birlstone, and Watson seized the opportunity to become involved in another case. They stayed that night in the local village inn, and the next night they solved the mystery by catching Cecil Barker in the act of removing a dumbbell from a moat, whereupon Edwards, alias Douglas, revealed himself and told his story. The sequel was not so happy: two months later, Barker made an appearance at Baker Street to tell Holmes that Edwards had died, lost at sea en route to South Africa.

Several weeks previously, in February 1890, Watson had had the pleasure of seeing his second written account published, thanks once again to his literary agent, Doyle. It was not by chance or accident that *The Sign of Four* told the story not only of the great Agra treasure, but also of Watson's courtship with

A Biography

Mary; he had chosen to fondly recount these personal reminiscences specifically in the hope of winning back Mary's affection, for he was genuinely distressed by their estrangement, and had, besides, tired of constantly travelling from Baker Street to his practice in Paddington. She was moved by his touching depiction of their meeting and engagement, and though she did not immediately capitulate, he eventually won her over when he revealed that he had purchased a new practice in Kensington that promised to be a great success, thereby proving his dedication to his medical work, and by April Watson was once again a rarity at 221B.

The spring of 1890 was full of mostly banal cases for Holmes, though the Dundas separation case did not lack originality. Watson, meanwhile, struggled with a dearth of clients at his new practice, which had not proven as successful as the seller had promised. In an effort to please his wife, who was not at all impressed, he minimised his visits to Holmes, but he still found his way to Baker Street on occasion. One such day was 16 June, when Miss Mary Sutherland happened to call upon Holmes to ask him to find her missing *fiancé*. Holmes set a rendezvous with the girl's stepfather, James Windibank, for 6 the following evening, and Watson promised to be present. Holmes spent the better part of the 17th in chemical analyses, while Watson was kept at the bedside of a gravely ill patient until nearly 6. He arrived in time, however, for the interview, in which Holmes demonstrated that Windibank was in fact the missing *fiancé*, and that he had treated his stepdaughter abominably.

Having started the week in his wonted old fashion, Watson could not help but call upon Holmes when he found himself with a little free time at the end of the week. On this Saturday, 21 June 1890, Watson arrived to find Holmes in the middle of an interview with a client, Mr Jabez Wilson. He shared his extraordinary tale of the League of Red-Headed Men, and Holmes and Watson, after a stop at Saxe-Coburg Square, attended Sarasate's third and final concert at 3 p.m. at St James's Hall. Watson had told Holmes earlier that his practice was slow and that he had nothing to do, but after the concert he reflected that he ought to return home and spend some time with Mary, though he assured Holmes that he would be back at 221B by 10 p.m. for the conclusion of the case. Upon arriving he found Jones of the police and Merryweather of the City and Suburban Bank already present, and the four men soon repaired to the bank, where they frustrated John Clay's attempt to steal the French gold. Watson then returned to Baker Street to discuss the case with Holmes over some whiskey and soda.

Watson's failure to return home at an even moderately reasonable hour brought him into renewed conflict with Mary, the upshot of which was that he agreed to completely stop solving crimes with Holmes. Indeed, it would be nearly a year before he joined him for another—and apparently final— adventure. Holmes remained relatively busy throughout the year 1890, handling, among others, a case for the royal family of Scandinavia (for the second time). Then, at the end of the year, he was called upon by the French government to investigate a matter of great import (in which he found himself pitted against Professor Moriarty), and it was not until he had solved it several months later that he returned to England and, on 24 April 1891, suddenly appeared at Watson's Kensington residence. Holmes asked him if he would join him for a holiday on the continent, and Watson, explaining that his practice was quiet and—more importantly—that his wife was visiting her aunt abroad, readily assented. The two men arrived in Brussels the next evening,

A Biography

progressed through Strasburg and Geneva to Interlaken, and finally arrived in Meiringen on 3 May. The next day they went to the Reichenbach Falls, into which Holmes cast Moriarty, though Watson, and therefore the world, believed his friend to have fallen as well.

Holmes chose to thus fake his own death in order to avoid the vengeance of Moriarty's associates, several of whom had escaped justice. Under the pseudonym of Sigerson, he went to Tibet, where he spent two years, then travelled back to Europe via Persia, Mecca, and Khartoum, finally settling for a time in Montpellier. Watson, meanwhile, spent his days perfunctorily tending to his patients and studying crimes, occasionally attempting to apply Holmes's methods to solve them. He also, as a tribute to his lost friend, published a series of twelve accounts of their past cases under the title of *The Adventures of Sherlock Holmes,* and they were so successful that not long afterwards he published a further series, *The Memoirs of Sherlock Holmes.* In the absence of any further adventures with Holmes, Mary was seemingly willing to overlook her husband's literary endeavours, and their marriage improved to the point that they again knew conjugal bliss by the time of Mary's unexpected and tragic death in late 1893.

Holmes—who returned to London to convict Colonel Sebastian Moran, the only remaining member of Moriarty's gang, of the murder of Adair—found Watson to be in a lonely and grieving state when he surprised him in his study on Tuesday 3 April 1894. Once Watson had recovered from fainting and Holmes had explained his miraculous survival, the two men settled down to discuss the past three years until 9:30 came round, at which point they made their way to an empty house across from 221B, where they captured Moran with the help of Lestrade.

Not long after his return, Holmes prevailed upon Watson to sell his practice—for which, though it was by no means flourishing, the young Verner paid handsomely (with Holmes's financial support)—and to return to his old quarters at Baker Street in order to devote himself once again to detective work. The first two cases which they handled were the papers of ex-President Murillo and the Dutch steamship *Friesland*, but they had had no others by July and Holmes was just beginning to complain of this lack of work when John Hector McFarlane burst into their sitting room on Monday the 2nd. After McFarlane explained his situation and was led away by Lestrade on the charge of murder, Holmes visited Blackheath and Norwood, returning late with no good news to report. The next morning Holmes and Watson both went to Deep Dene House in response to Lestrade's haughty telegram, where Holmes, to the astonishment of Lestrade, soon forced Oldacre out of his hidden retreat.

The ensuing months of 1894—a very busy year which afforded Watson enough material to fill three manuscript volumes—were replete with cases, including those of Crosby the banker and the red leech, the Addleton tragedy and the ancient barrow, the Smith-Mortimer succession, and Huret the boulevard assassin. A lull came in November, much to Holmes's annoyance, but on the 19th he received a letter concerning one Robert Ferguson, an old rugby acquaintance of Watson's who was asking for advice about a suspected vampire at his Sussex home. Ferguson appeared at Baker Street the next morning at 10 to tell his story and ask Holmes to visit his house; the men agreed to meet at Victoria Station at 2, and they arrived at Ferguson's home that evening. Holmes exposed the vindictive son Jack as the culprit, thereby effecting a rapprochement between Ferguson and his wife, who was not after all a vampire. Holmes and Watson stayed at the Chequers, Lamberley that night, and the next morning, having returned to Baker Street, Holmes sent a letter to Morrison, Morrison, and Dodd, who had referred Ferguson to him, to tell them that the matter had been settled satisfactorily.

About a week later, on a dark and stormy night, Stanley Hopkins, a newcomer to Scotland Yard during Holmes's protracted absence, appeared at Baker Street at midnight to ask for Holmes's advice about a murder at Yoxley Old Place. Hopkins slept on the sofa that night and with Holmes and Watson took a train at 6 the next morning and arrived at Yoxley Old Place a few hours later. Holmes eventually divulged the professor's sordid past, brought the woman Anna, who had accidentally murdered Willoughby Smith, out of hiding, and provided Hopkins with a solution to his mystery. Having returned to London, Holmes and Watson promptly delivered to the Russian embassy the letters and diary that would exonerate Anna's old friend Alexis.

Soon after this Holmes and Watson bested the criminal Colonel Carruthers, whom they had the satisfaction of seeing incarcerated. This had the adverse effect of initiating a period of inactivity which greatly irritated Holmes until Saturday 23 March 1895, when Mr John Scott Eccles called at Baker Street seeking the explanation of a most singular experience. He was followed shortly by Inspector Gregson and Inspector Baynes, with the latter of whom Holmes and Watson travelled to Surrey to visit Wisteria Lodge that same evening. They took rooms at the Bull, a local inn, and for the next four days they loitered in the town,

A Biography

Watson wondering why Holmes did not take action, Holmes clandestinely reconnoitring the house of High Gable. On the 27th, the case concluded when Signora Durando escaped from her captors and revealed all, and though neither Holmes nor Baynes succeeded in tracking down Don Murillo and Lopez, those two fugitives were murdered in Madrid some six months later.

Holmes and Watson, meanwhile, had turned their attention to the problems of other clients. John Vincent Harden came to Holmes seeking relief from a very peculiar form of persecution, and Holmes was busily engaged in clearing up this problem when on Saturday 13 April Miss Violet Smith called to ask for advice regarding a man who was following her when she rode her bicycle between Farnham Station and Chiltern Grange (the home of her employer, Carruthers). Holmes, busy with Harden's case, sent Watson to investigate on the following Monday, when the girl was returning to Chiltern Grange. Disappointed, however, in Watson's performance, Holmes went himself the next day; he returned with some wounds from his brawl with Woodley but had little new information to share with Watson. On Thursday the 18th Miss Smith informed them that she was leaving Carruthers's employment and returning to London on Saturday, on which morning Holmes and Watson went to Farnham to ensure her safe departure. They were too late to save her from the terrifying ordeal of a forced though void marriage to the odious Woodley, but they did apprehend the criminals and ultimately brought the girl safely out of the situation and back to London, where she soon after married Cyril Morton.

During the next two months Holmes investigated, at the request of the Pope, the death of Cardinal Tosca and also apprehended Wilson, the notorious canary trainer. Then at the beginning of July he began looking into the mystery of Woodman's Lee and the death of Captain 'Black' Peter Carey, though Watson did not hear anything about it until Inspector Hopkins came to see them on Wednesday 10 July. Together the three men went to Woodman's Lee that same day, and in the small hours of the following morning they caught young Neligan, who was trying to prove his father's innocence. Having spent the night at the nearby Brambletye Hotel, Holmes and Watson returned to London Thursday morning, and Holmes arranged the dramatic conclusion which took place at Baker Street on Friday at 10 a.m. and which saw the true murderer of Carey, one Patrick Cairns, arrested. Holmes and Watson spent the rest of the month in Norway.

Not long after their return to London, Holmes was presented with the most important political case of his career, solved due to the misalignment of a stain on a rug and a second stain on the floor beneath. On Tuesday 20 August Lord Salisbury, alias Bellinger, and Joseph Chamberlain, alias Trelawney Hope, entered 221B Baker Street and asked Holmes to recover a lost, indiscreet letter sent by Tsar Nicholas II of Russia in response to the annexation of Chitral by the British. Holmes went to Godolphin Street to investigate the death of Eduardo Lucas, suspected of having held the letter, but found nothing; the next two days brought no news. On the Friday, however, Lestrade summoned Holmes and Watson to the crime scene again, and Holmes quickly deduced that Hope's wife was in possession of the missing letter. He prevailed upon her to return it to her husband's despatch-box in order to deceive him into believing that it had never in fact been missing, thereby preventing, in all probability, a terrible war.

A Biography

In November 1895 Holmes and Watson settled into temporary lodgings in Oxford while Holmes devoted himself to an intensive study of early English charters. He was interrupted against his will by Mr Hilton Soames, who implored his assistance with a little problem concerning an examination for the Fortescue Scholarship that three of his students were supposed to take. Holmes questioned the students that evening, pursued a clue in the morning, and exposed Gilchrist as the student who had nearly cheated. Gilchrist had, however, during the night determined not to cheat but rather to leave England and join the North-Eastern Rhodesia Police, and he was accordingly not further prosecuted. Holmes, for his part, returned to the charters.

Holmes's studies in Oxford having concluded, he and Watson returned to Baker Street on Sunday 17 November. In the ensuing days they were confined to their rooms by a heavy, dense yellow fog, and Holmes, who had through his research into early English charters developed an interest in mediaeval music, spent his time studying this and cross-indexing his personal reference book. By the 21st he had tired of such mundane activities, however, and accordingly welcomed the problem brought to him that day by Mycroft concerning Cadogan West and the missing Bruce-Partington submarine plans. Having investigated the spot on the Underground line where West's body had been found, learnt from Colonel Valentine Walter that Sir James Walter had died that very morning, spoken with Miss Violet Westbury, West's *fiancée,* and stopped to see the location of the papers in the Woolwich office under the watchful eye of Sidney Johnson, Holmes and Watson returned to Baker Street, though Holmes left again shortly afterwards. Watson joined him that night to burgle Oberstein's abode, and the next morning they explained to Mycroft and Lestrade the trap that they had set for Oberstein. By 9 that evening they were back at Oberstein's, where they caught Colonel Walter, who had stolen the plans and sold them to Oberstein, who was in turn apprehended at the Charing Cross hotel the next day, Saturday the 23rd. Not long after this, Holmes answered a summons to Windsor Castle, from which he returned with an emerald tie-pin, a gift from Queen Victoria.

Cases were not plentiful during the holiday season and the beginning of the year 1896, but on 27 February, a Thursday, Mrs Warren came to ask Holmes's advice about a new lodger of hers who had remained locked in his room unseen for the past ten days. Holmes told her that nothing could be done at present but that she should send him word of any fresh developments; she returned to Baker Street herself the next day to inform him that her husband had been abducted (and rather violently released) that morning. Holmes and Watson arrived at Mrs Warren's lodging house at half past noon and discovered that the mysterious male lodger had become a woman, whereupon they returned to 221B to discuss developments. They went back to the lodgings before dusk and encountered Gregson and Leverton, of Pinkerton's, who were also involved in the mystery, and they soon found the corpse of Gorgiano of the Red Circle, the well-known murderer. Holmes then introduced them to Signora Lucca, the mysterious lodger, who rejoiced at the death of Gorgiano, and who told them the whole story of her and her husband's unwilling acquaintance with him. With the case neatly solved shortly before 8 p.m., Holmes, with Watson in tow, raced to the Olympia London concert venue to catch what remained of the Wagner performance that had begun at 7:30.

In the last quarter of 1896 a period of stagnation set in, and Watson began to fear that Holmes would once again resort to drugs for stimulation—a destructive habit off of which he had finally weaned him. Then came the little problem of the missing right wing three-quarter—brought by Cyril Overton, who had been sent to them by Inspector Hopkins, on the morning of Tuesday 8 December—to save Holmes from ennui and Watson from despair. Godfrey Staunton, the missing man, had disappeared the previous night, and without him, Overton assured Holmes, Cambridge would surely lose its rugby match with Oxford on the morrow. Holmes took up the case and immediately set off with Watson and Overton to investigate the hotel room in London in which Staunton was meant to have stayed. While there they made the acquaintance of the parsimonious Lord Mount-James, Staunton's uncle, then Holmes and Watson went to the nearest telegraph office, after which they took an evening train to Cambridge. They spoke with Dr Leslie Armstrong, who threw them out of his house; Holmes then attempted to follow him into the country, but he spotted him, and Holmes, defeated, returned to the local inn for the night. The following day Watson wandered aimlessly in Cambridge while Holmes visited neighbouring villages in a vain effort to track the movements of Armstrong. The next morning, with the help of Pompey the hound, they followed Armstrong to the cottage where Staunton was watching over the body of his deceased wife, and Holmes and Watson assured Armstrong that they would not disinherit the unfortunate lad by telling his uncle anything of what they had seen.

On 4 January 1897 the worst man in London, the master blackmailer Charles Augustus Milverton, entered the sitting room at 221B to discuss with Holmes the fate of Lady Eva Blackwell. Milverton refused to compromise and promised that on the 14th he would destroy the lady's reputation, thereby ending her engagement, if he had not yet received his exorbitant monetary demand. Holmes immediately set to work reconnoitring Milverton's house disguised as a plumber named Escott, and by the evening of the 13th he had taken the charade so far that he was engaged to Milverton's housemaid. That night he and Watson burgled Milverton's house, watched from behind a curtain as a mysterious woman shot him five times and fled, and destroyed his blackmailing papers before themselves fleeing. The next morning Lestrade came to Baker Street to ask Holmes to help him find the murderers of Milverton, but Holmes refused on the grounds that his sympathies lay entirely with the criminals.

Four days later, early on the morning of Monday 18 January, Holmes and Watson were summoned by Inspector Stanley Hopkins to the Abbey Grange in Kent to help with the investigation into Sir Eustace Brackenstall's death. They listened to Lady Brackenstall's account of what had happened the previous night, then had a look round the dining room, where Holmes was puzzled by three wine glasses. He was, however, beginning to suffer from something of a nervous breakdown at this time—the result of his arduous duel with Milverton—and he let himself be persuaded by the lady that it was the three Randalls, burglars from Lewisham, who had murdered Sir Eustace, in spite of the evidence to the contrary. He and Watson left to return to London, but while on the train Holmes suddenly realised his error, and they were soon back at the Abbey Grange. Holmes examined the dining room again to confirm his suspicions, gave Lady Brackenstall an opportunity—which she refused—to confess the truth, then left the house. Back in London, they visited the shipping office of the Adelaide-Southampton line to confirm that Jack Crocker was still in England, then returned to Baker Street, where Stanley Hopkins stopped briefly to discuss the case. Crocker arrived shortly afterwards and told the whole truth to Holmes and Watson, and though he was the murderer of Sir Eustace, Holmes believed that he had been acting in defence of the lady and told him that he would not pursue him further.

Following this case, the state of Holmes's nerves only worsened. Throughout the whole of February, he stubbornly denied that anything was amiss—though he resorted to his old habit of drug use in an effort to reinvigorate his constitution, much to the dismay of Watson—but after Watson brought Dr Moore Agar to see him, and he was told that he must surrender himself to complete rest lest he become permanently incapacitated, he finally consented to seclude himself for a time in Cornwall. Watson accompanied him and was pleased to see him settling into a study of the Cornish language when his rest was unceremoniously interrupted by a visit from Vicar Roundhay and Mortimer Tregennis on 16 March. These two men came to implore Holmes's assistance in solving the sudden death of Tregennis's sister and the inexplicable insanity of his two brothers. Holmes eagerly agreed, and they were all soon at Tredannick Wartha, the scene of the tragedy. After a brief investigation there, Holmes and Watson returned to their cottage, then took a walk and discussed the case, and finally returned to the cottage where Dr Leon Sterndale was awaiting them. A conversation with him convinced Holmes that he was implicated in the mystery, and he spent the rest of the day following him. The next morning, Wednesday the 17th, Vicar Roundhay appeared at the cottage in a frenzy and informed Holmes that Mortimer Tregennis was now dead, killed in the same manner as his sister, and they were soon at the vicarage where Holmes minutely investigated the dead man's rooms. He spent the next two days walking alone and performing experiments, the last of which, involving as it did the devil's-foot root, nearly killed him and Watson on that Friday. They survived the ordeal, however, and, not long afterwards, Holmes extracted a confession of murder from Sterndale, who had killed Mortimer Tregennis in revenge for that man's having killed his own sister. Holmes, who felt Sterndale's actions justified—just as he had those of Crocker—took no action against him and allowed him to return to Africa. Perhaps it was solving another mystery, or perhaps it was the cathartic shock from the *radix pedis diaboli,* but whatever the cause, Holmes's nerves and constitution were restored and he and Watson soon returned to Baker Street.

Mr Hilton Cubitt brought his cryptogram of dancing men to Baker Street on Wednesday 27 July 1898. Given the lack of additional dancing men messages, Holmes at this point could only tell his client to share any new developments, and this is precisely what Cubitt did when he returned to 221B on 3 August to show Holmes several new series of dancing men drawings. Holmes counselled him to be patient and said that he would soon visit him in Norfolk, but Holmes waited two days for a reply to a telegram he had sent to Chicago, and when he finally went to see Cubitt on 6 August it was too late—his client had been killed. He threw himself into an energetic investigation of the crime scene and very cleverly used the dancing men to lure Abe Slaney, the murderer, back to the house, where Inspector Martin arrested him. Holmes had caught the criminal, but for the second time in his career he had suffered the ultimate defeat of the loss of his client.

Holmes had no sooner returned from Norfolk than he became involved in solving the affair of the two Coptic patriarchs, but on the very day when he had every hope of concluding it, he was paid a visit by Mr Josiah Amberley, who claimed that his wife had run off with his money and her lover. Too busy to investigate the affair himself, Holmes asked Watson to visit Amberley at his house in Lewisham. Watson returned from his investigation that August evening and reported what he had found to Holmes, then the two men went to the Albert Hall to see Carina perform. The next day Holmes returned to Baker Street at 3 p.m. followed closely by Amberley, who soon left with Watson to visit the vicar of Little Purlington, from whom Amberley had received a telegram. This man denied, however, having sent any message, and Watson and Amberley, perplexed, were left to spend the night in the village as there was no return train available. They returned to Baker Street the next morning only to learn that Holmes was awaiting them at Amberley's house in Lewisham. There Holmes—accompanied by Barker, a private detective whom he considered a friend and a rival—revealed that Amberley had murdered his wife and her alleged lover, and the young Inspector MacKinnon led him away.

In 1899 Holmes and Watson were busy enough, but the cases which came to them were either too delicate in nature or too devoid of originality to be deemed worthy of publication by Watson. The next year, however, they had some of their most memorable adventures, including the strange affair of the six busts of Napoleon. Inspector Lestrade—whose attitude towards Holmes over the past six years had so much changed that he now openly acknowledged his genius and considered him a friend, visiting him not infrequently at Baker Street—appeared on the evening of 15 June and mentioned that three identical busts of Napoleon had been smashed in the same neighbourhood. The next morning, he sent a telegram summoning Holmes to Horace Harker's house, where a bust had been stolen and a murder

A Biography

committed the previous night. Holmes and Watson then attempted to discover the provenance of the busts by visiting the Harding Brothers, Morse Hudson, and Gelder & Co., and at 11 that night, along with Lestrade, they went to Chiswick, where they caught Beppo, the murderer and breaker of busts. Lestrade arrived at Baker Street at 6 the next evening to discuss the whole affair; soon afterwards Mr Sandeford, of Reading, arrived, and Holmes purchased the sixth bust of Napoleon from him. He promptly smashed it, revealing the black pearl of the Borgias hidden within.

On 24 September 1900 a Mr Mortimer called at Baker Street to ask Holmes's advice concerning the imminent arrival of Sir Henry Baskerville, the heir to an estate in Dartmoor, and the dreadful family curse of a hound from hell that threatened him. Holmes and Watson were out at the time, however, so it was not until he returned the next day that he was able to speak with them; Holmes asked him to come back with Sir Henry at 10 the following morning. After they all chatted that morning, they decided to reconvene for luncheon at the Northumberland Hotel at 2. Sir Henry determined to go to Baskerville Hall in spite of the family curse, and Holmes suggested that, as he was entirely preoccupied with a blackmailing case at the time, Watson should accompany Sir Henry. When Saturday the 29th came round, Watson joined Sir Henry and Mortimer at Paddington Station and took a train to Dartmoor, and they arrived at Baskerville Hall that evening. Watson spent his days observing all that occurred round him, and he wrote reports to Holmes on the 13 and 15 October detailing the strange behaviour of the Barrymores, the Stapletons, and Mr Frankland, among other things. Holmes, meanwhile, was not in London, but rather making his own observations incognito while living intermittently in a prehistoric hut on the moor. On the 18th Watson discovered Holmes, who then revealed himself to Sir Henry but declared that he would be returning to London with Watson. A disappointed Sir Henry then went to dine alone at the Stapletons' the next evening, and while walking home was savagely attacked by the hound from the jaws of which Holmes, Watson, and Lestrade only narrowly saved him. Stapleton, the would-be murderer, escaped Holmes's clutches but was apparently lost forever in the Great Grimpen Mire. Holmes investigated Stapleton's hideout in the heart of the mire the next day with Watson and Lestrade before returning to London.

Holmes spent the four weeks following Sir Henry's case solving two others of great importance: Colonel Upwood and the card scandal at the Nonpareil Club, and Madame Montpensier's alleged murder of her step-daughter. It was only after these had been brought to a successful conclusion that Watson prevailed upon Holmes to discuss in full the details of the Baskerville case. Sir Henry and Mortimer, en route to a voyage round the world meant to restore the baronet's health, had called upon them one day at the end of November, and that evening Holmes gave Watson all of the details that he needed to complete the account that he hoped to publish. Holmes then suggested dinner at Marcini's followed by a performance of *Les Huguenots*.

On 16 May 1901, shortly before noon, Dr Thorneycroft Huxtable stumbled into Baker Street and collapsed unconscious. Having recovered, he explained to Holmes that Lord Saltire, the young heir to the illustrious duke of Holdernesse, had disappeared from his priory school, and he beseeched him to help locate the missing boy. Holmes was busy at the time with the case of the Ferrers Documents and the trial concerning the

A Biography

Abergavenny murder, but he found time nevertheless to leave that same afternoon to visit Huxtable's school near Mackleton. The duke and his secretary, Wilder, were awaiting them at the school, and after they left Holmes examined Lord Saltire's and the German master's rooms, then went out alone to investigate the countryside round the school. The next morning Holmes continued his search of the grounds, then woke Watson and with him set out upon the moor. They found the body of the German master, stopped at Reuben Hayes's inn, and returned late to the school. The next morning, they went to Holdernesse Hall to see the duke, and Holmes extracted a complete confession from him; as he had already ensured Hayes's arrest for the murder of the German master, he agreed to say nothing of Wilder's complicity in the matter.

In the summer of 1901, while Holmes was attempting to solve the matter which gave old Abrahams such fear for his life, a Miss Dobney brought to his attention the disappearance of a certain Lady Frances Carfax. She had last been heard from in Lausanne, so Holmes sent Watson to investigate. From Lausanne Watson travelled to Baden and finally to Montpellier, where Holmes, who had finished his business in London, found him. They returned to England that same night to continue in pursuit of the lady and the man, Holy Peters, with whom she had travelled to London. They made no progress for a week, but then, with the help of Philip Green, the lady's lover, they tracked down Peters when he pawned a piece of the lady's jewellery. Holmes and Watson searched his house but failed to find the lady, but the next morning they stopped Peters from burying her alive, though Peters and his accomplice escaped.

Since his return from apparent death in 1894, Holmes had forbidden Watson to publish any further accounts of their cases.

Watson nevertheless kept notes of them in the hope that he might one day be allowed to publish them, as he eventually was. Indeed, in 1901 Holmes finally relented and permitted him to publish an account of Sir Henry Baskerville's extraordinary adventure, though he stipulated that Watson must write it in such a way as to avoid revealing to the public that Holmes was not in fact dead. Holmes had no desire to return to his former status of internationally-acclaimed detective, probably because this resulted in far too many of those socially important but intellectually dry cases which he so disdained. Watson's fifteen-chapter work *The Hound of the Baskervilles* was published in the *Strand* magazine from August 1901 to April 1902; in it, primarily in the opening chapters, he made a deliberate effort to obfuscate the date by inserting false years, having Holmes ask him to join him for the case, and referring to Stapleton as the most dangerous opponent that they had ever faced. He undermined his own effort to mislead his readers, however, by including many details throughout the narrative that betrayed the true date, and the perspicacious reader in 1901 might have divined that Holmes was in fact alive and well.

Not a single case of interest came to Holmes throughout the whole month of September 1901, the only development in his life being Mrs Hudson's decision to hire a cook because she had tired of dealing with his irregular eating habits. On 4 October 1901, however, began the case of Miss Grace Dunbar, accused of killing the wife of her employer, Neil Gibson. Mr Bates, Gibson's estate manager, called one morning in order to warn Holmes that Gibson was a villain. Then Gibson himself arrived at 11 a.m. precisely and rather haughtily asked Holmes to take up the case. Having initially demurred at Gibson's arrogant demeanour, Holmes ultimately agreed to investigate, and with

A Biography

Watson he went to Gibson's estate that afternoon to examine the scene of the murder at Thor Bridge. They then continued on to Winchester, where they spent the night, and the next morning they spoke with Miss Dunbar in prison, where Holmes suddenly realised the solution to the mystery. They returned to Thor Bridge to test his theory with Watson's revolver that evening, then passed the night at the local inn, where Holmes explained the whole affair to Watson. On the morning of the 6th Holmes met with Gibson and arranged for Miss Dunbar's vindication.

In the early months of 1902 Holmes spent his time rendering an inestimable service to the government in connection with the Boer War, an act for which he was offered a knighthood that he refused to accept. Watson, meanwhile, was eagerly courting the woman who would soon become his second wife. Then on Thursday 26 June the two men encountered a much different sort of problem involving three Garridebs. It began when one John Garrideb came to Baker Street to warn them not to interfere in his and Nathan Garrideb's affairs, though he was soon compelled to admit that any help finding a third man with the name Garrideb would be welcome. That evening they paid a visit to Nathan Garrideb, and John Garrideb appeared with a fictitious advertisement which led Nathan to Birmingham the next day. Holmes and Watson went on that Friday back to Nathan's house at 4 p.m. and captured John, better known as Killer Evans, who had broken into the house.

In July 1902 Watson married for the second time. He left Baker Street and moved into a residence in Queen Anne Street which doubled as his medical office, for in order to support his wife he had again entered civilian practice. On 3 September he found time to meet Holmes for a Turkish bath, and it was there that Holmes asked him to come to Baker Street at 4:30 p.m.

Watson readily complied and at the appointed time Sir James Damery appeared and on behalf of his illustrious client engaged them to try to save Miss Violet de Merville from the clutches of Baron Gruner. Holmes took the case and set off to speak with Gruner while Watson attended to his practice. The men reconvened at Simpson's for dinner, then repaired to Baker Street where Shinwell Johnson and Kitty Winter awaited them. Holmes went with Kitty to see Miss de Merville the next day, but the infatuated woman was unmoved by Kitty's denunciation of Gruner, as Holmes told Watson while they ate dinner at Simpson's once again. Two days later, on Saturday the 6th, Holmes was assaulted by thugs hired by Gruner. Watson read about the incident that evening, rushed to Baker Street, and at Holmes's request arranged for Johnson to hide Miss Winter to spare her the fate which had befallen him. For the next six days, Holmes and Watson spread false rumours that Holmes's wounds were far more serious than they actually were, and on Saturday the 13th Holmes ordered Watson to learn all that he could about Chinese pottery by the morrow. Watson studied for the next twenty-four hours, then Holmes sent him under the alias of Dr Hill Barton to Gruner's house, where Watson distracted his host with a piece of pottery while Holmes purloined Gruner's book of women, which Sir James showed to Miss de Merville to disabuse her of her falsely high opinion of Gruner. On the 17th, her engagement to Gruner was publicly broken off.

 Watson's second marriage, like the first, distanced him from Holmes as he devoted his time to his new wife and his new practice. Indeed, this tendency had only increased by the new year, for on Wednesday 7 January 1903 James Dodd of the Imperial Yeomanry came to Baker Street to ask Holmes for some help locating his missing friend, Godfrey Emsworth, and

A Biography

Holmes could not help but opine that Watson's marriage, which had led to his absence now, had been a selfish decision. Holmes agreed to take the case but told his client that he could not help him until he had completed his commission from the sultan of Turkey regarding the Dardanelles Incident which had begun on 5 January. Holmes brought the matter to a successful conclusion on Monday the 12th and averted a crisis, and as he had also cleared up the affair of the duke of Greyminster and the Abbey School, he was free to look into Dodd's case on the 13th. Together they went to Tuxbury Old Hall, where Holmes was able to prevail upon Godfrey's father to grant them an interview with the son. The young soldier's skin was blanched and it appeared that he was leprous, but Sir James Saunders, whom Holmes had brought, assured them all that it was a case of pseudo-leprosy and that Godfrey had nothing to fear.

On Tuesday 26 May 1903 Watson found time to pay a visit to Holmes. While he was there, Steve Dixie burst into the room and cautioned Holmes to stay away from Mrs Maberley and not to interfere in her affairs. She had already asked his advice regarding a peculiar offer to sell her house and quite literally everything in it, and Holmes, more interested now than before Dixie's visit, immediately set off with Watson for the Three Gables to see her. After speaking with her for some time, they returned to London, and Holmes went to see Langdale Pike to gather some information about Isadora Klein. Watson went home, but he was back at Baker Street the next morning when a telegram summoned them to Mrs Maberley's house, which had been burgled during the night. They learnt that some papers had been stolen from her deceased son's luggage, whereupon they returned to London and called upon Isadora Klein, who, Holmes knew, had taken them. The papers—which constituted a novel exposing the infamous conduct of Klein—being already burnt, he extracted from her the consolation of £5,000 for Mrs Maberley to use to travel round the world.

Watson was very busy with his practice and did not see Holmes again for some time, but one evening in the summer after a long day of work he called upon him, only to learn that he was expecting to be murdered at any moment for having dared to search for the missing Mazarin Stone. Count Sylvius and Sam Merton, the would-be assassins, showed up at Baker Street, and Holmes sent Watson off to bring the police. Holmes, meanwhile, recovered the stone from them through the use of a gramophone and a wax dummy, then handed them over to the police. Lord Cantlemere came to collect the stone from Holmes, and Watson stayed for dinner.

The next time Holmes and Watson saw each other was a morning at the beginning of September when Holmes requested his friend's presence. Watson arrived to find that a Mrs Merrilow was at Baker Street asking Holmes to come see her veiled lodger, Mrs Ronder. After she left, Holmes and Watson discussed the Abbas Parva tragedy of seven years ago, then went to see Mrs Ronder, who told them the whole truth of the incident. Holmes warned the unfortunate, disfigured woman not to take her own life, and two days later he showed Watson, who had called again, that she had overcome the temptation of suicide and proven it by sending her vial of poison to him.

A few days later, on the evening of Sunday 6 September, Holmes summoned Watson to Baker Street to discuss the problem of Professor Presbury and his wolfhound Roy, as explained to them by the man's assistant, Mr Bennett. The next day Holmes and Watson, the latter having frantically arranged for someone to take care of his patients in his absence, went to

A Biography

Camford to investigate, and they had a brief interview with the irascible professor. They stayed at the Chequers Inn where in the morning Bennett visited them, after which they returned to London. They could progress no further in the case until the next week, and they did not see each other again until Tuesday the 15th, when they returned to the Chequers in Camford and that evening spoke with Bennett briefly. Shortly before midnight they went to the professor's house where they found the man creeping about and tormenting his wolfhound, and they only narrowly saved him from the dog which nearly tore out his throat. The mystery solved, they had some tea at the Chequers while awaiting the earliest train back to London.

It was in this same month of September 1903 that Watson, having finally received Holmes's permission to publish the tale of his miraculous escape from the Reichenbach Falls, saw the account he entitled *The Empty House* appear in *Collier's Weekly*. Holmes had only relented on 3 August, but Watson immediately informed Doyle, who secured him publication of thirteen cases beginning in September, and Watson managed to finalise his first manuscript, which he doubtless had written many years earlier, in time. Over the course of the ensuing fifteen months, the public had the pleasure of reading twelve additional accounts of cases from 1894 to 1901.

Throughout the autumn of 1903 Watson was busy with his practice and did not see much of Holmes, but one Saturday morning in November Mrs Hudson appeared at his abode and begged him to come to Baker Street because Holmes appeared to be dying. Watson watched in despair as his old friend seemed to drift further and further into delirium until a few hours later he went to fetch Culverton Smith, an expert on foreign maladies, as a last resort. Watson returned and hid himself behind the bed,

Smith arrived and confessed that he had murdered his nephew, Holmes revealed that he was not sick at all, and Inspector Morton arrested Smith. Holmes and Watson went to the police station, then had dinner together at their favourite restaurant, Simpson's.

During this repast Holmes confessed to Watson that the strenuous role he had played to deceive Smith had seriously exhausted him and had starkly reminded him of his age. To Watson's ineffable astonishment, he went on to declare that he intended to retire from private consulting practice before the end of the year, and he elaborated upon his dream of living on the Sussex Downs and keeping bees. They spent the rest of the evening reminiscing about their many past adventures together.

Sometime in 1904 Sherlock Holmes left Baker Street. He moved into a villa near Eastbourne where he tended to his bees and lived a life of solitude in nature. On rare occasions Watson came to spend the weekend with him, probably only when his wife was herself away on a visit, but in general Holmes saw only his housekeeper and his neighbour, Harold Stackhurst. It was in the fourth year of his retirement, on 23 July 1907, that Holmes was confronted with a peculiar mystery very nearly on his doorstep: he and Stackhurst found Fitzroy McPherson dead that morning. They visited the Bellamys in Fulworth, and their suspicions settled upon Ian Murdoch. They made no progress for a week, but on the 30th McPherson's dog died, and Holmes investigated the bathing-pool where it and its master had perished. The next morning Inspector Bardle called upon him, but their conversation was interrupted by the appearance of Murdoch, horribly wounded. They rushed with Stackhurst to the bathing-pool, where they destroyed the murderous lion's mane jellyfish with a boulder.

A Biography

During his occasional visits Watson sometimes discussed with Holmes his publications, including what other cases might be of interest to the public. These conversations led to the sporadic appearance of additional accounts. In August 1908 *Wisteria Lodge* was released, followed four months later by *The Bruce-Partington Plans*. Next came *The Devil's Foot* in December 1910. In March 1911 he published *The Red Circle* and in December of the same year *The Disappearance of Lady Frances Carfax*. It was also in 1911 that Holmes published a *Practical Handbook of Bee Culture, with Some Observations upon the Segregation of the Queen*, the product of his preceding seven years of apicultural research.

In 1912, Holmes's tranquil retirement came to an abrupt halt when he accepted a commission from the Prime Minister himself to assume the false persona of Altamont in America in order to ultimately infiltrate a German spy ring. He told Watson where he was going to spare him from worry this time, and even gave him permission to publish the final case of his career, his duel with Culverton Smith. Watson's account, *The Dying Detective*, appeared in December 1913. After Holmes left for America, the two friends had no contact until the fateful evening of 2 August 1914 when Holmes summoned Watson to go with him to Von Bork's establishment, where they arrested the German spy master and reminisced about times past and yet to come.

When the Great War began, Watson returned to the army medical service, but Holmes had done his part already and remained firmly ensconced in his villa on the Downs. Doyle, meanwhile, secured the serial publication of Watson's account of the Birlstone tragedy, entitled *The Valley of Fear*, from September 1914 to May 1915. Watson, who was now quite busy, had fortunately already written this account before the war had begun; all the same, he found time to compose the patriotic *His Last Bow*, detailing Holmes's defeat of Von Bork in August 1914, for publication in September 1917. The following month Doyle arranged the compilation of the seven previous individually published accounts into a single volume also entitled *His Last Bow*.

Sometime before the new decade began Watson died. He bequeathed some of his case notes and several completed manuscripts to Doyle to have them published, though he stipulated that Doyle must first obtain Sherlock Holmes's approval. Doyle was compelled to fight for this for some time, but finally in 1921 Holmes agreed to let him write an account of the affair of the Mazarin Stone, of which he had Watson's notes only. Doubtless Holmes was deeply disappointed with the result and offered remarks far more scathing than any he had ever made to Watson. In any case, Doyle was for some time discouraged from again trying his hand at writing an account, and he contented himself with having manuscripts already completed by Watson published. *The Problem of Thor Bridge* appeared in February-March 1922, *The Creeping Man* in March 1923, *The Sussex Vampire* in January 1924, *The Three Garridebs* in October 1924, and *The Illustrious Client* in November 1924.

By 1926, Doyle had determined to again write an account based on Watson's notes, five years having now passed since his previous botched attempt. *The Three Gables*, published in September 1926, was the result, but it was no better than its predecessor, and he never again repeated this experiment. He did try something new, however: earlier that year, when he had discussed writing another story with Holmes, he had also proposed to him that he should write some accounts of his own adventures for which Watson was not present. Holmes refused utterly at first, but upon reflection he became persuaded that he owed it to his late friend and biographer, having mentioned to him more than once that he would one day write his own accounts. Doyle accordingly arranged the publication of *The Blanched Soldier* in October and of *The Lion's Mane* in November, both written by Holmes. In December he released *The Retired Colourman*, followed in January and March 1927 by *The Veiled Lodger* and *Shoscombe Old Place*, respectively, all three manuscripts of Watson's.

These were apparently the last of the accounts which Watson had left behind him, as no others have ever surfaced. Nothing further is known of the life of Mr Sherlock Holmes of Baker Street.

Conclusion

We have now reached the conclusion of our analysis of the dates of the sixty recorded cases of Sherlock Holmes and of our biography of his life. We have assigned a year, month, and day to fifty of the cases. For the remaining ten, we have found it impossible to select the precise day, but we have still determined at least the year and either the month (for seven) or the season (for three). We have not attempted to precisely date the many unpublished cases to which Watson refers throughout his accounts due to the lack of sufficient evidence concerning them.

Our chronology has the merit of rejecting only three of Watson's explicitly stated years. The first is in *The Engineer's Thumb*. Watson asserts that this case 'was in the summer of '89, not long after my marriage',[1] and because all of the other cases that closely followed Watson's marriage occurred in 1888, among other reasons, we place it in summer 1888.[2] We also correct the obviously erroneous year of 1892 that Watson gives for *Wisteria Lodge* by placing the case in 1895. Lastly, we move *The Veiled Lodger* from 1896 to 1903 since there is no satisfactory reason why Watson should have left Baker Street for any extended period of time in the year 1896 and, even if he had, the

---

[1] Short, ENGR, 201.
[2] Many chronologists keep this case in 1889, but in doing so they oblige themselves to alter many other years explicitly stated by Watson, including those of *A Scandal in Bohemia*, *The Five Orange Pips*, and *The Noble Bachelor*.

Conclusion

problem would remain that he would not have been living with Holmes seven years earlier in 1889.

For two cases we disagree with a less specific date given by Watson. He implies, through the date on Mortimer's stick, that *The Hound of the Baskervilles* took place in 1889, but 1900 is the actual year. He also says that *The Valley of Fear* occurred 'at the end of the 'eighties',[1] but we have shown that it was in 1890.

Besides these divergences, there are nine instances in which we disagree to some extent with Watson's stated season, month, or day:

1. In *A Case of Identity* Watson states that the wedding occurred on the 14th, but it is clear that the 14th was actually the day after the wedding.
2. Watson claims that *The Man with the Twisted Lip* occurred on 'Friday, June 19'[2] in the year 1889. Since 19 June was not a Friday in 1889, the case must have been on either Wednesday the 19th or Friday the 21st, and we choose the latter.
3. Watson mentions 'October weather'[3] in *The Resident Patient*, but we place the case in November.
4. In Watson's diary from his stay at Baskerville Hall in *The Hound of the Baskervilles* he has an entry which was published as '*October 16th*',[4] but the events described are clearly those of the 15th.
5. Watson mentions an August sun in *The Norwood Builder*, but the case occurred in July.

---

[1] Long, VALL, 467.
[2] Short, TWIS, 127.
[3] *The Original Illustrated Sherlock Holmes*, 282.
[4] Long, HOUN, 379.

Conclusion

6. In *The Dancing Men* Watson states that a fortnight elapsed when it is very clear that only one week had passed.
7. In *The Solitary Cyclist* there is no doubt that the day Watson calls the 23rd was a Saturday. As the 23rd was not a Saturday in 1895 but the 13th was, the actual day of the case was clearly the 13th.
8. *The Missing Three-Quarter* centres upon the rugby match between Oxford and Cambridge, and this event invariably occurred in December. Watson made an error when he recorded February as the month.
9. Watson says that *The Second Stain* occurred in autumn, but in fact it was in August.

Apart from these minor departures, we adhere to Watson's chronological indications. Note that we do not include Watson's botched transcription of newspaper articles in *A Study in Scarlet*—in which he wrongly asserts that 4 March was a Tuesday—in this list because it does not actually affect the dating of the case, which is determined by other more cogent factors. There are also several instances in which Watson gives conflicting evidence which seems to assign two different dates for the same case: July and September for *The Sign of Four*, June and October for *The Red-Headed League*, November and winter for *The Golden Pince-Nez*, and before and after Moriarty's death for *The Valley of Fear*. As we cannot possibly keep both dates, but do select one or the other and not something altogether different, we do not list these above either.

We trust that our chronology has been read and appreciated in the same spirit of serious study and critical analysis in which it was written. We have the greatest admiration for those

Conclusion

chronologists who have come before us, without the inspiration of whose works our own would not exist, and we have praised and criticised them, just as they have done to one another, in the interest of furthering an intriguing discourse to which it has been our aspiration to contribute. The discussion has endured for nearly a century, and it will no doubt persist until such time as the vaults of the bank of Cox and Co. at last release that fabled dispatch-box, the contents of which contain the solutions to those great chronological mysteries that our own best efforts, and those of our studious predecessors, have been insufficient to solve.

Appendix I: Chronological Table

Year	Day/Month	Event
1852	–	John H. Watson is born
1854	–	Sherlock Holmes is born
1872	October	Holmes begins studying at the University of Oxford
1873	July, September	The "Gloria Scott"
1878	18 July	The Musgrave Ritual
1880	27 July	Watson is wounded at the Battle of Maiwand
1881	1 January	Stamford introduces Watson to Holmes
1881	4–5 March	A Study in Scarlet
1881	6 March	Holmes and Watson discuss the events of A Study in Scarlet
1881	Late November	The Resident Patient
1882	24–25 February	The Beryl Coronet
1883	4–5 April	The Speckled Band
1883	6–7 May	Shoscombe Old Place
1884	7, 22 April	The Copper Beeches
1885	August	The Cardboard Box

Appendix I

1886	3 April	*The Yellow Face*
1886	7 July	*The Greek Interpreter*
1887	Mid-February–Mid-April	Holmes is working on a case in France
1887	26 April	*The Reigate Squires*
1887	Summer	Holmes suffers from a lack of cases, driving him to excessive drug use
1887	6–10 September	*The Sign of Four*
1887	9 September	Watson becomes engaged to Miss Mary Morstan
1887	Mid-September	Watson begins working part-time as a civil practitioner
1887	22 September	*Silver Blaze* begins
1887	23–24 September	*The Five Orange Pips*
1887	27 September	*Silver Blaze* concludes
1887	7 October	*The Noble Bachelor*
1887	November	Watson marries Miss Morstan and leaves Baker Street
1887	December	Watson publishes *A Study in Scarlet* through his literary agent, Arthur Conan Doyle
1888	March	Watson purchases the practice of Mr Farquhar near Paddington Station
1888	20–22 March	*A Scandal in Bohemia*

Appendix I

1888	16 June	*The Stock-Broker's Clerk*; this is Holmes's first visit to Watson's house
1888	19–21 June	*The Crooked Man*; Watson's neighbour Jackson helps with his practice when he is absent
1888	23 July	*The Engineer's Thumb*
1888	30 July–1 August	*The Naval Treaty*
1888	27 December	*The Blue Carbuncle*
1889	7–8 June	*The Boscombe Valley Mystery*; Anstruther has bought Jackson's practice and, like his predecessor, assumes Watson's professional responsibilities when he is away
1889	21–22 June	*The Man with the Twisted Lip*
1889	November–December	Holmes has no cases
1890	7–8 January	*The Valley of Fear*
1890	February	Watson publishes *The Sign of Four* through his literary agent
1890	16–17 June	*A Case of Identity*
1890	21 June	*The Red-Headed League*; Watson has acquired a new house and practice in Kensington
1890–1891	Winter	Holmes travels to the Continent to handle a case for the French government

Appendix I

1891	Spring	Holmes's sojourn on the Continent concludes
1891	24 April–4 May	*The Final Problem*
1891–1894	May–April	Holmes is presumed to have died fighting Moriarty at the Reichenbach Falls; masquerading as a Norwegian explorer named Sigerson, he spends two years in Tibet, travels through Persia, Mecca, and Khartoum, and performs research for several months in Montpellier
1891–1892	July–June	Watson publishes serially the twelve cases later collected as *The Adventures of Sherlock Holmes* through his literary agent
1892–1893	December–November	Watson publishes serially the twelve cases later collected as *The Memoirs of Sherlock Holmes* through his literary agent
1894	3 April	*The Empty House*; Watson's wife has died, but he still owns his house and practice in Kensington
1894	2–3 July	*The Norwood Builder*; Watson has moved back into 221B Baker Street and sold his practice at the insistence of Holmes
1894	19–21 November	*The Sussex Vampire*

Appendix I

1894	Late November	*The Golden Pince-Nez*
1895	February–March	Holmes suffers from a lack of cases following the incarceration of Colonel Carruthers
1895	23–27 March	*Wisteria Lodge*
1895	13–20 April	*The Solitary Cyclist*
1895	Early July	Holmes spends the first week of the month largely absent from Baker Street; Watson is unaware of his actions
1895	10–12 July	*Black Peter*
1895	Later July	Holmes and Watson are in Norway
1895	20–23 August	*The Second Stain*
1895	November	*The Three Students*; Holmes and Watson spend several weeks surrounding this case in Oxford
1895	21–23 November	*The Bruce-Partington Plans*
1896	27–28 February	*The Red Circle*
1896	8–10 December	*The Missing Three-Quarter*
1897	4–14 January	*Charles Augustus Milverton*
1897	18 January	*The Abbey Grange*
1897	February	Holmes is suffering from a mental and nervous breakdown, the result of demanding work throughout the previous month

Appendix I

1897	16–19 March	*The Devil's Foot*; Watson attempts to isolate Holmes in Cornwall to facilitate his recovery, but even there a case finds him
1898	27 July–6 August	*The Dancing Men*
1898	August	*The Retired Colourman*
1900	15–17 June	*The Six Napoleons*
1900	25 September–20 October	*The Hound of the Baskervilles*
1900	Late October–Late November	Holmes and Watson handle a number of difficult cases
1900	Late November	Holmes and Watson discuss Sir Henry Baskerville's case
1901	16–18 May	*The Priory School*
1901	Summer	*The Disappearance of Lady Frances Carfax*
1901–1902	August–April	Watson publishes serially *The Hound of the Baskervilles* through his literary agent
1901	4–6 October	*The Problem of Thor Bridge*; Mrs Hudson no longer cooks meals at Baker Street, having recently hired a cook
1902	26–27 June	*The Three Garridebs*

Appendix I

1902	Summer	Watson marries for the second time; he acquires a house in Queen Anne Street and returns to active medical practice
1902	3–14 September	*The Illustrious Client*
1903	7, 13 January	*The Blanched Soldier*; this is the first published case to be written by Holmes
1903	26–27 May	*The Three Gables*; this account was not written by Watson, and thus the evidence which points to this date may be unreliable
1903	Summer	*The Mazarin Stone*; again, this account was not written by Watson, and thus the evidence which points to this date may be unreliable
1903	Early September	*The Veiled Lodger*
1903	6–8, 15 September	*The Creeping Man*; this is one of Holmes's last cases before retirement
1903–1904	September–December	Watson publishes serially the thirteen cases later collected as *The Return of Sherlock Holmes* through his literary agent
1903	November	*The Dying Detective*; the extreme deprivations of this case determine Holmes to retire from active practice

Appendix I

1907	23, 30–31 July	*The Lion's Mane*; this is the second and final published case written by Holmes
1908	August	Watson publishes *Wisteria Lodge* through his literary agent
1908	December	Watson publishes *The Bruce-Partington Plans* through his literary agent
1910	December	Watson publishes *The Devil's Foot* through his literary agent
1911	–	Holmes completes his *Practical Handbook of Bee Culture, with Some Observations upon the Segregation of the Queen*
1911	March	Watson publishes *The Red Circle* through his literary agent
1911	December	Watson publishes *The Disappearance of Lady Frances Carfax* through his literary agent
1912–1914	–	Holmes accepts a commission from the British Government and assumes the persona of Altamont to infiltrate a German spy ring
1913	December	Watson publishes *The Dying Detective* through his literary agent
1914	2 August	*His Last Bow*; this is the last recorded meeting of Mr Sherlock Holmes and Dr John H. Watson
1914–1915	September–May	Watson publishes serially *The Valley of Fear* through his literary agent

Appendix I

1917	September	Watson publishes *His Last Bow* through his literary agent
1917	22 October	Watson publishes *His Last Bow*, a book collection of eight previously published cases, through his literary agent; both Holmes and Watson are alive, the former still living in retirement on the Sussex Downs
1921	October	Doyle publishes *The Mazarin Stone*, an account that he wrote based loosely on the notes of the case left to him by Watson; Watson is deceased, having bequeathed some of his case notes and manuscripts to Doyle for future publication
1922	February–March	Doyle publishes *The Problem of Thor Bridge*, a complete manuscript of a case written by Watson before his death
1923	March	Doyle publishes *The Creeping Man*, a complete manuscript of a case written by Watson before his death
1924	January	Doyle publishes *The Sussex Vampire*, a complete manuscript of a case written by Watson before his death
1924	October	Doyle publishes *The Three Garridebs*, a complete manuscript of a case written by Watson before his death
1924	November	Doyle publishes *The Illustrious Client*, a complete manuscript of a case written by Watson before his death

Appendix I

1926	September	Doyle publishes *The Three Gables*, an account that he wrote based loosely on the notes of the case left to him by Watson
1926	October	Doyle publishes *The Blanched Soldier*, a manuscript of a case written by Holmes
1926	November	Doyle publishes *The Lion's Mane*, a manuscript of a case written by Holmes
1926	December	Doyle publishes *The Retired Colourman*, a complete manuscript of a case written by Watson before his death
1927	January	Doyle publishes *The Veiled Lodger*, a complete manuscript of a case written by Watson before his death
1927	March	Doyle publishes *Shoscombe Old Place*, a complete manuscript of a case written by Watson before his death
1930	7 July	Sir Arthur Conan Doyle, Watson's literary agent of forty-three years, dies; no further cases are published

Appendix II: Comparative Chronology

Listed below are the dates chosen by the nine chronologists whose works we evaluated, as well as our own date, for each of the sixty cases. A range of years in brackets indicates that the given chronologist believes the case to have occurred in some year within that range, while a month or day in brackets indicates a guess by a chronologist. Note that Dakin in his book does not address the ending dates of the cases; thus, the dates shown below for him reflect only the first day of multi-day cases.

The Dates

1. A Study in Scarlet

              Bell: 1881 Mar 4–5
          Blakeney: 1881
            Christ: 1882 Mar 3–5
             Brend: 1881 Mar
     Baring-Gould: 1881 Mar 4–7
           Zeisler: 1881 Mar 4–5
            Dakin: 1881 Mar 4
         McQueen: 1882 Mar 4–5
             Hall: 1881 Mar 4–5
            Colpo: 1881 Mar 4–5

Appendix II

2. The Sign of Four

Bell: 1887 Sept 7–8
Blakeney: 1888 July
Christ: 1888 Sept 25–27
Brend: 1887 July
Baring-Gould: 1888 Sept 18–21
Zeisler: 1888 Apr 16–19
Dakin: 1888 Sept 27
McQueen: 1887 Sept
Hall: 1887 July 7–9
Colpo: 1887 Sept 6–10

3. A Scandal in Bohemia

Bell: 1888 Mar 22–25
Blakeney: 1889 Mar 20
Christ: 1889 Mar 20–22
Brend: 1889 Mar
Baring-Gould: 1887 May 20–22
Zeisler: 1889 Mar 22–24
Dakin: 1889 Mar
McQueen: 1888 Mar 20
Hall: 1888 Mar 20–22
Colpo: 1888 Mar 20–22

4. The Red-Headed League

Bell: 1890 Oct 4
Blakeney: 1890 Oct
Christ: 1890 Oct 18
Brend: 1890 Oct
Baring-Gould: 1887 Oct 29–30
Zeisler: 1889 Oct 19

Appendix II

Dakin:	1890	Oct	11
McQueen:	1890	Oct	11
Hall:	1890	Oct	11
Colpo:	1890	June	21

5. A Case of Identity

Bell:	1888	Sept	mid
Blakeney:	1889	(Apr or May)	
Christ:	1889	June	26–27
Brend:	1889	Apr	
Baring-Gould:	1887	Oct	18–19
Zeisler:	1889	Oct	9–10
Dakin:	1889	Sept	
McQueen:	1888	Sept	
Hall:	1888	Sept	17–24
Colpo:	1890	June	16–17

6. The Boscombe Valley Mystery

Bell:	1889	June	early
Blakeney:	1889	June	
Christ:	1889	June	7–8
Brend:	1889	June	early
Baring-Gould:	1889	June	8–9
Zeisler:	1890	June	27–28
Dakin:	1890	June	23
McQueen:	1889	June	early
Hall:	1889	June	6–7
Colpo:	1889	June	7–8

7. The Five Orange Pips

Bell:	1888	Sept	late

Appendix II

```
       Blakeney:  1889  Sept
         Christ:  1889  Sept  24
          Brend:  1888  Sept
   Baring-Gould:  1887  Sept  29–30
        Zeisler:  1889  Sept  24
          Dakin:  1889  Sept  24
        McQueen:  1887  Sept  late
           Hall:  1887  Sept  21
          Colpo:  1887  Sept  23–24
```

8. The Man with the Twisted Lip
```
           Bell:  1889  June  14–15
       Blakeney:  1889  June
         Christ:  1889  June  19–20
          Brend:  1889  June  late
   Baring-Gould:  1887  June  18–19
        Zeisler:  1889  June  21–22
          Dakin:  1889  June  21
        McQueen:  1889  June
           Hall:  1889  June  17–20
          Colpo:  1889  June  21–22
```

9. The Blue Carbuncle
```
           Bell:  1889  Dec  27
       Blakeney:  1889  Dec  25
         Christ:  1890  Dec  27
          Brend:  1889  Dec
   Baring-Gould:  1887  Dec  27
        Zeisler:  1889  Dec  27
          Dakin:  1889  Dec  27
        McQueen:  1889  Dec  27
```

Appendix II

Hall: 1889 Dec 27
Colpo: 1888 Dec 27

10. The Speckled Band
Bell: 1883 Apr early
Blakeney: 1883 Apr
Christ: 1883 Apr 4
Brend: 1883 Apr
Baring-Gould: 1883 Apr 6
Zeisler: 1883 Apr 4
Dakin: 1883 Apr 4
McQueen: 1883 Apr early
Hall: 1883 Apr early
Colpo: 1883 Apr 4–5

11. The Engineer's Thumb
Bell: 1888 Aug
Blakeney: 1889 summer
Christ: 1889 Sept 7–8
Brend: 1889 (July or Aug)
Baring-Gould: 1889 Sept 7–8
Zeisler: 1889 Sept 8
Dakin: 1889 Sept 7
McQueen: 1889 summer
Hall: 1889 (July or Aug)
Colpo: 1888 July 23

12. The Noble Bachelor
Bell: 1887 Oct 6
Blakeney: 1888 Oct
Christ: 1888 Oct 9–12

Appendix II

        Brend: 1887 Oct early
Baring-Gould: 1886 Oct 8
      Zeisler: 1888 Dec 7
       Dakin: 1888 Oct 12
   McQueen: 1887 Oct 7
         Hall: 1887 early autumn
       Colpo: 1887 Oct 7

13. The Beryl Coronet

         Bell: 1882 Feb
   Blakeney: (1881 – 1887)
       Christ: 1883 Feb 23–24
       Brend: 1886 Mar
Baring-Gould: 1890 Dec 19–20
      Zeisler: 1886 Feb 19–20
       Dakin: 1886 Feb 23
   McQueen: (1880s mid)
         Hall: 1886 Jan 8–9
       Colpo: 1882 Feb 24–25

14. The Copper Beeches

         Bell: 1890 Apr late
   Blakeney: (1896 – 1900)
       Christ: 1891 Apr 19 – May 4
       Brend: 1890 Mar
Baring-Gould: 1889 Apr 5–20
      Zeisler: 1890 Apr 7–22
       Dakin: 1885 Apr – May
   McQueen: 1890 early spring
         Hall: 1890 early spring
       Colpo: 1884 Apr 7, 22

15. Silver Blaze

Bell: 1881 early autumn
Blakeney: (1881 – 1887)
Christ: 1891 Sept 3, 9
Brend: 1887 Sept – Oct
Baring-Gould: 1890 Sept 25–30
Zeisler: 1888 July 12–17
Dakin: 1888 Oct
McQueen: 1887 autumn
Hall: 1888 Sept – Oct
Colpo: 1887 Sept 22, 27

16. The Cardboard Box

Bell: 1885 Aug 6–8
Blakeney: 1888 Aug
Christ: 1891 Aug 14–15
Brend: 1887 Aug
Baring-Gould: 1889 Aug 31 – Sept 2
Zeisler: 1888 Aug 10–11
Dakin: 1888 Aug 10
McQueen: 1890 Aug
Hall: 1888 Aug
Colpo: 1885 Aug

17. The Yellow Face

Bell: 1882 Apr 8
Blakeney: (1881 – 1887)
Christ: 1883 Apr 7
Brend: 1882 Mar
Baring-Gould: 1888 Apr 7
Zeisler: (1885 or 1886) early April

Appendix II

      Dakin: 1886 (Apr?)
  McQueen: (1880s early)
        Hall: 1886 early spring
      Colpo: 1886 Apr 3

18. The Stock-Broker's Clerk

          Bell: 1888 June early
    Blakeney: 1889 June 1
       Christ: 1889 June 15
       Brend: 1888 June
Baring-Gould: 1889 June 15
     Zeisler: 1889 June 15
      Dakin: 1889 June 15
  McQueen: 1888 June
        Hall: 1888 June
      Colpo: 1888 June 16

19. The "Gloria Scott"

          Bell: 1875 summer – autumn
    Blakeney: 1873
       Christ: 1876 Sept late
       Brend: 1873 Aug – Sept
Baring-Gould: 1874 July 12 – Aug 4, Sept 22
     Zeisler: 1876 summer
      Dakin: 1874 July – Aug
  McQueen: (1870s early)
        Hall: 1875 summer
      Colpo: 1873 July, Sept

20. The Musgrave Ritual

          Bell: 1878 Sept 26

Blakeney: 1878
Christ: 1880 June 24
Brend: 1878
Baring-Gould: 1879 Oct 2
Zeisler: 1879 Oct 2
Dakin: 1879 Oct 2
McQueen: 1877
Hall: 1879 summer
Colpo: 1878 July 18

21. The Reigate Squires

Bell: 1887 Apr 26
Blakeney: 1887 Apr
Christ: 1887 Apr 25–26
Brend: 1887 Apr
Baring-Gould: 1887 Apr 14–26
Zeisler: 1887 Apr 25–26
Dakin: 1887 Apr 26
McQueen: Undated
Hall: 1887 Apr 25–26
Colpo: 1887 Apr 26

22. The Crooked Man

Bell: 1888 Aug
Blakeney: 1889 summer
Christ: 1889 Aug 28–29
Brend: 1888 Aug
Baring-Gould: 1889 Sept 11–12
Zeisler: 1889 June 26
Dakin: 1889 Aug
McQueen: 1888 summer

Appendix II

         Hall: 1888 spring
        Colpo: 1888 June 19–21

23. The Resident Patient
                Bell: 1887 Oct late
        Blakeney: (1886 or 1887) Oct
             Christ: 1882 Oct 26–27
             Brend: 1887 Oct late
    Baring-Gould: 1886 Oct 6–7
           Zeisler: 1887 Oct 29–30
            Dakin: 1881 Oct
        McQueen: (1882?) Oct
              Hall: 1887 Oct
             Colpo: 1881 Nov late

24. The Greek Interpreter
                Bell: 1890 summer
        Blakeney: (1881 – 1887)
             Christ: 1888 Aug 29
             Brend: 1882 summer
    Baring-Gould: 1888 Sept 12
           Zeisler: 1888 Aug 15
            Dakin: 1884 Aug
        McQueen: Undated
              Hall: 1890 July late
             Colpo: 1886 July 7

25. The Naval Treaty
                Bell: 1888 July late
        Blakeney: 1889 July
             Christ: 1889 July 29–30

Appendix II

            Brend: 1888 July
   Baring-Gould: 1889 July 30 – Aug 1
        Zeisler: 1889 July 29–31
          Dakin: 1889 July 29
      McQueen: 1888 summer
           Hall: 1888 July
         Colpo: 1888 July 30 – Aug 1

26. The Final Problem

             Bell: 1891 Apr 24 – May 4
       Blakeney: 1891 spring
         Christ: 1893 Apr 14 – May 4
         Brend: 1891 Apr
   Baring-Gould: 1891 Apr 24 – May 4
        Zeisler: 1891 Apr 24 – May 4
         Dakin: 1891 Apr 24 – May 4
     McQueen: 1891 Apr 24 – May 4
          Hall: 1891 Apr 24 – May 4
        Colpo: 1891 Apr 24 – May 4

27. The Hound of the Baskervilles

             Bell: 1886 Sept 28 – Oct 19
      Blakeney: 1889 Oct
         Christ: 1897 Sept 28 – Oct 19
         Brend: 1899 Oct
   Baring-Gould: 1888 Sept 25 – Oct 20
        Zeisler: 1900 Sept 25 – Oct 19
         Dakin: 1900 Sept 25
     McQueen: 1900 Sept 25 – Oct 19
          Hall: 1889 autumn
        Colpo: 1900 Sept 25 – Oct 20

Appendix II

28. The Empty House

Bell:	1894	Apr	early
Blakeney:	1894	Apr	
Christ:	1894	Apr	2–3
Brend:	1894	Feb	
Baring-Gould:	1894	Apr	5
Zeisler:	1894	Apr	3
Dakin:	1894	Feb	
McQueen:	1894		
Hall:	1894	Apr	1
Colpo:	1894	Apr	3

29. The Norwood Builder

Bell:	1895	Aug	
Blakeney:	1894	Aug	
Christ:	1894	Aug	
Brend:	1894	Aug	
Baring-Gould:	1895	Aug	20–21
Zeisler:	1894	July	2–3
Dakin:	1894	Aug	
McQueen:	1894		
Hall:	1894	summer	
Colpo:	1894	July	2–3

30. The Dancing Men

Bell:	1898	July – Aug			
Blakeney:	1898	Aug			
Christ:	1898	July	27 –	Aug	12
Brend:	1898	July – Aug			
Baring-Gould:	1898	July	27 –	Aug	13
Zeisler:	1898	July	27 –	Aug	10

305

Appendix II

       Dakin: 1898 July
  McQueen: (Post-1887)
        Hall: 1898 July late
       Colpo: 1898 July 27 – Aug 6

31. The Solitary Cyclist

        Bell: 1895 Apr 13–20
   Blakeney: 1895 Apr
     Christ: 1895 Mar 23, 30
     Brend: 1895 Apr
Baring-Gould: 1895 Apr 13–20
    Zeisler: 1898 Apr 23–30
     Dakin: 1895 Apr 13
  McQueen: 1898 Apr 23
       Hall: 1895 Apr 13, 20
     Colpo: 1895 Apr 13–20

32. The Priory School

        Bell: 1901 May 16–18
   Blakeney: 1901 May
     Christ: 1901 May 16–18
     Brend: 1901 May
Baring-Gould: 1901 May 16–18
    Zeisler: 1900 May 17–19
     Dakin: 1900 May 14
  McQueen: Undated
       Hall: 1901 May 16–18
     Colpo: 1901 May 16–18

33. Black Peter

        Bell: 1895 July 3–5

Appendix II

       Blakeney: 1895 July
          Christ: 1895 July   3–5
           Brend: 1895 July
 Baring-Gould: 1895 July   3–5
         Zeisler: 1895 July   10–12
           Dakin: 1895 July   10
     McQueen: 1895
             Hall: 1895 July   2–10
           Colpo: 1895 July   10–12

34. Charles Augustus Milverton

             Bell: 1884 Feb   4–14
      Blakeney: (1896 – 1900)
          Christ: 1889 Feb   4, 13–14
           Brend: 1882 Dec
 Baring-Gould: 1899 Jan   5–14
         Zeisler: 1886 Jan   6
           Dakin: 1899 Jan   13
     McQueen: (1880s early)
             Hall: 1899 Jan   5–14
           Colpo: 1897 Jan   4–14

35. The Six Napoleons

             Bell: 1900 July
      Blakeney: (1896 – 1900)
          Christ: 1902 Aug   29–31
           Brend: 1900 late summer
 Baring-Gould: 1900 June   8–10
         Zeisler: 1900 June   11–13
           Dakin: 1900 July
     McQueen: 1900 (Aug or Sept)

Appendix II

Hall: 1900 June – July
Colpo: 1900 June 15–17

36. The Three Students
Bell: 1895 Apr late
Blakeney: 1895 Mar
Christ: 1895 Apr 18–19
Brend: 1895 May
Baring-Gould: 1895 Apr 5–6
Zeisler: 1895 Mar 27–28
Dakin: 1895 Mar – Apr
McQueen: Undated
Hall: 1895 spring
Colpo: 1895 Nov

37. The Golden Pince-Nez
Bell: 1894 Nov late
Blakeney: 1894 Nov
Christ: 1894 Nov 14–15
Brend: 1894 Nov
Baring-Gould: 1894 Nov 14–15
Zeisler: 1894 Oct 27–28
Dakin: 1894 Nov
McQueen: 1894
Hall: 1894 Nov late
Colpo: 1894 Nov late

38. The Missing Three-Quarter
Bell: 1897 Feb
Blakeney: 1898 Feb
Christ: 1897 Dec 7–9

Appendix II

           Brend: 1897 Dec
Baring-Gould: 1896 Dec 8–10
          Zeisler: 1896 Dec 8–10
           Dakin: 1897 Dec
       McQueen: Undated
            Hall: 1896 Dec 8–10
           Colpo: 1896 Dec 8–10

39. The Abbey Grange

            Bell: 1897 Jan
       Blakeney: 1897
         Christ: 1897 Jan 22–23
          Brend: 1897 Jan
Baring-Gould: 1897 Jan 23
         Zeisler: 1897 Jan late
           Dakin: 1897 Jan
      McQueen: Undated
           Hall: 1897 Jan early
          Colpo: 1897 Jan 18

40. The Second Stain

            Bell: 1894 autumn
       Blakeney: 1894 autumn
         Christ: 1889 July 15–19
          Brend: 1886 autumn
Baring-Gould: 1886 Oct 12–15
         Zeisler: 1889 July
          Dakin: 1894 Mar early
      McQueen: (1880s mid)
           Hall: 1888 July
          Colpo: 1895 Aug 20–23

Appendix II

41. Wisteria Lodge
            Bell: 1895 Mar late
       Blakeney: (1896, 1898 – 1902)
          Christ: 1892 Mar 21–25
          Brend: 1894 Mar
  Baring-Gould: 1890 Mar 24–29
         Zeisler: 1902 Mar 24–28
          Dakin: 1894 Mar late
      McQueen: (1890s mid)
             Hall: 1895 Mar late
           Colpo: 1895 Mar 23–27

42. The Bruce-Partington Plans
            Bell: 1895 Nov 21–22
       Blakeney: 1895 Nov 21
          Christ: 1895 Nov 18–23
          Brend: 1895 Nov
  Baring-Gould: 1895 Nov 21–23
         Zeisler: 1895 Nov 21–30
          Dakin: 1895 Nov 21
      McQueen: 1895 Nov
             Hall: 1895 Nov 21–30
           Colpo: 1895 Nov 21–23

43. The Devil's Foot
            Bell: 1897 Mar 16–19
       Blakeney: 1897 Mar
          Christ: 1897 Mar 16–19
          Brend: 1897 Mar
  Baring-Gould: 1897 Mar 16–20
         Zeisler: 1897 Apr 17–18

Appendix II

      Dakin: 1897 Mar 16
  McQueen: 1897 spring
        Hall: 1897 Mar 16–18
      Colpo: 1897 Mar 16–19

44. The Red Circle

         Bell: 1897 Jan
    Blakeney: (1881 – 1887)
       Christ: 1893 Jan
       Brend: 1896 Jan
Baring-Gould: 1902 Sept 24–25
      Zeisler: (1895 – 1902) winter
       Dakin: 1897 (Feb?)
  McQueen: Undated
        Hall: 1902 Feb mid
      Colpo: 1896 Feb 27–28

45. The Disappearance of Lady Frances Carfax

         Bell: 1895 summer
    Blakeney: 1896 spring
       Christ: 1903 Sept 2–9
       Brend: 1899 summer
Baring-Gould: 1902 July 1–18
      Zeisler: (1895, 1897 – 1901)
       Dakin: 1897 summer
  McQueen: (1890s late)
        Hall: 1901 summer
      Colpo: 1901 summer

46. The Dying Detective

         Bell: 1888 Nov

Appendix II

> Blakeney: 1890 Nov
> Christ: 1890 Nov 30
> Brend: 1889 Nov
> Baring-Gould: 1887 Nov 19
> Zeisler: 1890 Nov 29
> Dakin: 1890 Nov 29
> McQueen: (1888 or 1889) Nov
> Hall: 1889 Nov
> Colpo: 1903 Nov

47. The Valley of Fear
> Bell: 1887 Jan 7–8
> Blakeney: 1890 Jan
> Christ: 1889 Jan 7
> Brend: 1900 Jan
> Baring-Gould: 1888 Jan 7–8
> Zeisler: 1888 Jan 7–8
> Dakin: 1888 Jan 7
> McQueen: 1899 Jan 7–8
> Hall: 1889 Jan 7–8
> Colpo: 1890 Jan 7–8

48. His Last Bow
> Bell: 1914 Aug 2
> Blakeney: 1914 Aug
> Christ: 1914 Aug 2
> Brend: 1914 Aug
> Baring-Gould: 1914 Aug 2
> Zeisler: 1914 Aug 2
> Dakin: 1914 Aug 2
> McQueen: 1914

Appendix II

Hall: 1914 Aug 2
Colpo: 1914 Aug 2

49. The Mazarin Stone
Bell: 1903 summer
Blakeney: 1903
Christ: 1904 summer
Brend: 1903 summer
Baring-Gould: 1903 summer
Zeisler: 1903 summer
Dakin: 1903 June
McQueen: (1900 – 1903)
Hall: 1903 summer
Colpo: 1903 summer

50. The Problem of Thor Bridge
Bell: 1900 Oct 4–5
Blakeney: (1896 – 1902)
Christ: 1901 Oct 4–5
Brend: 1900 Oct
Baring-Gould: 1900 Oct 4–5
Zeisler: 1901 Oct 4–5
Dakin: 1901 Oct 4
McQueen: (1900 or 1901)
Hall: 1901 Oct 4–5
Colpo: 1901 Oct 4–6

51. The Creeping Man
Bell: 1903 Sept 6–8
Blakeney: 1903 Sept
Christ: 1903 Sept 6, 13

Appendix II

```
       Brend:  1903 Sept
Baring-Gould:  1903 Sept  6, 14, 22
      Zeisler: 1903 Sept  6–13
       Dakin:  1903 Sept
     McQueen:  (1900 – 1903)
        Hall:  1902 Sept
       Colpo:  1903 Sept  6–8, 15
```

52. The Sussex Vampire
```
        Bell:  1897 Nov  19–20
    Blakeney:  (1896 – 1902)
       Christ: 1896 Nov  20–21
        Brend: 1896 Nov  late
Baring-Gould:  1896 Nov  19–21
      Zeisler: (1896 or 1901) Nov 19
        Dakin: 1896 Nov  19
     McQueen:  (1890s mid)
         Hall: 1896 Nov  19–20
        Colpo: 1894 Nov  19–21
```

53. The Three Garridebs
```
         Bell: 1902 June  26–27
     Blakeney: 1902 June
       Christ: 1902 June  26–27
        Brend: 1902 June
Baring-Gould:  1902 June  26–27
      Zeisler: 1902 June  26–27
        Dakin: 1902 June  26
     McQueen:  1902 June
         Hall: 1902 June  26–27
        Colpo: 1902 June  26–27
```

Appendix II

54. The Illustrious Client
          Bell: 1902 Sept 13–23
      Blakeney: 1902 Sept
        Christ: 1902 Sept 3–14
        Brend: 1902 Sept
 Baring-Gould: 1902 Sept 3–16
        Zeisler: 1902 Sept 13–23
         Dakin: 1902 Sept 3
     McQueen: 1902 Sept
          Hall: 1902 Oct 3–13
        Colpo: 1902 Sept 3–14

55. The Three Gables
          Bell: 1903 May late
      Blakeney: 1903
        Christ: 1902 autumn
        Brend: 1903 summer
 Baring-Gould: 1903 May 26–27
        Zeisler: 1896 June early
         Dakin: 1903
     McQueen: (1890s mid)
          Hall: 1902 spring
        Colpo: 1903 May 26–27

56. The Blanched Soldier
          Bell: 1903 Jan
      Blakeney: 1903 Jan
        Christ: 1903 Jan 7, 12
        Brend: 1903 Jan
 Baring-Gould: 1903 Jan 7–12
        Zeisler: 1903 Jan 7–12

Appendix II

      Dakin: 1903 (Jan?)
McQueen: Undated
       Hall: 1903 Jan
     Colpo: 1903 Jan   7, 13

57. The Lion's Mane

         Bell: 1907 July 21–28
    Blakeney: (1904 – 1912)
      Christ: 1907 June 25–26
      Brend: 1907 July
Baring-Gould: 1909 July 27 – Aug (3?)
     Zeisler: 1909 July 27 – Aug (3?)
      Dakin: 1907 (July?)
  McQueen: (1903 – 1912)
       Hall: 1907 July late
     Colpo: 1907 July 23, 30–31

58. The Retired Colourman

         Bell: 1898 July
    Blakeney: 1898 summer
      Christ: 1898 summer
      Brend: 1898 summer
Baring-Gould: 1898 July 28–30
     Zeisler: 1898 July or Aug
      Dakin: 1898 (Aug?)
  McQueen: (1890s late)
       Hall: 1898 summer
     Colpo: 1898 Aug

Appendix II

59. The Veiled Lodger

Bell: 1896 autumn
Blakeney: 1896 winter
Christ: 1890 early autumn
Brend: 1896 Nov early
Baring-Gould: 1896 Oct
Zeisler: 1896 Oct
Dakin: 1896 (Oct?)
McQueen: Undated
Hall: 1896 early
Colpo: 1903 Sept early

60. Shoscombe Old Place

Bell: 1897 May
Blakeney: (1896 – 1902)
Christ: 1883 May 9–10
Brend: 1894 May
Baring-Gould: 1902 May 6–7
Zeisler: 1902 May 6–7
Dakin: 1902 May 6
McQueen: (1890s mid)
Hall: 1888 May late
Colpo: 1883 May 6–7

Appendix II

A Comparative Analysis

As is demonstrated by the above information, there are nine cases upon which all ten of us chronologists agree completely as to the year: SPEC, EMPT, BLAC, GOLD, BRUC, DEVI, LAST, 3GAR, ILLU. We are slightly less unanimous about the month and day. Most of us place EMPT in early April, but Brend and Dakin put it in February; Zeisler defies the general consensus that DEVI occurred in March and moves it to April; Hall similarly places ILLU in October rather than joining the rest of us in September. There are a further six—REIG, DANC, 3STU, ABBE, BLAN, RETI—upon which we all agree save McQueen, who does not give a year and therefore does not contest our collective choice.[1] Thus we are generally in agreement for the surprisingly high number of fifteen cases, a quarter of the total.

There are another fifteen cases for which there is a clear majority selecting the same approximate date, and in which we are in accordance with this majority. It is generally agreed that STUD was in 1881, only Christ and McQueen disagreeing with this year. Eight chronologists place REDH in 1890, though we are the only one to select June rather than October. FINA would be unanimously placed in 1891, where it obviously belongs, were it not for Christ's errant choice of 1893. The eight of us who put NORW in 1894 are divided between July and August. Christ joins eight of us in putting SOLI in 1895, but he diverges by choosing the month of March rather than April. He similarly chooses 1907 for LION along with five of us, but disagrees with

---

[1] The only dissension is that we place 3STU in November 1895, whereas all of the others put it in spring 1895.

Appendix II

our choice of July and moves it to June. SIXN is placed variously in June, July, or August by the eight of us who choose 1900. We agree precisely with the majority upon the dates of the following cases: BOSC, TWIS, NOBL, PRIO, MAZA, THOR, CREE, 3GAB. For a total of thirty cases, then, we are in agreement in our choice of date (or at least of year) with the majority, if not all, of the chronologists.

Our choice for a further five cases agrees with a plurality of the other chronologists. This situation is the direct result of Watson's ambiguity, which has led to great disparity of opinion in these instances. Dakin and Hall agree with us that YELL occurred in 1886; Blakeney and Brend date GLOR in 1873, as we do; and Bell and Hall join us in selecting 1895 for WIST. Improbably enough, Hall constitutes with us a plurality of two for LADY, placing it in 1901; no two other chronologists agree upon any other year. Regarding HOUN, four of us select 1900. Two others opt for 1889, but the rest all prefer a unique year.

There are nine cases for which opinion is evenly split. The most notable, and important for its chronological implications, is SIGN. We, along with Bell, Brend, McQueen, and Hall, opt for 1887, while the five others choose 1888.[1] Those of us who put it in 1887 all agree that STOC, CROO, and NAVA occurred in 1888, whereas those who prefer 1888 for SIGN inevitably place those three cases in 1889. We are pitted four against four for FIVE, while SILV is split three against three, with the other four all choosing a unique year. MUSG is also an instance of four against four, but as with SIGN there is disagreement in both camps as to the month and day. Four of us choose the exact

---

[1] As to the month and day, opinion is very widely divided between September and July, with no correlation to the choice of year.

Appendix II

same year, month, and day for MISS; four of the others agree upon a different year, though one of them opts for a different month than his fellows. As for REDC, it is a unique instance of a three-way split: Brend and we choose 1896 (though we disagree about the month), Bell and Dakin prefer 1897 (and also opt for different months), and Baring-Gould and Hall both select 1902 (yet again disagreeing as to the month).

For seven other cases, there is a consensus with which we do not agree. Five chronologists put SCAN in 1889, whereas only four of us choose 1888. Eight of them choose 1889 for ENGR, but as we have explained above this is impossible, and we, along with Bell, select 1888.[1] A plurality of them put BERY in 1886 while we have the support once again of Bell in choosing 1882. Four of them also form a plurality in placing CARD in 1888; Bell and we once more dissent, agreeing on August 1885. It is yet again a plurality of four that chooses 1887 for RESI, though this time it is Dakin who joins us in selecting 1881.[2] Only three of them agree that VALL occurred in 1888, but opinion is so divided that they have the plurality nonetheless; Blakeney places it in January 1890 with us. There is another plurality of three with regard to SHOS; dated 1902 by them, we, along with Christ, select May 1883. It is worth noting that of these cases for which our date is part of a minority, opinion is generally quite divided, and in only one instance is there a true majority opposed to us.

Finally, we choose an entirely unique date for nine cases. For IDEN, the other chronologists arrive at no real consensus and are as alone as we are in their opinions. For BLUE, seven chronologists choose 1889, but we prefer 1888. We select 1884

---

[1] Note, however, that while we choose July, he opts for August.
[2] We put it in late November, Dakin in October.

Appendix II

for COPP, against five in favour of 1890; we date GREE in 1886, while three others choose 1888; and for CHAS, the plurality of three opts for 1899, but we prefer 1897. Bell, Blakeney, and Dakin date SECO in 1894, but we choose the following year. DYIN is perhaps our most marked deviation. Four of the others select 1890, and all of the rest save us choose a date prior to that; we, contrarily, prefer 1903. Five of the others date SUSS in 1896, while we choose 1894; seven of them put VEIL in 1896 (disagreeing about the month), but we select 1903.

Appendix III: A Note on Holmes's University

Though this is a work of chronology and the many other intriguing conundrums of the Canon do not fall within its purview, there is one significant discovery which we made during our analysis of *The Musgrave Ritual* that, as it has the remarkable potential to settle the longstanding issue of which university—Oxford or Cambridge—Holmes attended, we feel warranted in including in this appendix. When Holmes began recounting the events of *The Musgrave Ritual* to Watson, he said that 'Reginald Musgrave had been in the same college as myself',[1] and other comments substantiate the fact that they attended the same university. Reginald Musgrave was clearly very proud of his ancestry, and he came from a long line of Royalists: 'My ancestor [he says], Sir Ralph Musgrave, was a prominent Cavalier, and the right-hand man of Charles II in his wanderings'.[2] During the English Civil Wars Oxford was a Royalist stronghold—King Charles I used it as his capital from 1642 to 1646—whereas Cambridge fell within the boundaries of Parliamentary power and control and served that faction, albeit unwillingly at first.

---

[1] Short, MUSG, 399.
[2] Short, MUSG, 415-416.

Appendix III

Reginald Musgrave—who had an 'exceedingly aristocratic'[1] appearance and was the proud descendant of staunch Royalists—would never, we may be sure, have so far betrayed his heritage and the memory of his ancestors, nor have forgotten the wrongs committed against them and their king by the men of Cambridge, that he would have condescended to attend the university there. He most unquestionably attended the University of Oxford, from which his ancestors had received staunch support, and as he and Holmes were at the same university, it follows that Holmes studied at Oxford.

We do not know for certain whether any other scholar has yet arrived at this momentous conclusion, though we may say that we have not encountered it in our researches. In any case, we can only suppose that no such theory has yet been propagated, for if it had been then it would have surely ended the debate concerning which university Holmes attended.

---

[1] Short, MUSG, 399.

Bibliography

Baring-Gould, William S. *Sherlock Holmes of Baker Street: A Life of The World's First Consulting Detective.* New York: Bramhall House, 1962.

Bell, H.W. *Sherlock Holmes and Dr Watson: The Chronology of their Adventures.* New York: Magico Magazine, 1984.

Blakeney, T.S. *Sherlock Holmes: Fact or Fiction?* London: John Murray, 1932.

Brend, Gavin. *My Dear Holmes: A Study in Sherlock.* London: George Allen & Unwin Ltd, 1951.

Christ, Jay Finley. *An Irregular Chronology of Sherlock Holmes of Baker Street.* New York: Magico Magazine, 1947.

'Concerts'. *Daily Mail,* 21 February 1900, No. 1,197. http://newspaperarchive.com/ (accessed 13 April 2018).

Dakin, D. Martin. *A Sherlock Holmes Commentary.* Newton Abbot: David & Charles, 1972.

'Dardanelles Incident'. *Daily Mail,* 16 January 1903, No. 2,105. http://newspaperarchive.com/ (accessed 3 April 2018).

Doyle, Arthur Conan. *The Complete Sherlock Holmes.* Vol. 1. New York: Doubleday & Company, Inc., 1930.

—. *The Complete Sherlock Holmes.* Vol. 2. New York: Doubleday & Company, Inc., 1930.

—. *The Complete Sherlock Holmes: Long Stories.* London: John Murray, 1929.

—. *The Complete Sherlock Holmes: Short Stories.* London: John Murray, 1928.

—. *The New Annotated Sherlock Holmes.* Vol. 3, *The Novels.* Edited by Leslie S. Klinger. New York: W.W. Norton & Company, 2006.

—. *The Original Illustrated Sherlock Holmes.* Secaucus: Castle Books, 1981.

'Grand Military and Household Brigade Steeple Chases'. *Bell's Life in London and Sporting Chronicle,* 5 March 1881, No. 3,166. http://newspaperarchive.com/ (accessed 2 February 2018).

Hall, John. *"I Remember the Date Very Well": A chronology of the Sherlock Holmes stories of Arthur Conan Doyle.* Romford, Essex: Ian Henry Publications, 1993.

McQueen, Ian. *Sherlock Holmes Detected: The Problems of the Long Stories.* New York: Drake Publishers, 1974.

'Music and the Drama'. *Brief: the Week's News,* 11 February 1881, Vol. VII, No. 172. http://newspaperarchive.com/ (accessed 2 February 2018).

'Olympia'. *The Standard,* 28 February 1896, No. 22,359. http://newspaperarchive.com/ (accessed 13 April 2018).

'Remarks on the weather from Feb. 27 to March 5'. *Lloyd's Weekly London Newspaper,* 6 March 1881, No. 1,198. http://newspaperarchive.com/ (accessed 2 February 2018).

Roberts, S.C. *Holmes & Watson: A Miscellany.* London: Oxford University Press, 1953.

Bibliography

'Russia and the Dardanelles'. *The Standard*, 7 January 1903, No. 24,505. http://newspaperarchive.com/ (accessed 3 April 2018).

'Sarasate'. *The Standard*, 19 June 1890, No. 20, 576. http://newspaperarchive.com/ (accessed 5 February 2018).

Taylor, A.J.P. *The Struggle for Mastery in Europe, 1848–1918.* Oxford: The Clarendon Press, 1954.

'The Dardanelles Question'. *The Standard*, 13 January 1903, No. 24,510. http://newspaperarchive.com/ (accessed 3 April 2018).

'The Future of Chitral'. *Lloyd's Weekly Newspaper*, 11 August 1895, No. 2,751. http://newspaperarchive.com/ (accessed 19 March 2018).

'The Future of Chitral'. *The Standard*, 12 August 1895, No. 22,187. http://newspaperarchive.com/ (accessed 19 March 2018).

'The Near East'. *The Standard*, 19 January 1903, No. 24,515. http://newspaperarchive.com/ (accessed 3 April 2018).

'The Position of Chitral'. *The Standard*, 3 September 1895, No. 22,206. http://newspaperarchive.com/ (accessed 19 March 2018).

Zeisler, Ernest Bloomfield. *Baker Street Chronology: Commentaries on The Sacred Writings of Dr. John H. Watson.* New York: Magico Magazine, 1983.

Printed in Great Britain
by Amazon